TWITCHERS

TWITCHERS

MALCOLM SUTTON

PUNCHER & WATTMANN

First published in 2024
Published by Puncher and Wattmann
PO Box 279
Waratah NSW 2298

https://www.puncherandwattmann.com
web@puncherandwattmann.com

ISBN   9781923099227

Cover design by Heath Riggs, Mono+
Edited by Ed Wright
Typesetting by Morgan Arnett
Printed by Lightning Source International

 A catalogue record for this work is available from the National Library of Australia

Australian Government

Creative Australia

This project has been assisted by the Australian Government through Creative Australia, its principal arts investment and advisory body.

LONDON PIRANHA ATTACK

Richard's piranhas found him at Barlett & Co, an 80-year-old advertising firm in London's West End. There was a problem with the Tampos campaign. The digital press had reacted with outrage to the concept of marketing a tampon brand to men.

'I'm all for gender equality,' one writer frothed in *The Independent* online, 'but sanitary products remain the domain of women and should not be ridiculed in demeaning marketing campaigns.'

'This is stupid and insulting,' *The Evening Standard* simplified.

But there were so many household applications for unravelled tampons. Fireplace kindling, spilled wine absorbers, water purifiers, even sound dampeners for drum-kits. It was a wonder no one had played the 'husband' card before. It was the punchline that pissed people off the most. A man asked his wife for a tampon to soak up engine oil from their driveway. She slapped him angrily and threw a tampon at his head. He unwrapped it and inserted it up his bleeding nose.

'Tampos. Not just for women.'

'I like you, Richard,' Old Man Stanley said after shuffling across the office carpet to give him a sermon. 'You're an innovator. But you can't mess with sanitary products, son.' He exhaled rotten coffee breath into Richard's face. 'You should have anticipated this reaction.'

'There's nothing printed in newspapers,' Richard said, pleased because he'd convinced Old Man Stanley to sign off on the disaster himself. 'It's just a digital headline for social media. Tomorrow it'll be forgotten.'

Stanley continued his sermon but Richard couldn't absorb a verse because he realised he was blinking … a lot. He tried to prolong the moments in between blinking but it was like trying to ignore an itch. It only made it worse and his eyes started watering.

'Understand?' Stanley said, frowning at Richard.

'Sure, sure, sure,' Richard said, needing to get away from the old man so he could wash his face, stick fingers in his eyes. By lunchtime, however, he was stuck into his next job. He forgot about blinking and by the time Lena swung past the office it seemed Old Man Stanley was ready to forget Tampos as well.

'Hello, darling,' Old Man Stanley said, his monobrow rising. 'Come to take Richard home?'

Richard's second wave of piranhas arrived two months later. The Big Cheese franchise wanted a campaign to sell their new range of burgers. They'd toned their buns black with vegetable dye, a direct copy of a KFC marketing gimmick. Big Cheese knew they were late to the party and wanted a risky campaign that stood out.

Richard's advert featured a young white couple sharing an elongated black burger that was too big for their mouths. They ooohed with the typical orgasmic joy people expected from food actors. They looked around with astonishment before spotting a group of black men sitting in a nearby restaurant booth. The men chuckled heartily and gave the white couple a knowing smile. The boyfriend wiped sauce from his chin and smiled back.

'Black Burgers. Once you go black, you'll never go back.'

'Big Cheese have drawn from stereotypes best left for pornography,' a commentator wrote in *The Times* online. 'It's puerile and I've lost my appetite.'

'Big Cheese have gone to all new lows,' *The Guardian* wrote. 'I'm shocked that in an era where racial typecasting is no longer acceptable, anyone could be this crass.'

A white fundamentalist group rose from the noise of social media to spit about Big Cheese's 'untoward glorification of the black man's anatomy'. They littered the franchise's Facebook page with pictures of large white cocks. At the same time, social media's hate crowd targeted Barlett for being 'out of touch', 'desperate dinosaurs trying to be hip', 'subversive lobbyists for the queer'. Richard rolled his eyes at that one. But then he swallowed, swallowed again and found himself thinking about the juices emerging from the pores of his tongue, trickling down the back of his throat. A dozen tiny piranhas, nibbly, perseverant, were tickling his tonsils, forcing him to swallow repeatedly.

Old Man Stanley, his frown bearing wrinkles so deep they resembled earthquake fissures, arrived at Richard's desk for another sermon. Richard tried telling Old Man Stanley that the controversy would blow over, that it was precisely the sort of exposure Big Cheese wanted. But his words were interrupted by his need to swallow. He couldn't string more than a few sentences together at a time. He needed the bathroom so he could fill his mouth with water, wash out the fish, the needle-teethed horrors.

'Their sales in South London have quadrupled,' he told Old Man Stanley. 'And how many … how many …' A globule of saliva fell from his mouth. All that talking and no swallowing had let a piranha pool fill his mouth.

Richard turned and lunged for the bathroom, turned on the tap, lowered his face to the waterspout, but then he hesitated. The tap serviced everybody in the office. They used it to wash their hands. A viral strand from somebody's finger could have already slid from the faucet onto his own hand.

Richard backed away and caught a glimpse of his lopsided face in the mirror. His left eye was slanted and his crooked mouth drooped. He had to go home. He had to see Lena. He had to get clean and crawl into Lena's arms.

'I'm sorry, Stanley,' Richard said after emerging from the bathroom, using his T-shirt to open the door so as not to risk more germs. 'I have to go home.'

'Wh … what?' Old Man Stanley spluttered. 'What do you mean?

I need you to—'

'It's Lena,' Richard said, cutting him off with the best weapon he had. 'She just called. She's in … trouble … I think.'

'Oh, dear.' Old Man Stanley's face wobbled, then softened, then twisted with urgency. 'Well don't stand here talking to me, son. Go.'

Later he lay in bed. Lena's clean scent filled their darkened room but the silence was killing him. In one minute he'd swallowed five times and Lena would have heard every contraction. He tried shifting focus to Lena's skin, the starch-scent she'd somehow managed to export from her parents' house in Adelaide to London. But the mouth juices kept flowing. He moved his head sharply on the pillow to mask the sound of swallowing. Less than 20 seconds later he did it again. This time he rubbed his face with his hand, attempting to hide the sound with the scratch of his stubble.

'Richard, what are you *doing*?' Lena said from the darkness.

'Sorry,' Richard replied, swallowing. 'I'm just a little nervous … about work, that's all.'

She rolled over and put her slender, perfect-smelling hand on his chest, right on top of his heart, an autonomous, pounding piece of flesh that accelerated when it wanted to, slowed when it wanted to, beat all day, every day, without fail, a mind of its own. He wondered if she could feel it beating, if she would notice it flutter, if the fact Richard was thinking such thoughts would make it flutter. He'd done it in the past, creating a lightning spark in his chest, sharp, like it was about to happen now. Her hand would make it happen now. It had to happen now. It was happening now.

'Stop,' Richard shouted, throwing Lena's hand from his chest, sitting upright so she bolted upright as well and turned on her lamp, the cute little ornament she'd bought along with all the other cute little things she'd bought to make their bedsit look nice, feel nice, smell nice.

'Richard?' Lena said, looking at him reproachfully. 'What is it?'

'Sorry, I'm just … I just …'

'What?'

He told her about work, about Tampos, about Big Cheese, Old Man Stanley and his putrid breath. He told her that he didn't like her hand on his chest, that he was feeling unsettled and nervous about work but it was okay because she smelt nice. Lena blinked at him, suggested it was time to go home to Adelaide. She said it too fast, too easily, like she'd been thinking it for weeks. But there were bushfires at home, real big fuckers in New South Wales, rainforests smouldering in Queensland, and Lena didn't know about Richard's arson conviction, the hermit artist who must hate him for burning his work, a master of symmetry who could paint better than Richard would ever paint — perfect, uninhibited, honest. She didn't know that their trip to London was an escape, that he'd never worked in advertising and his job was London luck. She only knew that he was good at advertising, too good. But it was a low form of art, the lowest, full of scumbags, rich hipsters and terrible pop music.

'Advertising isn't art,' Dad had declared last year. 'It's commerce.'

Lena didn't know that he wanted to quit but couldn't because he was afraid she'd leave him. Richard had been trying to get cancelled instead. But she was talking about leaving him anyway, so Richard decided to do something good. He would postpone his self-sabotage at work, at least for a little while, and do something good. He had to do something good.

'Let's just get some sleep,' Richard said, reaching over to turn off the lamp.

Richard's chance came with the arrival of Gold Dog, a cheap dog food brand from Russia. Word had spread about Barlett's fuck-ups and the Russians had come for a cheap deal. Old Man Stanley didn't want to give the job to Richard but the Australian had a good idea. It was cheap to implement and couldn't possibly offend anyone.

'Social Dog,' Richard said to the boardroom. Two crop-cut Russians in expensive suits stared at him. The shorter one dropped his eyes to Richard's jaw, smeared slime over his crooked mouth.

'We find a young, healthy, well-trained dog in a perfect family in a perfect home. We get the smallest high-definition webcam we can find. We strap it to the dog's head. We stream it live to the internet 24/7. We set up social media accounts, call it: Rexlife.'

The tall Russian grunted. Old Man Stanley pulled at the collar of his shirt.

'We post images on Facebook, on Snapchat, on Instagram with little videos and whatever else. And every time that cute little dog is fed by its perfect little family, it'll be fed from a giant can of Gold Dog, twice a day, every day, at the same time commuters are going to and from work, looking at their mobile phones.'

'But it's not healthy,' the shorter Russian said. 'To feed it Gold Dog, twice a day, every day, for weeks. It will get sick and—'

'This branding is subliminal,' the tall Russian said. 'Yes?'

'Completely subliminal,' Richard said. 'Like fish behind your eyes.'

'So,' Stanley interrupted, laughing nervously. Richard backed away from the table, rubbing his jaw, feeling the small Russian's stare. He forced a cheek-peeling smile and evacuated to the bathroom. He pulled out his bottle of antibacterial hand wash, washed his face, washed it twice, spat in the basin, spat again, punched himself in the left breast, coughed because he'd heard that coughing was the best way to stop cardiac arrest, and rubbed his eyes with alcohol fingers. It hurt like hell but it was clean. Anything that hurt was clean. But his chest was hurting again. He felt his pulse and its beat was sporadic, responding to his measurement, fucking with him, wanting to stop, wanting to throttle Richard with sudden death. He coughed. Coughed again. The emerging panic swelled and passed and he stumbled from the bathroom, poked his squirming face into the boardroom, mumbled something about Lena, and fled.

'Richard, please,' Old Man Stanley said a few weeks after Rexlife was up and running. 'How's Lena? What's happening? Is she okay?'

It didn't matter that Richard looked a wreck, that he was averaging three hours sleep a night, that the Gold Dog campaign was kicking goals.

What mattered to Stanley was Lena hadn't visited the office at the end of the day for two weeks. Lovely Lena, beautiful Lena with Brazilian heritage, caramel skin, thin but not too skinny, well postured, sharp-featured and clean, like pressing a warm plate from the dishwasher against your nose. The old bastard had been enchanted ever since Lena targeted him at an industry night, laid on the charm, flirted until he took the bait and offered her boyfriend a job.

'How is she?' Old Man Stanley persisted.

'She's fine,' Richard lied, feeling pieces of his lopsided face fall to the table where he'd been rubbing his stubble. Lena had moved out a week ago so he could 'act crazy on his own'. A beautiful, ambitious young physiotherapist who could ascend any ladder she wanted did not need a boyfriend pulling her backwards. 'It's just … the bushfires in the news … back home in Australia. It's got her upset, homesick even.'

The old man edged closer, wanting something, prompting Richard to suck in a breath and hold it.

'You know, Lena, she's a good asset for you, and …' Something about Richard's puffed-up cheeks made Stanley drop it. 'Anyway, I hope everything's okay because I need your A-game. We've got a big one, son. A real big one and I want your ideas.'

The big one was Warrior, a Chinese car company that had persevered from being a basket case in the '90s into selling respectable city cars across Europe by the mid-2010s. They were about to take on the sedan market for the first time. They wanted to break the mould of Asian-made hatchbacks and appear 'classier' to the UK's middle-class male demographic. They were also in a hurry to get things rolling.

'You heard about those pneumonia cases in Wuhan?' Old Man Stanley asked. 'Warrior think it might be something more serious, some kind of disease that's spreading. They want to beat that bad publicity. You reckon you could get something to me tomorrow?'

On the bus home Richard worked up an idea to pit a female driver against her male companion, dodging roadblocks, dodging men in white quarantine suits, doing their best to get out of Wuhan but arguing about which route to take, her reliance on the sat-nav, her willingness to let people into their lane.

At that point the car would become sentient, open its passenger door and hiccup the whinging male onto the open road.

'Warrior — take control.'

But it was too safe, too on-trend, too 'good'. Richard needed to switch it around, have the woman drive the car into a dead-end so the man could take over, save them from danger, exploit the car's power as only a male could.

'Warrior — maintain control.'

It would be 'sexist, crass, misogynistic', a 'pathetic display of big-otry', leave Barlett with no choice but to sack Richard and make peace with a 'progressive world that's done it's best to leave such tragic rednecks behind'.

Richard cringed as he imagined the insults, but his fingernails were broken, his jaw muscles ached. He was too tired to cause trouble and 'accidentally' get sacked and, now that Lena had left, couldn't care less about his future. He didn't need to. He could simply quit, much to the satisfaction of his dad, no doubt.

Richard binned the folder on the way home where he sat on the bed, wanting suddenly to paint his face, an expressionist self-portrait, a face sliding off the edge. But he hadn't painted anything since he'd made his escape from Adelaide and, at any rate, he didn't have any paint.

Lena surprised him by coming home. She brought wine and got drunk enough to love him, to care for him, to want to have sex with him. Later he lay above her, supporting himself on his elbows. She lay expectant beneath him, her breasts perky and pointed at his eyes. After a moment her face crinkled. She reached down to feel his lust and found a raw sausage defrosting, potatoes boiling soft. Richard panicked, did his best to hold on, but failure arrived in a piranha-pack frenzy and ripped his cock to pieces.

Lena extracted herself, put on her clothes and sighed. Richard sank into the aquarium she'd been banging her head against for months.

'I don't care about the sex, Richard,' she said resignedly. 'I care that you're losing it.'

'I'll see someone,' Richard offered, an urge to pick up the glass of water on his bedside table and glass himself.

'You always say that,' she said.

'I always mean it, but it's no good without direction. I thought it would be in advertising but it's not there. There's nothing for me here.'

Lena picked up some clothes and opened the door. She turned to glare at him one more time but shouted instead.

'Stop scratching your face!'

Richard's final wave of piranhas arrived at Barlett & Co's so-called 'Top Gear' party. It was tradition for Barlett to celebrate the resumption of business after the Christmas break, a period the old man described as 'swinging into top gear'. But business was slow. The Wuhan virus, which was now called coronavirus, had arrived in the UK at January's end with two Chinese nationals. A scout leader — dubbed the 'super-spreader' — had brought it back from Singapore and spread it to 11 Brits. The bug was out and advertisers were stalling.

Richard didn't want to go to the old man's party. But he hadn't seen Lena since she walked out the previous week and knew she'd be there. She'd bought an outfit last month and, once Lena invested in plans, she didn't like changes.

Richard arrived at the Kentish Town house with four cans of Red Stripe. The door opened and a wall of Top 40 tween pop music knifed his ears.

'Richard,' said a short intern called Matthew, his face sweaty and pink. 'Thank God you're here.' He pulled out his smartphone. 'I need to show you something.'

'Richard,' said Old Man Stanley from the open plan kitchen, surrounded by styled millennials, Generation Y hipsters, people like Richard but without the scratches, the police record, parents who could press charges against their only child for arson. He motioned Richard inside, took his elbow with a crab claw, and pulled him towards the fridge. 'How are you feeling, son? How's the Warrior advert going? You've got something, right? Tell me you've got something?'

He took Richard's beer and put it in the fridge.

'I need to tell you something about Gold Dog,' Matthew whispered in Richard's ear from behind him. 'There's been a—'

'Nooo,' Old Man Stanley said, opening a Red Stripe and handing it back to Richard. 'We don't need to talk about Gold Dog. We need to talk about Warrior.'

'Well, that's the thing,' Richard said, trying to straighten his back. 'I quit.'

At that moment Richard detected a familiar scent — starched cleanliness — and the door to his left crashed open to reveal a bathroom.

'Lena?' he said to a silhouette emerging from the entrance, watching which hand she used to pull the door closed. Lena took Richard's elbow and marched him through a laundry and outside into the cold night air.

'What are you doing?' she hissed.

'I can't do this anymore, Lena. I thought they'd sack me, but—'

'What do you mean, sack you? What have you done?'

'My adverts, they're *stupid*.'

'So you're quitting? But you're still only learning. They want you to stay.'

'But I wanted to be sacked.'

Her eyes hardened.

'What, do you mean, you *wanted* to be sacked?'

'Richard,' Matthew shouted, bursting through the door to stand next to them. 'You've got to listen to me.' Before either Richard or Lena could protest, the intern raised his smartphone to Richard's face and displayed a Twitter account. It was a meme, something about Gold Dog. Matthew pushed the phone closer to Richard's face. 'Look.'

The words were juxtaposed over a picture of sickly, horrible green slime on tiles Richard recognised. They were tiles in the backyard of the Rexlife house.

Gold Dog. Turning dogs green since 2019, the meme said.

'Rex is sick. He's got diarrhea. Look.' Matthew swiped his hand over the phone and brought up more Twitter images. Green slime covered the lounge room floor. Gifs showed the dog sniffing globules that appeared fluorescent green in the high-definition frame.

'He ate too much of that crappy dog food,' Matthew said, his voice breaking. Gold Dog cans shone in the background of nearly every shot, strategically located in various places around the house in an overkill of placement advertising. 'And they know it was us. They know it was you. And look.'

Matthew swiped his phone to show an Instagram clip of Rex's owners running about wiping up green vomit, slipping on green shit, picking up Rex and trying to escape. The dog's head flopped weakly, allowing his point-of-view camera to loll sickeningly across the goop-covered floor.

'They didn't turn off the feed for 20 minutes,' Matthew wailed as Richard backed away, edging through the door, faintly aware that Lena was moving with him, taking his arm and telling him to stop giggling.

'And I didn't even *try* to fuck that one up,' Richard heard himself snigger.

'Let's go home,' Lena's said sternly as she pushed him through the laundry, guided him into the kitchen, her hands warm but contaminated.

Old Man Stanley stopped them on the way through, but rather than question Richard, he put an arm on Lena's shoulder, around her waist. He drew her close to his face, latched onto the side of her Brazilian cheek and suckled and slurped with foul coffee breath. Richard backed away as the final layer of cleanliness was sucked from his starch-smelling girl-friend. He stumbled through the lounge room, its tween pop music, its small crowd of sharp-eared millennials, then hesitated at the front door, not wanting to touch it, not wanting to put his hand on the handle.

Lena arrived and opened the door. They stepped outside but when she went to pull him down the steps, he had to pull back, he had to pull out his pocket tube of antibacterial gel and tell her to 'use this to wash your hands, your arms, your face, all of your face where Old Man Stanley kissed you, where the old fucker kissed you. I can't look at you. I can't touch you. I can't see you. I can't be with you. Lena, I can't be with you.'

Lena shot her hand out and slapped Richard across the face.

'We're finished,' she said, and the piranhas disappeared from his mind, replaced by a sudden silence. He blinked, expecting them to return immediately, but nothing happened, no buzz, no blink, no swallow, no heart attack. All he heard was the footsteps of Lena disappearing up the road. The warmth of failure washed over his body and for the first time in months Richard felt himself relax.

'It's okay, Richard,' Dad's voice said on cue, all knowing, patronising and stable. 'You've had your fun and it's time to come back to reality. But this time, son, do us a favour. When you get home, try not to burn down the house.'

'Burn,' Pyro said to an exploding bush. 'Burn and know I'll be back.'

'Get on with it,' Mother's voice snarled from within his skull. 'Hurry up before you fuck things up.'

Pyro ran up the hill, legs pumping, smoke stinging his eyes, but it was the memories that hurt most. Stumbling across Ashleigh in her little blue car, fucking. Seeing his mother pushing around the babies, sneering. He wanted the memories fed to flames, eaten and erased, but there was no time. The running man was close. Somehow, he'd been waiting.

Pyro splashed more petrol on the paddock, a second violent arc between them. It took off faster than the first, fanned by the scorching northerlies, red, furious, dangerous. The smoke filled Pyro's lungs and he fell to his knees.

'Get up, you fool,' Mother shrieked. 'Get the fucker who bit my leg.'

Pyro clawed up the hillside and stumbled over the summit, inhaling the fresh air of Olave Valley. He froze as he saw the old Quaker's house among the gum trees and grapevines below, sensing the clown watching from inside his rotting building, licking his sharp teeth, ignoring Pyro's blaze like he'd ignored him banging on his door 20 minutes ago. Pyro was supposed to pour petrol over the walls, light it with a match. Instead he'd chickened out, creeping close enough only to throw a dead possum on the porch, shaved like the others, the dogs, the cats, the rats, taking their hair like his mother took his. She wanted Pyro clean, bare, nothing like his bearded father and everything like the babies she wanted to control, hold penned, confused, older kids astonished and frightened into submission, all of them except one, a kid who'd smiled like a clown, who never stopped smiling, who caught Mother off guard, strolled straight through the weeping children, and bit her on the leg.

'You coward,' Mother sneered, a distorted memory with a fat face. 'You had your chance and you fucked it up.'

Pyro heard a thump and a door opened to the stone cottage on the other side of Olave Valley. An old couple emerged to look at the smoke and look at Pyro in his hood. A black alpaca stood in their yard, an animal who'd attacked Pyro before. It started trotting up the hill towards him, its long neck supporting a taut face, honing in on its enemy. Pyro took another match and readied his can of petrol. But from inside the black smoke behind him somebody shouted. A confused section of Pyro's head buzzed him, prodded him, reminded Pyro he was a hunted man.

He spat the foam from his mouth, turned and ran across the hillside to the pocket of bushes that hid his car.

'Burn.' Pyro stopped among the banksias to pour his petrol. 'Burn and fucking know I'll be back.'

*

Constable Rory Sniles couldn't see anything behind the blaze. It was too hazy, too fierce, but somewhere behind them an arsonist was running. His prey was escaping, his first scalp since arriving in South Australia.

Sniles took a breath and leapt through the metre-high flames, fearing the worst. Instead he found unburnt stubble and rolled safely over the hilltop, emerging from the smoke to see a new valley, spot fires sparked by embers, a vineyard smouldering between two cottages at the bottom. A black alpaca was galloping across the valley, its head steady and pointed like a missile. Sniles followed its trajectory to a clump of bushes that looked more real than they should, a quality piece of realism in a shitty oil painting. Instinct told him this was where his scalp was hiding.

He was lucky to have been patrolling nearby when black smoke started rising into the sky. An arsonist was just what he'd been hoping for, an arrest to win respect from his new colleagues. But he had to check on the valley's two houses. Their occupants could be sleeping, oblivious to the bushfire coming. If somebody innocent got hurt while Sniles was chasing scalps he'd never hear the end of it. He couldn't risk another fuck-up like in Victoria.

Sniles ran down the hill towards the first of the properties, a dilapidated house, banged on the back door and looked through a main window. It revealed nothing but gloomy, antique-looking furniture. He ran around to the front porch and found a dead possum on the porch, its chest hair shredded, attacked by a fox perhaps. He hammered on the door, shouted, listened, heard nothing, started running towards the valley's second house, a stone cottage with a corrugated roof.

A thundering dark shadow appeared in the sky. A water chopper passed low overhead to survey the scene. Moments later an elderly man and woman emerged from the side of the cottage. They held a fire hose and were filling gutters with water. They looked calm and in control, unfazed by the spot fires flickering across the valley. It was as if they'd seen it a dozen times. When sirens sounded in the distance and the chopper dumped water on the hilltop, Sniles felt relieved of his protection duties.

He ran back up the hill towards the bushes, readying his baton to swing, arriving at the same time as the alpaca. But before either of them could enter, the bushes erupted into flames, a dirty orange ball of mockery blocking access to their prey.

'Motherfucker,' Sniles shouted as the alpaca turned and spat in the constable's face.

THE WATTLE BIRD

Chika chika CHEE CHAA chika chika CHEE CHAA chika CHAA

Drooping leaves mocked Richard from wrangled branches. A regiment of gum trees twisted and ancient guffawed with irony at the sight of Richard sitting alone on his steps. It was as if he'd never left. Bushfire smoke was in the air. He had a weapon in hand. He was scanning tree limbs for a noisy fucking wattle bird and, just like when he'd tried to remove the bird violently from his life the year before, his mind was filled with Lena.

They'd shared a flight home from London but she sat well away from him. They'd stopped in Singapore where she avoided him altogether. They'd arrived at Adelaide Airport but she didn't wait for him at the top of the terminal ramp.

His parents had shouted from an airport café, surprising Richard as he walked desolate through the terminal. It was early March and through the windows he could see the city shimmering in the heat. Behind it the Adelaide Hills loitered like unbreaking waves.

'Where's Lena?' Mum said as Richard approached. She seemed shorter than when he left, her brown hair noticeably thinner. There was a pile of hand luggage at their feet.

'Nice to see you too,' he said. 'Going somewhere?'

'We're going to China,' Dad said, his voice a little scratchy, a tall, white-haired baby boomer showing signs of age at last, or nervousness. They were leaving Australia the moment Richard returned home, having arranged their 'amazingly cheap' flights to coincide with his arrival.

'Otherwise we might not have *seen* you,' Mum added, her hands nervously entwined.

'Lena ran ahead to meet her parents. You're going to China *now*?'

'Here's the keys to the flat.' Dad pushed keys across the table. 'You can both stay there.'

'We had to get the carpets cleaned three times to get rid of the smell and—'

'Are you sure it's the right time to be visiting China,' Richard interrupted, 'you know, with that coronavirus thing?'

'It's just a bad flu,' Dad said. 'People will settle down. Commerce waits for no one.'

'Ashleigh called,' Mum said. 'She heard you were coming home.'

'He doesn't need to hear about Ashleigh yet, or any of that lot,' Dad said, blue eyes sharp as ever but unwilling to hold Richard's gaze for more than a few seconds. He stood up and towered over Richard, put a long arm on his shoulder. 'He needs to get organised, don't you son? Get back on your feet.'

'I am on my feet,' Richard protested. 'It's just that Lena needed a break from London, you know, the hustle and—'

'Take the Mitsubishi,' Dad said, letting go of Richard and fumbling car keys into his hand. 'You can set yourself up back in the flat, but I don't want any emails from the neighbours, son. You've got another chance, and you've got to respect—'

'Lena and I are thinking of finding a place in the city. We're—'

'Nonsense. You don't need to be spending that sort of money.'

'Where is she?' Mum said again, turning again to look through the crowd of airport people.

Chika CHEE CHAA chika chika CHEE CHAA

Richard stepped off his concrete steps and towards the solitary gum tree at the edge of his yard, an isolated patch at the edge of scrub occupied by his weatherboard granny flat. It was at the far end of a property occupied by a much larger house rented out by his parents to a 40-something couple who, like everybody else in his neighbourhood, never spoke to Richard directly but loved to leave him messages.

You've got a lot of nerve to come back here, a note stuck to his front door had said when he'd arrived home from the airport. *We'll be keeping a close eye on you. Any more of your 'accidents' and there'll be consequences.*

Chika chika CHEE CHAA chika CHEE CHAA chika CHAA

Richard peered into the leaves of the tree, its crown blurred by a layer of bushfire smoke moving across the sky. Barbed wire wrapped its lower branches, metal cats dangled from others, a plastic owl with a rotating head moved in the breeze from a higher perch. It was everything he'd used in the past to try and remove the wattle bird. His parents had left it all in place to remind him of his 'accident'. It wasn't necessary, however. The scorched black trunk said it all.

Chika CHEE CHAA chika CHAA

'Shut up,' Richard shouted, spotting the bird's taut little body stretching upwards to bark at the smoke, a fucker who'd woken him every morning since he returned. Richard lifted his slingshot, pulled back on the powerful rubber, aimed, let fly. The ball bearing *cracked* into the bird's perch so it flapped away squawking. He heard his mobile phone ringing from inside the house and ran inside, hoping it was Lena, praying it was Lena, but the caller display showed a number he didn't recognise.

'Hello?'

'Where've you been hiding, man?' Lars said.

'Ah, I just wanted to settle in quietly, you know.' Think about Lena. Never call Lena. 'Hey, where's the bushfire? There's smoke in the air and—'

'Fuck the fire. Come over for a few drinks tomorrow. Donnie will be there, and …' Lars paused. 'Ashleigh's hoping you'll come.'

'I don't know, man.' Her name prickled over Richard's skin. 'I've gotta find work.'

'Don't you think you ought to see some of your friends? You've been back from London a week and you haven't seen any of us.'

'Well, you know, I've gotta hit it while I'm hot. You know, drum up some work from advertising agencies.' It was a lie of course. He was done with advertising. He'd been trying to get work in some of the few art galleries left in Adelaide, without success.

'We'll pick you up at 11,' Lars said.

'I'll drive,' Richard sighed.

'Don't be stupid. See you tomorrow.'

AIR CONDITIONING

Richard was barely out the shower when he heard Lars and Donnie banging at his door, calling his name. He wanted to do his hair, look his best, find the aftershave he knew Ashleigh liked. Lars had said 11am but they were half an hour early, leaving the front door open while Richard pulled on his shoes.

Donnie seemed larger, his face chubbier with unkempt stubble, his head freshly shaved to a centimetre of his skull. Lars too had changed. He still had a white face with stoned, bloodshot eyes, a mop of black, rock-star hair, but there was stitching at the sides of his eyes, wrinkles from laughter, age, too much smoking, or all of the above.

'Come on,' Donnie said, as Richard hesitated at the doorway, touching his hair. 'You look pretty enough.'

They took off in Donnie's Holden VT, Richard in the front passenger seat with a box of beers at his feet, Lars in the back with a dog panting on his lap. The red heeler whimpered at passing banksias and gum trees lining Richard's access lane. Its breath stank with decay. Richard opened his window with a push of a button but Donnie overruled him from the centre console.

'AC, Richard,' he said. 'Remember that?'

Richard's skin started to tighten as the guts of three men and a dog were redistributed in the cabin, chilled by air conditioning. He breathed from as close to his window as possible, watching 1960s houses enclosed in a mix of European trees, gum trees, flowers and lawns pass as they travelled through Belair and Glenalta. He wondered how many of their occupants had signed the petition to kick him out of the district, what they'd say if they saw him back from London, which one of them had thrown horseshit at his front door last year.

'So what's been happening?' he said.

'I've been learning Mandarin,' Lars said. 'I'm practically fluent.'

'Really?' Richard turned around. The dog licked its lips and watched him anxiously. 'When did you—'

'It's the Asian century, man,' Lars said, holding onto the dog's collar. 'I'm getting the jump on all you cunts.'

'Yeah, you and their bat virus,' Donnie said. 'That's how it started, you know. They were eating raw bats.'

'Don't be stupid,' Lars shot back. 'And anyway, coronavirus isn't as bad as the flu. Everyone's freaking out about nothing. It's just new, you know?'

'There were four *new* cases the other day, two in Queensland and two in WA, that's 22 in Australia already—'

'Who's counting?' Lars leant forward in his seat, prompting Richard to hold his breath and push his face against the window seals. 'There's gonna be tonnes of jobs for people who speak Mandarin. Could help you too, Richard.'

'I don't need any help.' Their voices were jarring. Richard had grown accustomed to UK accents and their Australian twang bludgeoned his ears. 'Advertising's a Westerner's game.'

'Why'd you come back then?' Donnie asked, slowing the car for a raised chicane, one of several installed to stop teenagers getting airborne and killing themselves on the rises between Hawthorndene and Coromandel Valley. 'If you're doing so well?'

'Visa ran out.' They drove through another chicane and to his surprise Donnie turned the car left onto a dirt road. *The* dirt road. 'Where are we going?'

'Just a little detour,' Donnie said. 'You'll see.'

Olave Valley emerged. The road's twisting passageway sucked them upwards into its guts. At the same time Lars' red heeler erupted barking, agitated by a second dog that had appeared in a junk pile in somebody's front yard. Richard yanked his antibacterial gel wash from his pocket, squirted it onto his hands, rubbed them together, rubbed his face. He hit the window button again and pushed his head out the car, gasping for fresh air, but instead inhaled the charged stench of a nearby bushfire site. It was strong, acrid, familiar. He coughed and retreated, squirted more gel onto his hands, turned to stare at Donnie, the round-faced bastard who was already messing with him. One year away and the fucker was already playing games.

'You haven't changed a bit,' Donnie said, laughing. 'But keep the window shut, yeah?' He pushed a button in the centre console to close it. 'You're not in Pommyland anymore.'

The car turned a corner and the valley widened to their left, two properties with a vineyard between them. The horrible old Quaker's house looked as dilapidated as always, its blank windows seeming to stare at Richard, accusing, hating. It made his skin prickle, a sensation that worsened when he noticed the little pockets of charred earth scattered across the hillside. They drove the valley road over the summit and the hill to their left fell away into a paddock freshly blackened by fire.

'This is it,' Lars said, leaning all the way forward so his head was between Richard and Donnie. 'Pull over, man.'

'Nah, it's further up,' Donnie said. 'In the forest.'

'We said we'd never come back here,' Richard said, pain emerging in his left breast so his voice squeaked a little. 'Tell me why we're here.'

'Settle down,' Donnie said. 'In case you haven't noticed, there was a bushfire here, just yesterday.'

'It was deliberately lit,' Lars said from the back. 'And we think it's the—'

'And on one of those trees in the paddock, there's a drawing of a butterfly, right near where the fire started.'

'Bullshit.'

'It's the clown, Richard,' Lars said, jerking on the dog's collar, holding the impatient red heeler as it wriggled on his lap. 'We pissed him off.'

'What the fuck are you talking about?'

'You know, the Blackwood Clo—'

'I know who the Blackwood fucking Clown is.' Another flash of pain struck Richard's chest. He was some guy who used to dress up as a clown and scream at bushwalkers in the forests, or so the legend went. Apparently he always wore white. Apparently he got away with killing his parents too, or so the kids used to tell each other back in high school. 'But what the hell has that got to do with anything?'

'Pass me a beer,' Donnie said, parking the car next to a low drooping fence from where the black paddock rolled away towards a clump of pine trees. Richard picked up a beer and held it out, annoyed, confused, but Donnie didn't take it. Instead he watched Richard's face. 'I was down here this morning, checking out the fire ground, and I saw this tree, with one of his butterflies drawn on it.'

'Bullshit. You guys are just fucking with me,' Richard blabbered. 'I've only been back a week and already you're fucking with me. Do you want this beer or not?'

Donnie continued to smile but didn't take the beer. Richard cracked it open himself and swigged. The earthy flavour of Coopers Pale Ale slid down his throat, but it was horribly warm.

'Why the hell are you drinking warm beer?'

Donnie laughed and reached behind his seat to retrieve a small cooler bag filled with cold beers and took one out.

'I thought you Poms liked warm beer,' Donnie said before climbing out the car so it rocked on its suspension. Lars opened his own door and was almost pulled outside by his excited red heeler. The dog whimpered and squatted in the kerbside dirt, laying a sudden turd that made Richard want to puke.

'For fuck's sake,' he warbled as he leant out the car to dry retch, spilling warm beer into the earth, prompting Donnie to laugh again.

'Still the same Richard,' Donnie said. He hoisted himself over the fence, cracked his beer, and started walking across the scorched pad-dock towards the pine trees. 'Come with me and I'll show you the tree.'

'Sorry, Richard,' Lars said, lifting his haphazard dog over the fence. 'It's my uncle's dog. He shits when he's excited, that's all.'

Lars scaled the fence himself and motioned for Richard to come close.

'You remember last year, when we went in the old Quaker's house and found the paintings and you burnt—'

'How could I forget,' Richard spat, averting his eyes from the dog's shit.

'Yeah, yeah, of course. Well, Donnie worked it out. It was the *clown's* work you burnt. The Blackwood Clown. *He's* the artist.' Lars stared at him with wide eyes, then continued in a hushed voice. 'And don't worry about Donnie. He's just bitter 'cause he lost his job. Car indus-try's fucked. Manufacturing's fucked. And there's no jobs around the place, you know, for cunts.'

He crunched away through the stubble, leaving Richard to flick his throat where a disturbing pulse was starting to thump. They'd known each other since Year 8 — Lars a quiet kid who'd gone to Hawthorndene Primary, one of the smallest of the district's primary schools. Donnie a domineering force from some primary school in the south, returning to the district where he was born. They'd been fucking around with stupid shit like this for years, but the last time it landed Richard in trouble, real trouble.

'Hurry up, Richard,' Donnie shouted from halfway across the hill.

Richard swore and climbed over the fence to clump after them. Ash powder engulfed his suede shoes from Oxford Street, his chinos from Camden Town, reclaiming the ridiculous, overdressed fool who'd actually believed he could escape this place for London. He joined his old friends at the edge of the pine tree plantation where whistles, thousands of them, sounded from above—a breeze cut to ribbons by millions of pine needles.

'See this?' Donnie said. He slapped the spiny trunk of a tree. 'This is where he put it.'

28

The butterfly was painted on the jagged bark of the tree, crudely, without finesse, somewhat slanted where the artist had been overcome by the uneven surface. It resembled nothing of what they'd seen in the old Quaker's house last year — perfect, uninhibited, honest.

'No,' he said. 'This isn't anything. It doesn't mean anything. I don't think it was even him.'

But Donnie was waiting for Richard's attention, little beads of light at the centre of his eyes.

'Check this out.' He slapped the trunk of an adjacent tree and stepped aside.

BURN IT ALL RICHARD

The words — splashed over its bark with the same yellow paint — swirled and spun before Richard.

'I don't understand ...' His voice faltered.

'I told you,' Donnie said, his eyes glowing. 'It's the clown.'

Richard felt his mind crumbling as Donnie turned away and took a few steps into the whistling pines. The dog whimpered and tried to follow but Lars tugged him back with his leash.

'The clown's been screaming and shit, from outside our house, from Blackwood Forest,' Lars said. 'He wakes me up at night. That's why I got Thompson, for a lookout. And he knows you're back, man. He *knows* it was you.'

'Hey,' Donnie suddenly hissed. 'He's right there. I can see him!'

Donnie stared into the trees, rows of craggy trunks made dim by the canopy above, eliciting another nervous whimper from Thompson. Richard followed his gaze but there was nothing but pines. They whistled and ebbed, until from somewhere in the orange-brown gloom there was the sudden *crack* of a twig snapping underfoot.

Thompson leapt forward but was nearly garrotted by the leash attached to his collar, rearing backwards on his hindquarters, trying to bark but choking.

'Get him,' Lars hollered, unhooking Thompson so he bolted into the trees, followed by Lars and Donnie.

'We were supposed to be getting a drink,' Richard shouted as everybody crashed through the branches and twigs and disappeared. 'We were supposed to be seeing Ashleigh!'

'We'll see your precious Ashleigh soon,' Donnie yelled back, his voice growing distant as the breeze sucked it into the canopy to be shredded by pine needles.

'Son of a bitch,' Richard snapped. 'I didn't ask to see Ashleigh. You rang *me*.'

Richard turned and scratched frantically at his name on the bark, memories of the fateful night that had caused so much trouble rushing through his mind, their drunken walk through Olave Valley, the alpaca attack, breaking into the old Quaker's house and finding dusty paintings in the gloom, static butterflies in differing colours, differing sizes, but always exact, always symmetrical, save for a little gap in their right wing where the paint strokes were left unjoined, a deliberate flaw that seemed to mock Richard's own failure as an artist, an accountant who couldn't paint symmetrically to save his lopsided face.

A bark fragment slipped under his fingernail. It was sharp and drew blood, bringing him focus, direction, anger. Richard continued clawing at the yellow paint until the bark crumbled from the trunk and fell to the ground. From behind him came a sudden thump. Richard turned but could only see drooping needles. He heard a crack to his left and spotted a flash of white disappearing behind a tree.

'Hey,' Richard called out, running to the tree. But no one was there. He heard feet pattering away on dried needles, a crack and snap in the forest. Richard swore and ran after the sound, shielding his face as branches clawed at his arms. Something white sparkled briefly across an open patch of forest, a fire track separating the pines from an orchard.

'Hey,' Richard shouted. 'You need to know what happened. It wasn't me who stole your paintings.'

Richard leapt across the fire track and into the orchard where pears occasionally knocked against his head. He zigzagged through them, seeing nothing in the dappled shadows, eventually stopping again to listen. But all he could hear was the heartbeat in his head. There were no more footsteps, no more forest crackles. Richard wondered briefly if he'd imagined the whole thing, if he'd let his mates' stupid game about an urban myth claw under his skin, until there was a sudden thump behind him, rustling grass, rapidly approaching feet. The clown had backtracked. The clown had him in his sights. Richard started turning but it was too late. The clown had him and he never meant to burn a thing.

'I didn't even want to be there,' Richard screamed as he was knocked off his feet.

Two months before Gold Dog and their London evacuation, Richard and Lena went to the cinema to see a re-screening of Alfonso Cuarón's *Gravity*. Lena didn't want to go. She wanted to do something more social. She said Richard was hiding from his work colleagues, her friends, even his own friends, which was ridiculous because he didn't have any in London. He argued they just needed a break from the stress, that it would be good for them, good for him.

Richard scanned the auditorium when they arrived, spotting two central seats next to the stair aisle. There was a quiet-looking couple sitting further along in the row behind it. He led Lena to the row, checked the couple weren't holding popcorn boxes or a bag of crisps, gave them a brief glare to warn them against talking and other disruptive behaviour, and sat down.

A Christmas advert for Big House started on the screen, a clothing label for larger people. Richard knew of the advert because DCK, the low budget agency that had taken him on at extortionate wages when he'd first arrived in London, had been raked over the coals for it. Obesity was a sensitive issue and agencies generally considered the concept too difficult. But ever since Mattel launched more realistically proportioned Barbie Dolls, large person labels were getting more popular. Public opinion was changing and Big House wanted to seize the day.

DCK's advert featured a typically plump Santa Claus. He parked his sleigh in the West End and bent over to pick up a sack of toys, causing his trousers to tear, exposing Santa's undies and leaving his ruddy face flushed. He rode his sleigh to Oxford Street where skinny, scantily clad mannequins posed in a shopwindow advertising 'Xmas specials'. Santa shook his double chin disapprovingly.

He passed another shopwindow displaying slightly larger mannequins. They looked like Barbie's 'curvy' doll — voluptuous, sultry, cleavage popping out like hardened balloons. They were advertising *Xmas* clothes for the 'robust individual'. Santa puffed his cheeks and moved on. He approached a third shop with custom-made extra-large mannequins on display. One of them proudly presented a big arse in tight red jeans. 'Merry Christmas, from Big House. Xtra large size clothes for Xtra big people.' Santa wobbled off his sleigh and entered.

'Big House has unapologetically dragged Santa Clause into the sewers of commercialised sexuality and hyper body awareness,' *The Guardian* wrote online. 'Think of the children.'

'Santa Claus is too fat and it's time he went to the gym.' *The Daily Mail* added.

DCK itself was targeted for 'normalising' obesity, 'thoughtlessly sending yet another reckless message to children in an era where childhood obesity was at an all-time high.' The PC brigade joined the feeding frenzy, finding offence in Santa's rejection of the word *Xmas* in favour of the word *Christmas*. They said they had a right to celebrate the holiday season without 'invoking Christ'.

Richard remembered giggling at his office desk while reading the abuse on DCK's Facebook site. After all, it was Richard who'd inspired the factory agency to take an 'edgier' approach to its campaigns, but this was a giant misstep. Fashion followed trends, which followed social media, and there was no way fashion-savvy customers were going to wear the Big House label while the internet was ripping it to shreds. But watching the advert now with Lena, he felt sad. Fake. Alone.

Richard hadn't enjoyed Christmas since he was six. That year he'd asked Santa for a new easel because the one he'd been given three years ago had disappeared. He'd been using it every day to paint Mum, to paint Dad, short and tall parents standing together, to paint the strange beings and landscapes he saw in his dreams at night. But then it disappeared from his bedroom one day and he had to draw on newspaper with pens instead. He didn't like it because it wasn't as colourful, and his dad didn't seem to like the pens either. Whenever he walked past, Dad made an agitated swallowing sound in his throat, accompanied by a click.

A week before that Christmas, Richard had heard his dad criticising his mum for 'encouraging the boy'. He overheard the conversation because he'd woken from a nightmare. His parents didn't know he was awake because by then he was so used to bad dreams that he didn't scream anymore.

'He's off with the fairies,' Dad said. 'And he's been drawing on my newspapers with bloody pens. It's gotta stop, Cherise. Enough's enough.'

Richard thought he heard Mum crying but the main thing he remembered was that he didn't like drawing in front of Dad anymore. He wondered if he had hidden his easel. He didn't ask. Instead he wrote to Santa and requested a new one.

Christmas morning came but there were no presents under their little tree. Mum and Dad drank eggnog and gave him hot chocolate before they all went to lunch at his aunty and uncle's house. To Richard's joy, there was a little box waiting under tree with his name on it. Unlike the tree Dad put up — small, proportionate, plastic — this tree was real, messy and large, full of decorations with a beautiful angel on top with silver hair.

Dad collected the box but rather than give it to Richard in front of everyone and the angel, he took him out back to where his uncle had built a small fishpond in the concrete yard, a fishpond Dad always liked to inspect whenever they visited.

'Santa didn't come this year,' he said to Richard, watching goldfish rise slowly to the surface to look at the tall man and his 10-year-old son.

Something stung inside Richard's little chest. He felt betrayed, either by Santa or Dad, he wasn't yet sure. The fish in the pond could tell something was wrong too. They flapped and splashed in the water, trying to swim away, but there was nowhere to go.

'Do you know why?' Dad said, his head inadvertently shifting with the movements of an agitated goldfish. 'Because he doesn't exist.'

Dad pulled his gaze from the pond and stared at Richard, pupils slitted like a hunting cat. He handed the parcel to Richard and asked him to unwrap it. Inside the wrapping was a calculator, a Casio, but before Richard could open its packaging, Dad took it from him, opened it himself, exhaled a great breath and held out the calculator like it was a sacred object.

'Numbers, son,' Dad said as Richard took the Casio. 'Numbers are everything. Santa Clause is nothing but a number, something they made up for the sake of retail. It's *all* about commerce, son, and the sooner you realise that, the better.'

Dad turned his gaze back to the pond where Richard saw that the fish were no longer moving. They were floating as if dead, all except one that rose to surface and bared tiny little teeth that had no place on a goldfish. Richard jumped, turned to his dad but he was stepping inside the house. He told Richard to wait until they were home before switching the calculator on and closed the door.

As soon as the door latched, the little piranha splashed away and the rest of the fish sprung back to life. It was as if they'd been playing dead. Richard wished then that he could play dead as well. It seemed the only way Dad would leave him alone. He dragged himself inside with the calculator in his hands and looked up at the silver angel but her eyes were no longer smiling. Her eyes were sad and worried like Mum's.

Feeling just as empty in a London theatre some 21 years later, Richard watched the beautiful girlfriend he'd known less than a year shake her head at the movie screen.

'I'm just glad you didn't do that advert,' Lena said.

'I could have,' Richard said, rubbing his cheeks with the backs of his hand, wanting suddenly to bury his face in her neck and cry. 'Santa

Claus has been getting screwed by advertising ever since they turned Christmas into a shopping mall. This is nothing different.'

'But it's stupid,' Lena said as the lights went down. 'It's obviously going to annoy people.'

'DCK got it wrong,' Richard agreed, watching latecomers enter the auditorium. 'But sometimes it's best to annoy people. It's the only way they pay attention.'

Lena gave Richard a weird look and started talking about a barrel-tasting event in West London, a start-up wine label he should pitch his work to.

'At least with alcohol adverts you can afford to be daring.'

Richard nodded and agreed, but more latecomers were skipping up the stairs. He linked his hands behind his head, raising his elbows to discourage anyone from sitting directly behind them. Lena continued to murmur in the background and he continued to nod and agree, but his eyes were on a group of teenagers who'd entered at the last minute. Richard's chest tightened. He rose his elbows as high as possible until two orbs glowered at him in the screen's reflected light. It was Lena. She hit Richard's leg and said he wasn't listening, that he couldn't just say 'yes'. He started to protest and claim otherwise, that she'd misunderstood.

'Of course I was listening,' he said. 'I was just thinking, alcohol advertising's on death row anyway. They're comparing it to smoking, you know, they want us to print rotten livers on wine labels.'

The teenagers were having a hard time finding a seat in the darkness. The couple behind them whispered loudly, told the kids there were seats next to them, moved further down the row to give them space. The teenagers sat directly behind Richard and he lowered his hands, defeated. The opening credits scrawled across the screen but it created an atmosphere Richard couldn't concentrate on because another teenager had entered the room, a boy loaded with two popcorn boxes and a Santa Claus gut. He stood at the base of the stairs, his silhouette outlined by the movie screen light.

'Oi, Darryl,' a teenage boy behind them shouted. 'We're up here.'

Darryl ascended a couple of steps and stopped, finding it difficult to see his friends in the dark.

'Oi,' his mate said again. 'Up here, ya tit.'

The teenagers laughed, as did a couple of other youngsters in the auditorium.

'Well I couldn't see yas 'cause it was dark, could I?' Darryl protested.

The back of Richard's neck prickled. He wanted to move to another seat. He looked at Lena but her eyes remained focussed on the screen. He risked a glance at the kids, watched the last teenager pass a box of popcorn to the girls sitting directly behind Richard. He slumped lower into his seat, using the top of the backrest as a sort of soundwave deflector, and then it started — the popcorn munch. The first crunch punched his eardrum. The second gripped his brain. The teenagers' plastic fingers clicked and tapped at the cardboard container. From behind Lena he heard Darryl get stuck into his own box of popped kernels, fingers ploughing into the cardboard box, rummaging, extracting a handful and shoving it into his mouth. *Crunch crunch crunch, munch munch munch.* Spilled popcorn pitter pattered to the floor. Richard convulsed but Lena ignored this. She was focussed on a movie that had made the point of starting quietly in the vacuum of space where sound couldn't travel. There was no music, no bass, nothing to block out the kids feasting, rummaging, munching, throwing popcorn around like it was confetti. It was all they'd come for, not the film, not the escapism, the thrills and special effects, just the munching and the fucking crunching. He looked at Lena again and still she was staring at the screen, ignoring his pain. On screen astronauts were talking quietly about numbers. Richard pleaded for something to happen, some kind of noise, explosions, a spaceship crashing, calculators blown apart through nuclear fission. Instead an astronaut was floating in a chair. It turned into George Clooney pontificating, and behind Richard the kids ate and ate and ate and he heard them swallow, snort, slurp those kernels like they were fucking drugs and he was standing up, jumping over Lena, hightailing it out of the auditorium with bleeding fingernail cuticles and his chest was stinging where his heart was failing and he ran to the bathroom and splashed water over his face and nearly vomited with the bugs that came with it but he had to get it together and he had to calm down and he couldn't breath and he punched his chest once, twice, three times, four times, to stop the pain, to keep his heart beating, to keep the air coming in but it hurt and Richard hurt and all he wanted to do was somehow fall asleep, wake up in space and have his brain sucked out through his eyes.

Lena eventually texted him from the auditorium and asked where he was. Richard wrote back and said he was outside on the verge of leaving. Among other things, she called him a crazy freak.

The next morning he woke her by moving his head around the pillow, trying to mask the sound of his throat as he swallowed, then swallowed again. A fish from his uncle's pond was swimming in his neck, teeth clicking with Dad's disapproval. But Lena didn't ask him what he was doing, what was wrong, why he couldn't just be normal. She suggested he rethink going home to Adelaide, that they could 'just go for a visit'.

'We don't have to stay,' Lena said.

But she didn't know about the fire Richard had started in Pony Ridge Scrub by burning another artist's paintings, the sessions with his court-appointed psychologist, the hatred of the neighbours. She only knew this man she'd travelled with overseas was showing signs of serious weirdness, and if it didn't stop, she'd have to wash him away with a load of her starch-smelling washing.

Constable Rory Sniles bowled into the screaming man in the pear orchard, slammed him to the ground, a piss weak, curly-haired scoundrel who was trespassing on a crime scene, *his* crime scene.

'What the fuck are you doing on my property,' Sniles growled, using his elbow to push the man's face into the dirt.

'Don't touch me don't touch me don't touch me,' he wailed, a whining, pathetic little voice breaking with fear.

Sniles rolled off the curly-haired fucker and ordered him to stand up. Leaves and grass stuck to the man's designer T-shirt. He was tall, at least three inches taller than Sniles, with a slightly gaunt face and earnest green eyes — the kind of artistic face that made girls gooey. It was ruined by two clusters of half-healed scratches on either cheek.

'What's your name?'

'Richard.'

'Why were you screaming?'

''Cause I … I thought I was being chased.'

'By who?'

'By … ' The man's tired green eyes blinked repeatedly. His Adam's apple wobbled up and down. 'Just some farmer. I was picking pears.'

'Bullshit. In those clothes?'

Richard looked down at himself and brushed leaves from his shirt. Sniles pulled an expandable baton from his belt.

'Listen, mate. The last time I caught a kid on my crime scene, it didn't end too well for them, you hear? You'd better start telling the truth.'

'I swear, man,' Richard said as Sniles extended the baton with a flick of his wrist. 'I was just picking pears, for my girlfriend, and I thought … I thought, you know, that you were an angry farmer and—'

Sniles jabbed his baton into Richard's gut so he folded over. He patted him down, finding nothing but a wallet, phone and a tube of antibacterial gel. Sniles threw them onto the ground.

'Tell me what you were doing out here, you little fuck.'

'There was a clown,' Richard stammered from the ground, wretched eyes filling with water. 'The Blackwood Clown. He lit yesterday's fire. He's after me.'

Sniles slammed the baton across Richard's knuckles.

'Shut the fuck up. You're the only clown around here. Where'd you get those scratches on your face?'

'I did it,' Richard wailed, his lips quivering. 'With these.' He twiddled his fingers in Sniles' face. Their nails were chewed, jagged, ruined. 'I've got issues.'

Sniles rose his baton, ready to strike. Yesterday's grassfire had destroyed an empty shed, a bit of grass, burnt a few vines in an out-of-commission-vineyard. The damage bill was so small nobody gave a shit, not after the catastrophic bushfires they'd faced earlier in the summer. Forensics spent barely two hours on the scene here, finding matches at ignition points, footprints from a man in sized seven work boots. Sniles had come back in the hope of finding something, anything, that might lead him to his prey. But Richard's shoes were too big for the footprints, even if they were covered in crime scene ash.

Sniles sighed and lowered his weapon. He had to act professional. He'd just found what he'd hoped to find, a lead, a suspect, a potential motherfucking scalp. The last thing he needed was to lose his temper and fuck things up like he had in Victoria.

'Your girlfriend, hey?' he said, collapsing his baton. The lunatic nodded, a strange hope flashing in his eyes. 'Pick up your shit. I'll give you a lift.'

Pyro's finger shook as he scanned the 'full body massage' listings in the newspaper, the Thais, the Chinese, the European 'beauties' offering Swedish massage. His index finger, singed in yesterday's fire, traced the print, separating the genuine from the happy enders. His other hand rubbed his beard, pulled at hairs.

'Idiot,' Mother declared in his head. 'You had your chance.'

'Shut up,' Pyro said to the steering wheel of his car where he'd parked in the Foodland carpark. It was that fucking policeman, that annoying son-of-a-bitch. He'd arrived at the worst possible moment, foiled everything. Pyro's finger landed on an advert.

ABSOLUTELY AWESOME F/B MASSAGE. Swedish. Soothing. Private.

'And that old couple saw you,' Mother said. 'You need to go back.'

'Shut up,' Pyro shouted, gripping a tuft of his stubble and yanking it out.

'You need to—'

'I'm not getting cornered like you, *Mother.*' Pyro took out his cigarette lighter and set fire to the tuft so it filled his car with the putrid stench of memories. He pulled the jar of hair from his pocket, possum hair, horsehair, kangaroo fur, memories of every animal he'd ever killed, a collection he'd started as a child when he'd taken beard trimmings from Father's razor. He shook it about, watching the memories tumble, rubbed his cheeks where Mother had once washed him clean with acetone. Pyro returned his attention to the adverts but noticed a man walking past his windscreen with a white fluff ball on a lead. He stared over the newspaper at the dog's hair, fingers twitching, his other hand flicking his lighter.

'Burn them,' Mother said, her lips curled and ugly. 'Burn them all.'

Pyro clambered from his Commodore and slammed the door, walking in the direction the man had taken. He pulled on his hood, kept his eyes straight, avoiding eye contact with those who were shopping, strolling, chatting. He spotted the fluff ball tied to a pole outside the bank. He approached and saw its owner lining up in a queue inside. He bent down and patted the dog, felt its hair, soft, long. He resisted an urge to pluck a piece out right there and then and instead let the dog lick him, trust him. Then he unhooked its lead and turned quickly away, led the little Maltese towards the station, turned left and followed the tracks to the old water tower at the railway station. The dog walked happily alongside, every now and then looking back as if it expected to see its master but not caring enough to stop. Pyro took it to a clump of bushes underneath the tower where the dog suddenly started to whimper. Pyro pulled on its lead, dragged it howling into the bushes where he strangled the mutt with the chord, pulled out his knife and hacked some hair from its torso, which he stuffed in his pocket for his collection of memories, burning a little so it shrivelled, flamed, smoked. Then he thought of Ashleigh, of her dirty friend, and wanted to burn.

The clown stories started when Richard was in Year 12. A student was walking her dog at Frank Smith Dam when she heard a 'horrible squeal'. She looked up to see a red-headed man in a white jacket step out from an olive tree. The teenager screamed and shouted at the 'fucking weirdo', threw stones, set loose her dog and ordered it to attack. The chihuahua pissed on her foot.

Another kid said they saw the Blackwood Clown while taking a shortcut across the football club oval. In those days it sat on the edge of civilisation with scrabbly scrub and cows on three sides, a black expanse that sucked up the night's light. But on this evening a person was shimmering from a sideline bench, wearing white. As the kid drew closer, a man lifted a face that looked like it had been painted on, 'like some weird fucking bird-face,' before he slumped and resumed staring at the ground.

'Man, that dude was *depressed.*'

Most stories came from Blackwood Forest, a hillside covered in pine trees planted from the late 1950s to replace an orchard. Students said the clown would shriek from the trees, never closer than 30 metres and, if anyone approached, he would piss off via rabbit tracks and disappear. The forest was also home to what they called the Clown House, an old building abandoned to rot in the pines. Kids hung out there on Friday or Saturday nights to drink beer and get stoned. The place was covered in graffiti. Broken beams and nails stuck out. They said the clown grew up as an only child in the house, a loner who dressed like a clown before he snapped one day, killed his parents and burnt their bodies in the basement.

Richard never believed that. It was just an old orchard manager's house, rented out for years until it was abandoned. But there was something horrible about the building all the same, something dark and hateful, and Richard didn't like hanging out there. Nor did he like that he was back in the mix with such stupid shit after just one morning with Lars and Donnie. Worse, he was back in the hands of the law, a violent policeman who'd practically dragged him by the ear to the house of woman he'd done his best to leave behind.

The door opened and Ashleigh appeared, her blonde bed hair a mess. She wore an oversized Primus T-shirt and possibly nothing else. She looked incredibly alluring to Richard. Her eyes lit up as she saw him for the first time since he left for London, flittered over the scratches on his cheeks, the dirt and ash covering his clothes, the angry policeman at his shoulder.

'Sleeping late, Miss?' Sniles asked.

'Sure. I worked the night shift.'

'Honey, this is a policeman,' Richard said quickly, before she could say anything or dare to act like she hadn't seen him in a year. 'I was on my way over and stopped to get pears from Magarey Orchard and—'

'Richard, you've gotta stop doing that,' Ashleigh said suddenly, stepping forward and sliding her arms around his midriff. 'One day they'll catch you.'

'And …' he hesitated, her green eyes peering up at him, smiling, sharing the joke. Unlike everyone else, Ashleigh hadn't changed a bit since he left. She looked radiant, flushed cheeks, a face bursting out of its skin with vitality. 'There was a fire.'

'Another one?' Ashleigh asked, a flash of concern. She slid a hand across Richard's stomach, warm, familiar, dangerous.

'Yesterday's fire, over at Olave Valley.'

'Not two kilometres from here,' Sniles said, his wolf mouth seeming to grow and extend towards her. 'Where were you at 11am yesterday?'

'I was at Richard's, of course,' she said, recovering her smile, waiting for Richard to acknowledge an alibi that didn't exist.

Sniles stepped past to peer into the orange-lit lounge room, a neat, well-kept space despite its faded 1960s carpet. He pulled out a notebook and demanded Ashleigh's phone number, her details, raised his eyebrows when Ashleigh said she lived next door to one of Richard's friends, Lars, and that he was out with Donnie. The constable took their names as well but then his walkie-talkie crackled with police talk, something about a dog. He stepped outside to respond. Richard started washing his hands with antibacterial gel but Sniles called them both outside.

'You two been paying attention to what's happening in this bloody country? Look how bloody dry it is out there.'

He pointed at the Blackwood Pine Forest reserve on the other side of Ashleigh's cul-de-sac where several hectares of Monterey pines stood in disorderly rows up the hillside. He pointed to Archibald Reserve next door, a grassy, scrub-covered corridor running behind a strip of houses to connect Blackwood Forest with Turners Avenue and, beyond that, Olave Valley where the fire was lit yesterday. He pointed at Ashleigh's unkempt yard, its long, dirty grass, its banksia bushes, the bark littering the ground from gum trees in the reserve, and then the unkempt mess of Lars' house on her far side where a dead lawn was nearly consumed by a massive bottlebrush shrub.

'You're in the thick of it. One bloody spark around here and the whole place goes up, you hear?' Sniles assessed Richard's face for a moment before climbing into his car and starting it with a supercharged roar. 'Clean up your fucking yard.'

He tore away and Ashleigh took Richard inside, gave him a glass of water and settled him into an armchair. She sat in the chair opposite and strummed her unplugged electric guitar. Richard kept his eyes on a gap in the orange curtains, pretending not to notice her glancing at him. He rubbed his hands together. Their skin was dry and red.

'Thanks for vouching for me,' Richard said.

'Mmm hmm,' she said.

'I needed a reason to be out there, you know, because of—'

'I know.'

'Fucking Lars and Donnie,' Richard blurted out. 'I left this shit, you know? I fucking left it, but those idiots had to take me back to their forest, didn't they? Just so I could get chased by some bloody freak dressed as a clown.'

'The Blackwood Clown?' Ashleigh asked, her blonde hair more buoyant than ever. 'He's harmless.'

'Oh, yeah. Real harmless. He started a fire and wrote my name on a tree.'

'He what?' Ashleigh lowered her guitar.

'My name, right next to the bushfire, telling me to burn it all.'

'Why would he do that?'

'Because he's got it in for me, that's why, because he thinks I …' but Richard stopped. They'd never told Ashleigh anything about what they'd done, how they'd trespassed inside the old Quaker's house and burnt the paintings of some artist who'd apparently turned out to be the Blackwood Clown.

'Richard?' Ashleigh put her guitar aside and stood up, pulled the centre table towards him, sat on it so she was directly in front of him. Richard wanted to close his legs but couldn't because hers were between them. 'Are you okay?'

'Not now, Ash,' he said, gripping the armchair, its surface sweaty under his palms.

'I can tell you're not okay.' She paused and her scent stood up, stepped from her body, and settled upon Richard. It invoked sweet memories of their past — kissing behind the art building at school, losing their virginity on her parents' couch. She frowned and above her right eyebrow a tiny little scar revealed itself, the one she'd received years ago from her little brother wielding a toy Star Wars lightsabre. 'Is it Lena?'

The name smacked Richard in the forehead.

'I don't wanna talk about it. I got chased and that constable thinks—'

'She left you, didn't she?'

'Yes,' Richard said, deflating, prompting Ashleigh's eyes to glow greener and her cute scar to disappear.

'Was it bad?'

'We're taking some … time out, I guess,' Richard continued. 'I just needed to get back on my feet. Get a job and get over the, you know, the disappointment.'

'In Lena?'

'In me,' Richard said, Ashleigh's familiarity, her scent, tugged him along, urged him to talk. 'Things in London … they were going well but then … I got a chance to hit it big but I didn't want it, you know? Advertising isn't art and it was a mistake to get involved and I just … wanted to destroy it, I guess, and my boss was a sleaze who wanted to fuck Lena and—'

He stopped when Ashleigh grasped his hands, warm fingers prising his own from the armchair, bringing his hands together, clasping them inside her own. She leant forward and peered up at him again from below her blonde hair, one of her knees resting gently against his inner thigh.

'What about the rest, Richard?'

'Hmm?' It was all he could manage. Ashleigh's reckless, gorgeous spell was stronger than ever.

'What's happening inside your head, Richard. Your face, your hands.' She turned them over, exposed their backs. They were decorated with tiny cracks where his skin had dried and pulled apart.

'Not now, Ashleigh.' He jerked his hands out of her grip and wiped them against his jumper.

Affection crawled over her face. He wanted to run outside and peel skin from his body, stand under a garden hose on full pressure, cleansing, disinfecting, repeating, but she leant forward and put her hands on his cheeks, pushing her bare knee closer to his crotch.

'Richard,' Ashleigh breathed with sweet, steady, undeniable power, swallowing him with warm eyes, a far cry from everything he'd lived with Lena, ambitious, flabbergasted, disappointed Lena.

'Is it …' She straightened her back so her T-shirt lifted and Richard saw she was wearing underwear, white underwear. 'The *piranhas?*'

Richard reeled backwards, his head dunked into an aquarium and shamed, angry with Ashleigh for daring to *verbalise* them, angry with himself for revealing so much in that damned court room a year ago. But just as quickly his anger collapsed, a plug pulled from a piranha-filled bath. Emotion rose in his chest, sadness, defeat, depression and tiredness, such tiredness. He realised he was about to cry. Tear ducts started to release moisture. His nose started to fill. He would upend himself into Ashleigh's T-shirt and be snagged by Blackwood forever.

'I'm fine,' he said, standing up, realising with dismay that he had a semi-erection.

Ashleigh had seen it too.

'I've gotta go.'

Richard walked to the front door and made the mistake of turning to look back. She remained seated, the curl of a satisfied smirk on her beautiful thin-but-not-too-thin lips. He realised that even though he'd walked away from her, even though he'd resisted the urge to fall into her sweet-scented trap, she'd taken control of the greatest autonomous function of them all and they both knew it.

Richard left the door ajar on his way out.

BLACK MOZZARELLA

According to court transcripts Constable Sniles found in Richard's file, the lanky man burnt 'intellectual property' in the yard of the property he rented from his parents in December 2018. A gust of wind lifted the burning pages and blew them into Pony Ridge Scrub to the north of his property. Grasses dried by summer ignited. Flames gripped onto bushes and within ten minutes it had spread 60 metres on a trajectory parallel with the access lane to his house and the backyards of much bigger houses on Fourth Avenue.

By the time it was contained the blaze had burnt four hectares of uninhabited reserve and threatened at least three properties, one of which was Richard's. All were saved, which was lucky considering where the lanky fucker lived. Fourth Avenue houses were on a slope that led up to Sheoak Road and, beyond that, the Belair National Park — 835 hectares of scrub and European tree plantations. If the wrong wind had blown, the whole place could have gone up.

Richard was raked over the coals for starting the fire. Letters to the editor in the local newspaper suggested his house should have been left to burn.

'That way the dirty fire bug would take his arse out of the district,' a local wrote. 'Nobody up here's gonna give him a place to live now, nobody of sound mind that is, although maybe that's the problem. There's just too many damned nutbags up here.'

Their hatred for Richard wasn't surprising, considering the Adelaide Hill's long history with disasters. Sniles had researched them all, figuring they were the greatest threat to the district, and his greatest chance at earning respect by catching anyone who lit one. The worst was the Ash Wednesday fires of 1983, labelled that way for occurring on the first day of Lent. They killed four people in the hills and another 24 elsewhere in the state. It occurred after a 10-month drought and during a heatwave where temperatures rose to 43 degrees Celsius. Sniles remembered as a 10-year-old the same conditions across the border in Victoria. They fuelled fires that killed 47 people, creating a total of 75 fatalities — the deadliest bushfire in Australia's history at the time. It was made more severe by a gale-force wind change that occurred just before nightfall. It pushed a corridor of flames that stretched in one direction all day to the north-east and created a massive fire front kilometres wide that tore through the land at 110 kilometres per hour. Tests based on melted metal later suggested temperatures of 2,000 degrees were produced — conditions similar to those created by the Hiroshima atomic bomb.

The Black Sunday bushfire of 1955, which had come as close to Blackwood as Upper Sturt just eight kilometres further up the hill, was the next deadliest fire. It killed two people, laid ruin to 40 homes and, bizarrely, seemed to target Adelaide's high society. Governor in Residence, Robert George, and his family escaped incineration by sheltering outside under wet blankets while their summer residence, the Marble Hill mansion, was destroyed. Just over a kilometre away, Premier Sir Thomas Playford had to take shelter with five other men in a patch of hoed earth at Cherryville.

It was the region's most dangerous fire since the Adelaide Hills Bushfires of 1939, which occurred during a 14-day heatwave where the city of Adelaide recorded its highest ever maximum temperature of 47.6 degrees Celsius. It was the biggest bushfire the settlers had yet seen and authorities were shocked by its ferocity. Thirty fires raced across the district, destroying about seven houses in Crafers and Upper Sturt, and ripping through sections of the Belair National Park. It had drawn an unprecedented response from the city as 5,000 volunteers arrived in 300 lorries to fight the blaze with tree branches, wet sacks and bucket brigades.

Blackwood itself had been given its own taste in 1934 when a blaze tore towards it from Belair, moving at speeds too fast for some 450 firefighters to stop. Articles reported flames 150 feet high and a heat so intense that firefighters regularly had to retreat. Outhouses and cottages were destroyed, most notably the homestead property of 'Wittunga' — owned by imminent naturalist and ornithologist, Edwin Ashby. Firefighters and helpers managed to retrieve the elderly man's collection of bird skins, eggs and butterflies just in time, along with his invalid wife, who was unable to escape on her own.

Other prominent buildings lost to fire in Blackwood included the Parade Childcare Centre in 1986, which burnt to the ground after a former staffer named Helen Lawson lost her mind and set it alight, killing herself in the process after the kids escaped with another staff member. Caddy's Tavern, a two-storey colonial style building made from recycled jarrah at the edge of Belair National Park, went up in a spectacular blaze six years later in 1992.

So when Richard burnt four hectares of Pony Ridge Scrub in 2018 and risked the properties of his neighbours, the fact it was accidental drew little sympathy. It happened just three months after he deliberately set fire to a tree in his front yard, which also brought out the CFS. His lawyer argued on that occasion he was trying to remove an annoying bird that had been disrupting his sleep. Residents argued it was proof of prior intent for Richard's latest attack and wanted him jailed. He was ordered to undertake a full psychiatric assessment and diagnosed with acute obsessive compulsive disorder. He was fined $3,000 for the fire and ordered to visit a psychologist every fortnight for three months. Local residents sent him nasty letters and, on at least one occasion, threw horseshit at his front door. They even petitioned to have him sent from the district. Authorities dismissed that request but for a time they got their wish anyway. Just three months after the fire Richard left on a plane to London. One year later in 2020, however, he was back, and within a week Blackwood was burning.

To make matters worse, people were already on edge thanks to the previous month's Cudlee Creek bushfire. Bigger fires had swallowed half of Kangaroo Island, demolished parts of the eastern seaboard interstate where a megafire spread into places that hadn't seen fires in hundreds of years. More than 24 million hectares went up in smoke and 33 people died. The media were calling it 'Black Summer'. A fire historian had gone so far as to declare it the beginning of a 'Pyrocene' age, a 'fire epoch' brought about by climate change and a lack of rainfall. With such theories circulating, Richard's neighbours would stone him to death if they heard he was suspect for arson again.

'What kind of parents press charges against their own son, for fuck's sake?' Sniles said aloud in the office as he closed Richard's file. Unfortunately Constable Dawksted wobbled past at the same time.

'Your shift finished three hours ago,' he said, a double chin flapping under his jaw. 'And it's Sunday, Sniles. Don't you have a partner—'

'She's busy,' Sniles said, noticing the look in Dawksted's eye, a rude son-of-a-bitch searching for weakness. But he checked his phone and the fat fuck was right. It was 9pm and he'd been researching for three hours. Worse, he'd missed a text message from Jenny, a simple question mark. No call, no show of concern, just a strong indication that she was pissed off.

Sniles stuffed the phone back in his pocket and reminded Sniles he'd found a convicted arsonist on the site.

'There's a lot of maniacs in the hills, Sniles.' Dawksted pointed at his head and rotating his finger. 'It's all that wacky weed they smoke.'

'Yeah, and this one's an arsonist.'

Sniles brought up the SAPOL pyromaniac database. Most pyros were sneaky fuckers who used delayed incendiary devices, or targeted thick, isolated bushland that allowed them to sneak away unseen. Of the 237 pyromaniacs on SAPOL's database, none had ever splashed petrol over a hill in full view of a road, then done it again as a policeman approached.

Sniles mentioned this to Dawksted but he looked at him with a small smile on his lips.

'Playing detective, are we?'

'Piss off.'

'You said it yourself,' Dawksted laughed, leaning against the wall. 'Your suspect's feet were too big for the footprints they found and he was too tall to be whatever prick you think you saw.'

'The old couple saw him too.'

'At that distance those old codgers couldn't tell the difference between an alpaca and an elephant. You ain't got shit, mate. What about the dog?'

'What dog?'

'You know, the one you're supposed to be investigating? Stolen, strangled, shaved. C'mon Sniles, we've all got a job to do, no matter how unglamorous.'

Sniles ignored him and concentrated on the computer monitor. He wouldn't be lectured by the likes of Dawksted. A couple weeks ago, he'd been sent to the Yorke Peninsula for a weekend country roads blitz. Dawksted pulled farmers over for dirt on their number plates, crossing the road in tractors, possession of a loaded weapon for shooting foxes. By the end of the weekend the local police station had three cartloads of sheep manure dumped on its doorstep. The fat fuck didn't know anything about community work, about *real* police work. Instead he'd knocked up more speeding fines and traffic infringements than anyone else in the division, not because he worked hard, but because he lacked discretion, lacked intelligence, was everything the public referred to as a 'pig' when they discussed the law.

'Did you check the CCTV?' Dawksted persisted. 'Foodland's security channel? The dog-napper was probably recorded.'

'I'm not interested in the fucking dog.'

'Hey, don't bite *my* head off.' Dawksted pushed off the wall he'd been leaning on with a flappy chin smile. 'I'm just trying to get you started. There'll always be pyros to catch, don't worry about that.'

Sniles left Dawksted chuckling and went home to find Jenny already in bed, her black hair a silent creature on the pillow. He ate some two-minute noodles, watched 20 minutes of shit on TV, climbed into bed and pulled her close, held her tight, did his best to be covered in her scentless embrace. She sighed with irritation and pulled away.

In the morning Sniles woke gasping, anxious he'd slept in. He listened for wind outside. There was no movement, no northerlies scattering the leaves of trees, just the sound of magpies warbling in the still air. Jenny murmured from the covers beside him and nudged him.

'Go on. Get up,' she said, pushing her partner towards the edge of the bed. 'I can't sleep while you're thinking so loud.'

Sniles changed his clothes, watching Jenny's shape rise and fall beneath the covers as he threaded his belt. He was working too much, mostly in his own time, getting lost in efforts that were probably futile. Jenny knew he needed a scalp, to make his mark in a new town, and she hadn't been able to find work herself. Despite being a highly respected psychologist back home in Mildura — with a never-ending list of depressed farmers and ice-hooked teenagers on her books — Jenny couldn't even get an interview. Talk of a potential pandemic had apparently put the job market on hold.

Sniles touched the covers tenderly. He would offer her a holiday after he took his scalp, a trip to the Barossa Valley. He'd suggest it tonight when he came home. But in the meantime, he had to keep it together. He couldn't risk losing his temper and fucking things up like he had in Victoria.

Sniles started his car and moved it gently down the driveway. Once he was away from the house he floored it. Warm air pushed through the vents — another hot day was brewing. He drove towards Belair National Park, a bushland playground separated from hundreds of houses by a single road around its perimeter. He'd spent hours patrolling the park since they moved here, usually out of work hours, and always when the northerlies blew. Such winds brought pyros to bushland like flies to shit.

Sniles reached the road where grey box gums overhung his passage in ways he didn't like, twisted, non-conforming umbrellas that turned the road into a tinderbox snake hole. He stopped at a T-junction, momentarily unsure which direction to go, but then the CB crackled. There was another fire back at Olave Valley, a structure in flames.

'Motherfucker.'

Sniles punched the ceiling of his VF Commodore and floored the engine so it scratched over loose gum leaves and gum nuts. He descended a steep hill into Hawthorndene and saw smoke in the distance. He roared through the chicanes of Turners Avenue, up the valley road, down the long driveway and past the old Quaker's house. Red CFS truck lights flashed alongside what was left of the second cottage, a smouldering wreckage that only two days ago had been protected by an elderly couple and their fire hose.

Sniles skidded to a halt, leapt out and flashed his badge at the nearest firefighter. A leather-faced man stepped backwards and nodded at the wreckage solemnly. Its iron roof was fully collapsed and resembled melted mozzarella that hissed and steamed.

Another volunteer stood next to smouldering iron where a broken brick chimney protruded through the mess like a devil's horn. The volunteer had death in his eyes and said nothing but pointed Sniles to the back of the wreckage. Here the roof was not so much melted cheese, but a flat, low-to-the-ground tomb encasing what Sniles already feared was an improvised coffin. He could see something hissing amid the mess, bubbles of oily fat steaming down its sides. Sniles leant in for a closer look, expecting to see the roasting corpses of two old people, but it wasn't. It was a four-legged animal, its mouth open, caught in the act of screaming, its long neck twisted backwards and agonised.

The alpaca would never spit again.

The old couple limped from around the other side of the house, led by a paramedic. They were wearing pyjamas covered in soot. Sniles marched towards them.

'It was same arsonist as Saturday, right?' he said, prompting the old man to splutter into a coughing fit. 'Did you see him?'

'That bloody bastard,' the old man wheezed. 'He killed Lucy. The bloody bastard killed our Lucy.'

'She was squeaking and shrieking,' the woman said. 'You ever hear an alpaca squeak? Got me right out of bed or we would have been done for.'

'Yes, but was it the same guy? Can you confirm it was the same—'

''Course it was the same guy,' the old man snapped. 'I don't need to see him. He poured petrol all over the doors. It was only 'cause—'

'Of our darling Lucy,' the woman interrupted, nostrils flaring. 'She saved us. She burst inside and woke us up. It's just as well she did or we'd be cooked.'

Sniles looked them over. They were covered in soot, but not *that* much soot. He noticed too that the woman's hair lacked the curled ends synonymous with the kiss of flames, and even the man, who was mostly bald, had tufts of white hair sticking out from his temples unsinged by fire. There was something they weren't telling him.

'You were real lucky,' Sniles suggested, 'to escape unscathed.'

'Yeah, well Lucy didn't.' The old man erupted with another fit of coughing, his eyes red with tears. 'I'm going to miss the old spitter.'

The couple turned to look at the cooking alpaca. The hissing grew suddenly louder, changed into the wail of hot steel freezing. Inside the alpaca something popped, let off pressure and threw a pint of steaming fat over its roasting body. The CFS volunteer behind them vomited and staggered away.

Sniles ground his teeth so hard he felt a filling dislodge and crumble. He spat the broken piece from his mouth and told the couple to call their insurance company, find shelter for the night. He would call them later, talk further, press the old woman for whatever secret she was hiding. Sniles pulled out his phone and dialled the number of the only suspect he had and dared him, begged him, to have a blonde fucking alibi this time.

THE APPOINTMENT

Pyro needed to be taken away, distracted from the horror between his ears. Echoing screams, two old people trapped beneath a steadily heating corrugated roof that had collapsed too quickly, surprising Pyro as he stood outside drooling. He'd done what he was told. They should have burnt with their rotten alpaca but then *he* turned up. *He* came from nowhere and screamed his horrible scream, the horrible clown in white, the freak Mother really wanted Pyro to burn but couldn't because Pyro was a 'coward'.

Pyro wanted distraction, oil on his skin, a woman's dirty hands. Swedish. Soothing. Private. He drove out of the foothills to Mitcham in the city flats where he'd booked an appointment with a woman who'd turned out to be from New Zealand. She brought him into her scungy massage parlour and rubbed his back, his thighs, prattled on about the quality of her oils, asked where he liked to be touched, pushed deep within his legs, pretended to sigh, pretended to enjoy him.

'You want to turn over, honey,' the Kiwi asked, her blonde hair hanging flat over her naked, sagging breasts. It was nothing like Ashleigh's buoyant gold locks, Ashleigh who'd never so much as let him kiss her.

The Kiwi crawled up on the massage table, kissed Pyro's neck, let her hair fall on his face. She touched his hips as his mind switched between images of Ashleigh's beautiful face, the clown's stupid grin, the way he turned up at the last minute to save the old couple from their burning home with his magical fucking scream.

'You with me, honey?' the Kiwi panted, working harder, trying to tug his mind clear of rotting animal fur, if only for a moment, an intense, spine-contorting moment. But nothing happened, he remained as use-lessly floppy as ever.

Swedish. Soothing. Impotent.

'Awww,' the Kiwi sighed as Pyro let go of her hair and brushed away her hand. 'That's okay, darling. You're probably just a little stressed, that's all.'

He hated it when they called him honey, or love, or sweetie, or any-thing fake. They said it as if they cared, as if they knew each other, would ever be anything to each other but a transaction and a memory Pyro had to burn. He covered his shame and pulled on his underwear, ignoring her false, unloving, contemptuous eyes that would light-up only if he suggested another appointment.

'I have something for you,' he said, pulling on his jeans and hoodie.

'Oh?' Her beady eyes shone with triumph.

'Hold out your hand.' He reached into his pocket and pulled out a jar of memories, pre-mixed with petrol.

'What is it?'

He poured memories onto her hand and lit a match.

'Numbers, Richard,' Dad said. 'It's all about numbers. They'll keep you honest and they'll keep you occupied.'

'It's good to be occupied,' Mum said. 'We don't want to see you lost, you know—'

'Like that useless kid Lars,' Dad said. 'Kid's not gonna know what hit him when he grows up. At least that Donnie's got himself sorted.'

It was 2007 and Richard was starting Year 11, the first of his senior school years, two years his parents were convinced were the be-all and end-all of his life. Donnie had made a 'smart move' by leaving school to start a trade, a fitter and turner, whatever the hell that meant.

'Plenty of work here,' Dad said. 'He could have made the parts for my Mitsubishi.'

Of course he had to mention his brand new, locally made Mitsubishi 380. He hadn't been able to stop talking about it since he bought it a month ago.

'That boy always did seem level-headed, despite his past,' Mum said.

'He knows his limits and that's the point,' Dad said. 'We can't all have our head in the clouds. You need to continue with mathematics, son. It'll keep you on the straight and narrow.'

'But people say the car factories are gonna close, Mitsubishi, maybe even Holden, and there won't be any cars made in Australia at all,' Richard said, standing as tall as he could. He was already taller than Mum but Dad still towered above him. 'I've heard everything's gonna come from Japan, or China.'

'Don't be smart,' Dad snapped, taking Richard's arm and leading him towards the aquariums. Twice a year they went to a restaurant in Chinatown. Dad liked to stand at the side of the restaurant, peer into the aquariums, point out to the Chinese waiters what fish he wanted to eat. If it was a new waiter, they'd look at him in surprise. The fish were supposed to be for ornamental purposes only.

'We subsidise auto-manufacturing in this country,' Dad said. 'For every buck the government puts in, they get three back on income tax from workers, and not just from the car manufacturers, but from the component industries like Donnie's, the service industries, all the flow-on industries. No government's gonna be stupid enough to let that go. Trust me.'

Dad turned to look at the fish swimming in circles. Sometimes he would use the ritual for a father-son connection moment — his version of taking Richard fishing. Mum would sit alone at the table, looking over the menu, glancing up nervously from time to time. The fish themselves would become unsettled, speed up their relentless circles, open and close their mouths and watch Richard's dad nervously.

'Your mother and I, we were disappointed you chose art as a contribution to your education certificate,' Dad said, bending his knees as he followed a fish to the bottom. It picked up some gravel and spat it back out. 'All that work I've put into your maths homework.' Watching over Richard's shoulder, forcing him to do more homework than necessary, unaware Richard was often stoned after smoking pot with Donnie and Lars after school. 'And you want to throw it away on something as flippant as art?'

Dad's head turned sharply as another fish, slightly smaller, flapped near the surface of the aquarium, agitated by its audience. It swam to the other end of the aquarium and looked back at Richard, gobbing. Richard realised he was pushing his thumbnails against the cuticles of each finger, one at a time, the same pressure for each, the same length of time. It was a little habit he'd caught himself performing recently. He shook his hands and stepped back from the aquarium.

'I don't know, Dad. I like art, but maths … I don't feel like it's me, you know? I just … I don't like it.'

'You don't like it?' Dad leant over Richard, looking him up and down. 'The world's full of things we don't like. I don't like having to work every day. I don't like picking you up at midnight from your friends' houses on Friday nights. I don't like paying bills, paying for your clothes, paying for food, this fish, this Chinese dinner you're about to be treated to. But I do it, don't I? We all do it. That's life, and I tell you what, if you take that course, follow your airy-fairy art tripe, you're gonna find yourself in a whole world you don't like. You'll have no direction, and without direction, a person gets real lost, real quick. Trust me. Waiter?'

A young Chinese waiter who'd been standing by the kitchen door hurried over.

'I want that one.' Richard's dad jabbed his finger against the aquarium so hard a fish nearly jumped from the water.

'But I don't like numbers,' Richard protested, his young voice breaking.

'And what are you gonna do with art, huh? You think you're gonna be famous? Who gave you that idea? That girl, Ashleigh? My advice to you, son, is to ignore the praise of bottom-feeders. People who aim low don't count for much.'

The waiter retrieved a net from the cabinet beneath the aquarium and dipped it into the water.

'Listen.' Dad pulled Richard aside and spoke quietly in his ear. 'You're in a very privileged position. You're one of the very few people who are lucky enough to have a job waiting for them after school. You finish Advanced Maths, Year 11 and 12. You study commerce at university, and you work for me part-time at the firm. After you get your degree, if you want a year or two to follow this art *hobby*, fine. But you get your career underway first, got it? You've gotta get something solid underfoot *first*.'

He backed away and behind him Richard got a glimpse of Mum wringing the menu anxiously.

'Direction,' Dad said, moving towards his wife. 'It's more important that you realise.'

At that moment there was a splash and drops of water hit Richard's cheek. The Chinese waiter was lifting dad's squirming fish from the aquarium.

'Good fish,' he said to Richard, nodding approvingly. The fish stopped twisting and contorted its suffocating head to stare at Richard, baring its little teeth as if it hated him, as if it blamed him for its imminent death.

'Fuck you,' the fish said.

Richard stumbled backwards in surprise and bumped into a table of diners. The waiter lunged forward to stop him from falling but instead smacked him in the face with the fish. He dropped the net and apologised profusely, dabbing Richard's face with a tea towel. The fish flapped about on the carpet, opening and closing its mouth.

'Fuck you fuck you fuck you fuck you fuck you.'

Another waiter swept in and rushed the swearing fish through the kitchen doors. Richard shook off the waiter and ran to the bathroom, washing his face with soapy water for five minutes. Fish didn't talk. Fish didn't bare their mouths like angry piranhas. That skunk Lars had been buying was bad news. He washed and washed but couldn't get rid of the fish smell. It seemed to be inside his nostrils. Eventually he gave up and dried his face with paper towel, staring at himself in the mirror. He would call Lars tomorrow and say he couldn't come to his party on the weekend. He needed a break from weed. But that was when he noticed his face was asymmetrical. His left eye was slanted and his mouth drooped to the left. Perhaps it was the mirror. Perhaps it was cheap. He brought his face closer but his mouth drooped even lower. Richard shook his head and backed away. He was about to throw the paper towel into the bin when he spotted blood on it. Startled, he saw that his fingers were bleeding from their cuticles. He'd been subconsciously digging his thumbnail into each of them again, one at a time.

'Fuck me,' Richard said to himself, looking in the mirror again. 'I've gotta stop smoking so much pot.'

But he didn't. He went to Lars' party. He smoked more skunk. He told Lars about the fish and he laughed. Everyone laughed. Everything crazy in high school was funny. But there was something wrong with Richard's throat. He could feel his heart pounding against his collar bone, accelerating, getting harder. He jumped to his feet and started walking in circles, did his best to keep up with his pulse. Lars laughed, everyone laughed. It was funny to see Richard walking in circles, faster and faster, his heart descending into his stomach, beating too fast, pounding too hard. Something was wrong. Maybe it was a heart attack. Maybe he was about to die. The air gushing in his ears told him he was about to die. He said he had to go and his voice was so deep, so distorted, so disconnected that its isolation panicked Richard further. His soul was leaving, austral projection at the moment of death. Richard ran from the party, expecting pain, expecting to drop dead, yet he made it home, then hesitated outside the front door because he could see Dad reading the *Financial Review* in his armchair, ready to sermon Richard about numbers, make him count how many beats per minute his heart was travelling, multiply it by days wasted in school studying art. Richard backed away and walked half an hour back to the party, his pulse regulating, his heart rate decelerating. When he got there Lars said he was just freaking out. He'd smoked too much skunk and had a panic attack and it would pass.

Lars was right, but two nights later when Richard smoked again, he lost his shit even worse. And this time it didn't go away, not completely. In the morning he had an autonomous terror in his chest, accelerating, decelerating, threatening to explode at any minute, a nutty fish banging its head against his rib cage. It dematerialised and re-materialised into a variety of different piranhas that attacked all his autonomous functions in the weeks, months, years that followed, swallowing, blinking, deflating, panicking, and nobody knew about it. Richard concealed it from everyone. He kept it secret until his lawyer advised him to come clean to avoid being jailed for arson and tell the court about his piranhas, the relentless little fuckers that came with a panic attack that never really stopped, and his dad was so disappointed, so embarrassed. Everything he'd wanted for Richard had dissolved with the fish food in one of Chinatown's aquariums. But while Dad had been wrong about the car subsidy — the government threatened to drop it in 2013, prompting Holden to say it was pulling out of Australian production altogether by 2017 — he was right about direction. People went fucking nuts without direction.

'Where are you right now, Richard? Hey? Right fucking now?'

Richard stood motionless as Currie Street swarmed about him. People going to work, a small Australian city filled with bustling direction. It was everything Richard didn't have. All he had was a constable who'd surprised him by calling from an unknown number, squeezing a wolf snout through the handpiece.

'I'm in Adelaide, in the city.'

'Bull-fucking-shit. You're in the hills and you've just tried to kill two people, you psychotic son of a bitch, only they got out, sonny. They got out and they're gonna point you out.'

It was his own fault. He should never have answered an unfamiliar number, certainly not when he was on his way to an impromptu job interview. But that was the problem. The director of Cedar Desk had called him late yesterday on an unknown number. Richard had only answered because there was a chance it might be Lena. Instead it was an agency he'd doorknocked with his resume a year ago, asking if he'd drop by their city offices on Monday morning. They'd heard about his work in London and, bizarrely, wanted to speak about a potential job offer. After all that time trying to get attention a year ago, it had taken a trip to the UK, a disastrous expedition that had cost him his girlfriend, to get it. Richard tried to refuse, but the agency director wouldn't have it.

'I've just got here,' Richard told the angry constable. 'I've got an interview.'

Sniles stopped spitting long enough to listen to the city traffic surrouding Richard.

His voice grew angrier when he realised Richard was telling the truth. He warned Richard that he was a suspect, that he was being watched, that he was gonna call his 'blonde fucking girlfriend', but then there was shouting in the background, something about an attack on a massage parlour, an emergency siren starting up.

'Just don't you fucking go anywhere, lad,' the constable said in an ultra-throaty voice, as if he was swallowing the phone. 'You or your *girlfriend.*'

The line went dead. Richard dropped his phone to the pavement, covered his head with his hands, a ball closing in on itself among people who wouldn't stop hassling him.

'Are you okay?' a female voice said as somebody rested a hand on Richard's spine. He stood up, throwing the hand from his back. A middle-aged lady in loose black clothes and a leopard-pattern scarf looked back at him with kind eyes, but they were ragged, tired, beaten, possibly a victim of a piranha-like affliction herself.

'I'm fine,' Richard said. 'I have an interview.'

He picked up his phone, smiled, and walked onwards towards the offices of Cedar Desk, racing a dark cloud of piranhas that had been congregating in the air above. He found the glass doors of the advertising agency and entered an open-plan building filled with colourful plastic chairs, designer tables, young creatives at work with their heads down.

'Richard?'

It came from a man in his late 40s. He had heavy dark stubble, short grey hair, lines of hard work in his face.

'Thanks for coming in at short notice,' the man said, holding out his hand with a wicked smile that should have included a silver tooth. 'I'm Max.'

Max didn't wait to see Richard wipe his hand on his pants but led him to a boardroom in the back corner of the room equipped with a coffee machine. Richard declined the offer for a coffee. Max made one for himself while Richard stood wondering what this man wanted with him, if Constable Rory Sniles would ring him again, if he should call Ashleigh to tighten the alibi.

'You're in the wrong place, Richard,' Max said, operating a milk steamer that shrieked.

Richard blinked, brought suddenly from his thoughts.

'Adelaide's fucked, mate. Why'd you come back?'

'I … err,' Richard stammered, surprise, discomfort and the aroma of fresh coffee forcing him into the present moment. 'My girlfriend was homesick.'

'Homesick?' Max glanced at him with astonishment before approaching the table. 'Take a seat.'

They sat down and Max pulled a leather coaster across the redwood for his mug of coffee.

'This place is one decade away from being a desert outpost between east and west. You should have gone to Sydney.'

'I wasn't aware it was so hopeless,' Richard said, hearing his father somewhere in China yell with protest, slam a hand on a desk, threaten to ground this entrepreneur for speaking ill of Adelaide.

'Holden's gone, Mitsubishi's gone, mining's fucked, manufacturing's fucked. Everything's getting made in China. Shit, there aren't even any jobs in agriculture. They use machines for that.'

'Yeah, my friend's just lost his job. He was a fitter and turner in a factory that—'

'Went belly up after Holden left,' Max said, sipping his coffee, taking in the scratches on Richard's face, looking at his hands, his fingernails. 'That fucked everyone up. Did you hear that General Motors is culling the brand for good? What a disaster.'

'Well, you're probably right about Sydney,' Richard said, clasping his hands together. 'But Adelaide's—'

'Run by a bunch of stiff old baby boomers mate.' Max's face flashed a passionate red. 'A bunch of old cunts stifling progress, stifling youth, buying up everything and blocking everyone. Anyone young with any sense is moving to Sydney, or Melbourne. You could have gone to Melbourne.'

Max sipped his coffee again, eyeballing Richard, sizing him up.

'Still,' he said before bursting into sudden laughter, deep, hearty, loud. 'You sure as shit couldn't stay in London.'

Max's eyes shrunk with humour.

'I, er …' Richard heard himself saying, feeling saliva form in the back of his throat. 'Why did you ask me here?'

'You really fucked up over there,' Max laughed, sipping his coffee again.

'Yes, I know I … I messed up, but—'

'The world's changed, son. Your ads, they would have been okay ten years ago, but it's all PC now, mate, the New Morality. You can't fuck with that, not in print, not in broadcast, and definitely not online. Shit, social media's the great judging room of the 21st century. There's no room for satire or social commentary anymore. Forget it. And heaven forbid you poke fun at the sacred sanitary product.' Max chuckled again, swigging at his coffee. 'You gave me a good laugh, son. And man, that Gold Dog campaign. No wonder you bailed out to let the old bastard deal with *that*.'

'Old Man Stanley?' Richard asked in a small voice. 'You know him?'

'Yeah, I know him,' Max said. 'He still got those crusty old blinds on his window?'

Richard nodded.

'I used to work there too, you know. I wrote the Smart Phone campaign.'

Richard's mind crawled through a pile of stupefaction as Max looked at him like he should know what he was talking about.

'You know, the $1.5 million contract that got the old bastard back in the game?'

'Yeah, it was something to do with—'

'The talking fucking phone, before Siri and Cortana, before smart-phones themselves. That was mine and it went berserk, made them millions, put Barlett & Co on the circuit.'

'So what happened?' Richard asked, scratching his neck, clawing for some kind of anchor. 'Why'd you … when did you come back to Adelaide?'

Max stopped smiling, sipped his coffee, set it down decisively.

'You're an eccentric son-of-a-bitch, aren't you?' he said. 'All these scratches and shit on your face, you're messed up, right?'

Richard didn't answer but for a second thought he saw some kind of desperate fish swim across Max's own eyes, a sad, unhealthy fish.

'It's okay. Let me ask you something. If I had to come up with an idea to market crisps, what's the first thing that comes to your mind?'

'Make them sound healthy,' Richard heard himself say. 'It's the only way to cut through.'

'And if they're not?'

'Put truth in the small print. Nobody has time for the small print.'

'A new chocolate bar?'

'Palm oil free. The chocolate's made from a sustainable cocoa bean plantation.'

'Is there any such thing?'

'In the wording. It's all in the wording. Who's gonna travel to the Congo to find out?'

'A small car?'

'Market it to professional 20-year-olds, hipsters, city people who generally—'

'Don't know shit about cars?'

'That's right,' Richard said, feeling himself in a daze, unsure what was happening.

'What about furniture?'

'As in—'

'Kits you take home to put together yourself, you know, Ikea kind of shit.'

'Market it to the same demographic, only throw a few heterosexual men into the adverts, you know, but take the Mickey out of them. The woman wears the pants in the store, makes the choice because the man's choice is daft. When they get the kit home, the man struggles to put it together, but the woman hands him the right tool, and he finishes it, not because she couldn't do it, clearly she could, but because she knows that she has to let him feel useful, because at the end of the day, while it's obvious men are useless, a smart woman knows it's better to make them feel useful.'

Max beamed and started clapping.

'See?' he said, clapping some more. 'You do know what's going on out there. Advo-culture, that's what I call it. Stories that pander to whatever social movement is swinging on any given day. Which is why,' Max stopped clapping and looked dead into Richard's eyes, 'what you did in London was genius.'

'What?' Richard said, coughing sharp. 'No. I was trying to get out. I was trying to—'

'Oh, come on, Tampos, Big Cheese, I know what you did. It was perfectly subtle. Just enough to create outrage but not bad enough to be banned by the ASA. Your clients made a point of apologising publicly, but we both know they were very happy. Their sales went through the roof. And don't tell me any of it was Old Man Stanley's idea. He isn't nearly that sophisticated. How the hell did you get the old bastard to sign off on Big Cheese?'

Richard blinked. 'My girlfriend … he was into her.'

''Course he was, the dirty old jerk. Shit, did you ever smell his breath?'

Richard choked with surprise, let slip a little laugh, his first real laugh in months. Everything he'd done to exit the industry in London had impressed this guy. He was actually smiling as if Richard had something to offer.

'Here's the thing, Richard. I want you to come work for me. Adelaide, we're fucked mate. Nobody here's got any money, not to advertise, that's for sure, and now that this … this coronavirus thing is coming, it's going to make it even harder. That's why your strategy is perfect. I want to create campaigns that cost our clients fuck-all, but have high penetration on social media. I want to do that by pissing people off, with style, with subtlety, just the same as you did in London. I want patriots, radical feminists, bitter vegans, hardcore lefties, right-wing nut-fuckers, all of them smashing away at keyboards, sharing shit on Facebook, Twitter, in newspaper op-eds, making memes for Instagram, giving our clients more exposure than they could ever pay for, for free. Our clients will apologise and appease the populist press, do whatever they have to do to calm the outrage. Then I'll tell them to sit back and watch sales go through the roof as our target market, the silent *majority*, you know, those who can actually take a fucking joke, for fuck's sake, go out and buy what we want them to buy, not because our campaign was particularly good, but because the brand's been pummelled into their head, outraged across social media, regurgitated in the news thanks to an army of social media warriors who are too precious, too self-righteous, too fucking short-sighted to realise they've just been played, hook line and sinker, to advertise our shit for free.'

Richard blinked at this silver-toothed devil, this crazed man who wanted to harness whatever lie he'd lived in London, who was slapping his hand on the table and laughing.

'It'll be fucking brilliant.'

'I … ' Richard resisted another urge to laugh and felt the amassing piranhas outside hesitate. 'I kind of wanted a break from advertising, you know. It's a little … '

'Fake?' Max said curtly. 'Of course it's fake. That's the point. You're an artist, right? A musician who didn't make it, an unrealised writer perhaps, or a painter?'

Richard shrugged.

''Course you are. And that, my tall and edgy fucking protégé, is exactly why you're perfect. Nobody who actually believes in this shit does anything worthwhile.'

Max abruptly held out his hand for Richard to shake again, which he did, and it felt like a near-dead octopus, warm and limp.

'Take some time to think about it,' he said, standing up and kicking his chair backwards. 'I'll be in touch.'

Max led a confused Richard back through the white room, the fresh coffee smell, the colourful chairs, the ugly designers and mad fucking creatives. They lifted their heads as Richard passed, faces a little worried, eyes a little skittish. But then he was in the foyer and Max remained in the doorway, watching Richard, waiting for him to leave.

'Thank you … for being interested, I guess,' Richard said, feeling a little saliva rise in the back of his throat. 'I'll … I'll think about it.'

''Course you will,' Max said again, pushing the door open for him, looking again at the scratches on Richard's face. 'That much is patently fucking obvious.'

Max spun about and returned to his creative ugly.

WHITE ICE

The Asian slid her hands over Pyro's oiled back. She ran them down the back of his legs, upwards within his thighs. Pyro widened his legs, screamed silently at the masseuse to go lower, deeper, take him away.

'Turn over now please,' she said with broken English.

The Asian placed a cloth over his weeping eyes, hid his pathetic face, a coward who couldn't get it up — twice in the same day — who couldn't even get warm.

'You fucking pussy,' Mother said.

A coward who'd been too scared to burn the clown's house, who'd burned the old couple's instead. A coward who couldn't even ask Ashleigh out, a girl who'd been available for at least a year and a half. He had a chance two weeks ago when she hugged him, smothered him in perfume, but now her dirty lover was back and they were probably fucking in her little blue car right now, her shitty Hyundai Getz from South Korea, its little wheels bouncing, her perfect smile panting, hungry, unbearable, breaking open to show clown-teeth, white biting clown-teeth.

'No,' Pyro shouted.

'Eh?' the Asian said, grabbing his cock.

'Do it,' Pyro snarled.

The masseuse squeezed and pulled but he was all rubber with no spine. She frowned and grabbed Pyro's hand, pressed it against her breasts, 'oohed' and 'aahed' but it was useless. She clicked her tongue and gave up. Pyro got off the table to get dressed and collect his backpack but then she said something she shouldn't have: 'You been at bonfire?'

She motioned to Pyro's clothes and waved her hand in front of her nose, screwing up her face with mock disgust, before smiling at him.

Pyro grimaced back, avoiding her horrible, hard, paid-for eyes. She took his money, said goodbye, kissed him on the cheek and closed the door.

Pyro retrieved a jar of memories and a 10-litre can of petrol from his backpack. He sprinkled hair on the massage parlour doorstep, cat hair, rat fur, a few strands of his mother's hair. He threw petrol against the front door, splashed it against a side wall, and lit it with a single match. It created a percussive smash and the woman screamed from inside, a terrible mixture of surprise and mortal fear. Pyro doubled over, vomiting, suddenly crying, spitting snot from his mouth, and wondered if his father had shed the same tears when his mother went crazy, when his mother cut him off from his son, when his mother tried to cook the babies. But then a louder shriek rattled the building — an orchestra of flutists squeezed together by wire. The flames curled, shrivelled up and retreated, and from behind Pyro a gust of fresh wind flattened his shirt to his skin. A flash of white tore through the black smoke, a wailing spear with the power to turn fire to ice and the flames evaporated, the shrieking stopped, the white noise of conquered heat sizzled and suddenly the clown was standing between him and the parlour, staring at him, puffing as steam billowed behind him, a widening smile that could engulf Pyro, a fucking superhero gloating as the door behind him opened and an unscathed Asian starred gingerly out the door.

'Run, you useless cunt,' Mother loomed in his mind, fat, angry, hideous. 'Get the fuck out of here before he bites your knee.'

Pyro sprinted down an alleyway and clambered over a backyard fence. He ran down the side of the house and onto a footpath, down another side street, through another backyard where a large black dog barked in the curtains. He made it to his Commodore, started its locally made V8 with shaking hands and drove away into a crisscross of Adelaide's foothills, avoiding main roads and CCTV cameras. At one point he needed to pull over and vomit, but it was too violent, too fast, and all he could do was stop in the middle of the road, open his door, and let it all out onto the bitumen.

Dawksted walked passed the kitchen, stopped, poked his fat head through the door. 'Didn't get the call-up, Sniles?' he said, eyes glinting.

'For what?' Sniles said, pulling his milk out of the fridge. It was almost empty and he'd only bought it two days ago, using just a few splashes for his tea. He slammed it onto the kitchen bench for Dawksted's benefit.

'What? You haven't even heard,' Dawksted's eyes shone. 'Shit, Sniles. You've gotta pay more attention. The taskforce? Operation Dark Horse?'

'What, for the pyro?' Operation Dark Horse. South Australians loved their stupid operational names.

'Not the pyro, Sniles. A serial killer. That's two massage parlours in the same day.'

'Both of them burnt with petrol, just like at Olave Valley.'

'Will you give it up about your damned hills pyromaniac, Sniles? You're meant to be investigating the dead dog.'

'Fuck the dog. This guy tried to burn those two old *people* in the valley to death. Before he even got to the first massage parlour.'

'Well shit.' Dawksted clicked his tongue. 'Imagine if you'd caught him, you know, the day you were *there*.' A conniving look spread over Dawksted's face. 'What did you say the name of that weirdo you found out there was—'

'I didn't.' Sniles turned his back and continued making his tea.

'Because if you give me his name I might recognise it and—'

'If I need your help I'll ask.'

'No wonder you fucked up in Victoria,' Dawksted said, a hurt tone in his voice. 'You're a one-man-band. I've gotta go. I'm on the taskforce.'

Sniles hocked up a loogie and spat it into what was left of his milk, shook it up and placed it back in the fridge. If they wanted to drink his milk, they could have it. He stomped down the office hallway towards the briefing room where Dawksted's sizeable bulk leant against the doorway, blocking it.

Dawksted looked over his shoulder at Sniles' approach, an intolerable lizard-slit grin for a mouth. Sniles imagined for a moment leaping onto his shoulders and gauging out his eyes. Instead he planted a minor uppercut into Dawksted's left kidney. Dawksted ricocheted in surprise and nearly fell over.

'What the fuck, Sniles?' he whined with his pathetic high-pitched voice. The doorway was free and Sniles pushed past into the room where about six officers were seated facing an address from the superintendent.

'We'll conduct a doorknock of the street's residents and … ' The superintendent, a stocky crewcut man, stopped as Sniles stepped into the room. 'Sniles? What do you want?'

'I want to be on the taskforce.'

'I've enough resources already, Sniles, and—'

'I've seen the suspect,' Sniles said. 'I'm the only one who's gotten close.'

'I saw nothing from your grassfire report that offers a reliable description of anyone. You were too far away.'

'The arsonist I saw had a heavy build. That much was obvious, and the old couple gave a similar description. If you can find the surviving masseuse, she'll confirm it, I know it.'

A couple of the seated officers groaned with impatience. The masseuse had high-tailed it out of there before emergency crews arrived, more than likely a prostitute who wanted nothing to do with the law. They only knew it was a woman of Asian appearance because an irate neighbour across the road had seen her and her clients coming and going for a year. The lease for the building was in the name of a Chinese man, based in Shanghai, but he'd been difficult to reach.

'Sniles,' the superintendent sighed. 'This taskforce's purpose is to find a serial killer, a man with a fetish for burning sex workers. The Olave Valley fires are a separate investigation.'

'Listen,' Sniles said, a pulse in his forehead. 'Saturday's grassfire at Olave Valley was lit with petrol, right? The second fire at Olave Valley this morning, where both *witnesses* nearly died, was also lit with petrol.' The seated officers looked at him agitated eyes. 'You see what I'm getting at? Both parlour fires were lit with petrol. And with the exception of the Mitcham parlour fire, which is only 10 minutes' drive away, they were all in the same district. They're connected. I'm sure of it.'

'You're *sure*, are you, Sniles?' the superintendent said, relaxing his jaw.

'Well ... ' he faltered. 'I can't be *sure*, but petrol isn't commonly used by bushfire arsonists, is it? It's too sudden, leaves them no time to make their escape. It's violent and sporadic, right? Like this parlour killer, and ...'

'Give it up, Sniles,' Dawksted said from the door.

'And I have a lead,' Sniles said, facing the room's hostile eyes. 'A convicted arsonist I found on-site the day after the fire at Olave Valley. His own parents pressed charges.'

'His parents?' the superintendent said, looking suddenly curious.

'I ... I don't think he's the pyromaniac himself. His feet are too big for the footprints forensics found and he has alibis.' Another impatient murmur swept through the room. 'But it was odd that he was there. And his girlfriend too ... something about her doesn't stack up.'

'This isn't the bloody movies, Sniles,' Dawksted said, eliciting a guffaw from an officer or two. 'What sort of crap do you Victorians—'

'Shut up, Dawksted,' the superintendent said, returning hard, glimmering eyes to Sniles. 'Fine. Sniles, you lead the investigation into the valley fires, okay? We'll call it, Operation Hunch.' The officers sniggered. 'And Dawksted? You're with Sniles.'

'What?' Dawksted said, his voice high-pitched again. 'You're kidding. This guy's a—'

'That's all. I want this shit tidied up. We've got a potential pandemic situation on the way and the last thing we need is a bloody serial killer on our hands.' The superintendent glared at Dawksted, at the seated officers, at Sniles. 'Now get the fuck out of my briefing, both of you.'

Dawksted's frame moved backwards from the door, his fat face sweating with anger, beady little eyes marking out Sniles with contempt. Sniles couldn't help but grin. Victories, however minor, were few and far between.

'And Sniles,' the superintendent said. 'You find anything else, anything at all, that you think connects your investigation to Dark Horse, you give me a call, got it?'

Sniles nodded.

'Straight away, son. I don't wanna hear about any *heroes* with a point to prove.'

*

' ... any *heroes* with a point to prove,' Sniles' superintendent had said, uttering the word with a wicked grin.

The *Sunraysia Daily* had printed that word right above that damned nurse's picture of the unconscious teenager in Mildura, his face so swollen and purple that you couldn't see the red-head's freckles.

Hero.

It had pushed Sniles out of town, to an appearance in a Melbourne court. It nearly cost him his relationship with Jenny, and now his superintendent was driving in the nails like everyone else, denying him a blank canvas, ensuring Sniles couldn't forget his damned past for a minute.

'Motherfucker,' Sniles said under his breath, following Dawksted down the hallway.

But he didn't follow the fat fuck to the desks. Instead he slipped down the stairway to the basement, climbed into his car and tore out of the station. He raced an orange light and sped up Shepherds Hill Road, a duel carriageway back to the Adelaide Hills, a place without the headlines, hatred and shame of Mildura, a land that baked hotter than hell during summer and sizzled with fire-ready eucalyptus.

His new colleagues could laugh all they want, mock Sniles and drink his milk, but when he came in with a scalp bigger than their collective heads, they wouldn't be able to laugh. He'd shove it down their throats 'til they choked.

He pulled into the access lane for Richard's house behind Fourth Avenue. To his right was Pony Ridge Scrub, the trunks of scraggly gum trees black and scorched, their branches emerging with rejuvenated green leaves — the site of Richard's second fire in 2018. To his left were the backyards of houses fronting the upper side of the block. Richard's house was really just a box at the back of a large block, and the blocks were deep.

Sniles killed the ignition and sat quietly for a moment. The shutters of Richard's weatherboard box were closed and there was a Mitsubishi sedan in the yard. He wondered briefly if a man troubled enough for his own parents to press charges against him was secretly training a gun on him. Sniles dismissed the idea and opened his car door to be confronted with a guttural birdcall overhead.

Chika CHEE CHAA chika CHAA

'Bloody hell,' Sniles said, gritting his teeth and scanning a gum tree at the centre of the yard. The lower part of its fat trunk was scorched black — Richard's first fire, the one his parents said proved he had prior intent to burn Pony Ridge Scrub three months later.

The bird screeched again. Sniles looked up but was distracted by three flat pieces of black metal. They were fashioned to look like cats and dangled from the lowest, thickest branch. Sniles climbed out his car and saw that its entire length was wrapped with barbed wire.

'Fucking nut case,' he said before sucking in his breath. The trunk of the tree was littered with what looked like fresh axe marks, chunks thrashed from its side. The exposed flesh was starkly white compared to its black exterior. An axe head was wedged into the tree and fresh sap leaked from around its edges. Its estranged wooden handle lay at the base of the trunk.

Chika CHEE CHAA chika CHAA

'Damn, you're a noisy fucker,' Sniles snarled, spotting an ugly brown bird in the leaves, complete with a fleshy red wattle wobbling at its ears. His fingers twitched over his gun in its holster.

'Do me a favour and shoot it,' a voice behind him said. He turned to see Richard — tall, lanky and weird-looking — watching from his porch.

'You broke your axe,' Sniles said, reaching down to pick up its wooden handle.

'Fucking thing didn't work.'

'You're a real *hero*, aren't you?' Sniles said, feeling the weight of the axe handle in his hand.

'The bird's the hero. Shoot it and I'll be just fine.'

'Why would I shoot a little bird?' Sniles said, stepping towards the porch, slapping the axe handle against his palm. He noticed scorch marks at the base of the front window frame. Richard's second fire had spread to his house but the CFS had arrived in time to save it. ''Cause it bothers you? Do old people bother you too? Your parents perhaps?'

'My parents are in China.'

'No alibis there then, huh?' Sniles reached the first step. 'Not like Ashleigh, or *Cedar Desk*.'

'You rang *them*?' Richard stepped backwards on his porch as if Sniles had walloped him in the stomach. 'But he wants to give me a job. Why would you do that?'

'Because I don't like you.' Sniles slid up the concrete stairs. 'You or your girlfriend. I think both you little fuckers need to be cracked right open.'

Sniles raised the handle.

'I don't even want to be here.' Richard's lanky legs gave out and he crumbled onto the concrete.

'I can help you with that.' Sniles touched the axe handle to the side of the man's curly hair, marking the spot he'd like to hit. Jenny's angry face flashed through his mind and he hesitated, pulled back. But then Richard grabbed the handle and slapped it against his own face instead.

'Don't do that,' Sniles said, trying to pull the axe handle from Richard's grasp.

'Hit me,' Richard said, slapping himself again in the cheek with the handle.

'I said don't do that,' Sniles repeated, yanking the handle from Richard's hand.

Richard crawled after him on his knees. 'Hit me so it fucking stings.'

Sniles flung the handle away. The tall man crumpled into a heap, his back shuddering. For a moment Sniles felt empty, unsure how to proceed, the fuzzy rage that had welcomed him now in retreat. But his phone buzzed in his pocket. He pulled it out to see a text message from Dawksted.

Leaving a little early, aren't we?

'Motherfucker,' Sniles said, picturing himself swinging police boots by their laces into Dawksted's flappy double chin. He shook his head as Richard convulsed on the concrete before him, a twisted knot of anxiety with feet too big for Sniles' pyro. The pathetic sight drained what was left of Sniles' violent impulse.

'Just … take me inside for a quick look around, okay? Then I'll get out here.'

'Yes. Good.' Richard sprung to his feet and retrieved from his pocket the tube of antibacterial gel wash, held it out, eyes blinking, cheeks wet from tears. 'But do me a favour first, yeah? Clean your hands with this before you come in. I don't know where you've been.'

SUPER SNOUT

Richard's nose turned hyper-sensitive while he was working for Dad as an accountant in 2018. He would sit at his desk, the weight of his body pushing through his hindquarters, blood vessels flattening against the office chair, and smell the chlorine in his glass of Adelaide water. He'd smell the body odour of a co-worker from across the room, the perfume of the secretary by the door, ink in the printers, warm dust inside computer casings, the sweaty feet of a guy who rode his bike to work every day.

His strengthening sense of smell bothered him outside the office as well. Coffee addicts drove him crazy. They had breath like rotting fish. Smokers were more self-aware but no matter how much perfume they used, he could still smell the ash in their lungs. He was dating a girl called Matilda from his night classes at art college. She used charcoal to draw ballerinas in box-like cages. She had black hair, long eye lashes, laughed about things like accounting. But there was an issue with her mouth, a sweet, slightly rotten odour on her breath. It was intermittent at first but became more and more pronounced. Eventually Richard could detect it the moment she entered a room and smiled, opened her mouth to say hello. He would offer her gum, offer it whenever they caught up, when they walked to the college café together, when they hung out on weekends, every hour, then every half hour — all the time.

'I don't want any gum, Richard,' she said just before they broke up. 'Why are you always offering me gum?'

Matilda dropped out of art college and told Richard it wasn't because of him. She said she'd scored a job in an advertising agency. Student life was too hard and she couldn't see herself ever making money from art, but there was money in advertising.

'You can be creative with advertising,' Matilda had said.

A few days later he went to a café to drink tea during his lunchbreak from Dad's office. The moment he stepped into the café he was struck with a clean, starch-like scent transcending the coffee aroma, clothes pressed with an iron after drying on a warm spring day. He followed his nose and spotted the source immediately. It was a brunette in a green, long-sleeved top, her tanned profile and sharp nose facing the barista, waiting patiently for her order.

Richard approached the counter and ordered tea, turned to look at her face and met her eyes, two curious brown balls staring back into his own, eliciting a smile from his mouth, from her own mouth.

'Hi,' he said before knowing why.

'Hi.'

They turned their attention to the barista for a moment, a man who eventually raised an eyebrow and gave Richard a bemused look.

'It's good coffee here,' he blurted out. He was actually buying tea. Coffee made him nervous, a sense of impending doom as if a bomb was about to drop.

'Yes, I know.' She smiled a gorgeous, symmetrical smile that revealed perfect white teeth. 'I work nearby.'

'Oh, me too,' Richard said. 'I work at Caruso Accountancy.'

'An accountant?'

'Well, yes, for the moment, but I'm also studying art … at night.'

'Oh?'

'Your cappuccino's ready, Lena,' the barista interrupted, putting a takeaway cup on the bench between them. Clearly the barista thought an accountant wasn't good enough for this woman.

'Advertising. I plan to work in advertising … as a copywriter. It's creative, you know, and it pays well.'

The brunette called Lena slowly leant forward to collect her cup. Her action swamped Richard with another wave of starch. It was intoxicating. She was so clean.

'Well … ?' Lena paused, raising her own eyebrow.

'Richard.'

'Richard,' she nodded. 'Perhaps we'll bump into each other again.'

She smiled and bobbed her head, a deliberate act of coyness, he was sure of it, and exited. Richard blinked, barely aware of himself as he collected his tea, burning his hand because the malicious barista had filled it to the brim with boiling water and just a drop of milk, and stepped outside to see Lena enter a building just two doors down. He followed her scent down the sidewalk and saw her inside a physiotherapist's studio.

Richard made a point of buying tea from the same café every day at the exact same time for the following few weeks. But she was never inside the café, nor did he ever see her inside the physio again, despite walking past it and staring inside, subtly at first, not wanting to look like a stalker, but more and more recklessly as the days went on, searching for this beautiful brunette who wanted to know his name and had led him to believe she worked nearby.

He was also nearing the end of his art diploma and the graduation exhibition was coming up, his final works for his final grade. He'd been working his arse off at night, painting an abstract series on numbers, but his tutors were unimpressed, and now that Matilda was no longer about he didn't even have her to draw encouragement from. He considered giving Ashleigh a call but he'd been avoiding her for months. His sense of smell was continuing to develop. He could smell the air-conditioner at the office, its chlorofluorocarbons penetrating his brain like Vicks VapoRub. His nose could identify what people ate at their desks for lunch, if their rolls were wholemeal or white, what meat was inside, if their pasta was sprinkled with pepper, if their soup had asparagus in it. He'd hear the accountants crunching away at their desks at lunch time, *crunch crunch crunch, munch munch munch*, teeth grinding into rolls, fresh carrots, apples, swallowing, slurping, and all the time he would smell body odours developing with the hour of the day, perfumes fading, computer dust getting warmer, printer ink melting. His dad would produce one of his tuna cans and head to the kitchen. He would spoon the tuna into a bowl, mix in whatever leftovers he brought from Mum's fridge, soft avocado that smelt like internal organs, lettuce that smelt like dirt, and put the entire mix into the microwave to heat so the stench slammed Richard's nose, grabbed hold of his sinuses and licked out his brain. What kind of a motherfucker heated up *fish* in an office kitchen? It was worse because Richard's final artworks were due in two days and they were shit. His series on numbers was born of fear rather than passion, hatred rather than love, and it wasn't coming together and it was too late to start afresh and again, he thought about calling Ashleigh. There was always encouragement from Ashleigh, but Dad had turned him away from her. Dad said she was a 'bottom-feeder' who didn't count.

Richard sat at work with tired eyes hanging out his asymmetrical face, upper legs aching in the office chair. Dad walked past with his can of tuna in hand. Richard sprung to his feet and followed him into the kitchen, told him he was thinking about advertising, that there was creativity in advertising.

'At least I'd be able to make a bit of money, you know, from my … art.'

'Art?' Dad said, stopping to blink at him, astonished. 'Advertising isn't art. It's commerce. And you're not just gonna walk into an advertising job around here. Do you realise how lucky you are to have a job at all?'

'Matilda did it. And there's good money in advertising, and they need creative people.'

Dad set his tuna can down on Richard's desk and stood over him.

'We're supporting your art college,' he said, exhaling a fish cloud that crept into Richard's lungs, made him swallow, swallow again. 'But it's time to get real, son. You've either got it, or you don't. If you can't make money from it, let's just call it a hobby and be done with it, okay?'

Dad walked off, a brown streak of tuna dragged through the air after him, a stench that flicked Richard's nose. The bastard didn't even recognise that Richard's works were about his precious bloody numbers, numbers that hid among the abstract, somewhat painful scenes of Richard's nonsensical nightmares.

Three weeks later, after his exhibition flopped, after Ashleigh turned up unannounced and bought one his paintings, after Richard caved into old friends, agreed to 'celebrate' with them but ended up at the old Quaker's house and its butterfly paintings, he was being charged with arson. He was being assessed by a psychiatrist. He was being advised by his lawyer to tell the world about his piranhas, his issues, his OCD symptoms and anxious thoughts. It was apparently the only way he could avoid jail. His lawyer then proceeded to disclose *everything* to the court about Richard's psyche. He said Richard grew up controlled, bullied by his father, that he'd basically been trained 'to cut himself down', to repress himself 'with ridiculous obsessions'. He said Richard's 'piranhas' were to blame for his dangerous behaviour, that they led him to burn Pony Ridge Scrub, but if he continued to get counselling and learn how to deal with his condition, 'I've credible advice to believe he'll never offend again'.

The court ordered Richard back to work while he underwent counselling. Dad responded by taking back his car and forcing Richard to take four weeks annual leave. Richard used the time to run about the city knocking on the doors of Adelaide advertising agencies, talking himself up, telling them he was a creative after a start — just like Matilda did. Directors gave him the time of day smiled and liked his enthusiasm. But there was no work for tall accountants with art diplomas, a lopsided face and anxiety issues. They told him he should try some freelance work, work up a portfolio, perhaps get a position as an intern with another firm and be prepared to work for free. He visited the café near Dad's office for a tea and to his surprise there *she* was, ordering coffee, as beautiful and clean-smelling as ever. Richard marched right up to Lena and started conversation, said something inane like, 'so you really do like the coffee here', and she gave him an amused look, a brown gaze that ripped straight through his mind and into his heart. He heard himself talking about advertising again, how he might start looking for opportunities overseas in London, 'you know, just to get a start. It's pretty hard around here,' and those eyes of hers grew wider, interested, drawing closer so he was throttled with starch, with cleanliness, with a world different to the shitty smoke he occupied, and he swore to himself right there and then that if got her number, if she gave him a chance, he would do everything he could to make it work, everything to make her believe he was the person he wanted to be: better, smart, efficient, a good catch.

She gave him her number and he took sleeping pills. He took Viagra. He concealed his piranhas and they became an item, gave his parents hope. Richard was so doped up on anti-piranha pills he almost believed in it himself. But ultimately, of course, it wasn't just his raging lust that held Lena's interest. It was his frequent use of the word London. She liked it so much that within just four weeks of seeing each other she'd organised visas and they were on a plane to the UK.

Thankfully Sniles didn't search his house for long. He looked around the lounge, sniffed the air, and studied a ceramic garden gnome on Richard's windowsill. He put the gnome back and checked Richard's room, his cupboards, looked out the back door at the much bigger house his parents had tenanted about 50 metres away up the slope. He asked questions about Richard's face, the scratches, what he did after his interview at Cedar Desk, how long he and Ashleigh had been together. Richard played it down and said he'd been overseas, that they'd just always sort of stayed in contact and it was too soon to say if they were an official couple.

'Looks pretty serious to me,' Sniles said, staring hard into his eyes.

'What about the clown?' Richard asked.

'What?'

'The Blackwood Clown. The one who really lit the fire. Did you look into it?'

'Richard,' the constable said after studying his face for a moment. Richard's left cheek twitched at the insult. 'Right now I'm after a killer. Do you understand that? A fucking killer.'

The constable received another text message and swore even more vehemently at his phone than he did the first time. He stepped off the porch to climb into his car.

'I'll be in touch.'

Richard sat at his desk, squeezing his eyes shut, cringing as the car growled away through gum tree streets. Once the noise disappeared, he lifted the lid on his laptop. The confirmation for his flight booking to

Sydney was red and bold on the screen. He swallowed, swallowed again, rubbed his face where the constable's eyes had bothered him. He would call Max tomorrow to say thanks but no thanks, his self-destructive work was designed to get him sacked, not to make sales. Then he would fly to Sydney and pound the pavement, go to the art galleries, the art museums, ask for a different job, something to do with real art, something that would get him the fuck out of Blackwood. He'd call Lena, tell her the ball was rolling, that he'd moved to Sydney and she could join him if she wanted.

Richard's phone buzzed and he jumped, snatching it up quickly, hoping it was Lena, but the caller ID showed a number he didn't recognise.

'Hello?' he said cautiously.

'Hello, Richard,' Ashleigh said. 'What are you doing?'

'Oh, it's you.'

'Geez, don't sound so excited to hear from me. Will you come over? I was just thinking, with all this coronavirus stuff, and you know, your problems with—'

'I couldn't give a shit about coronavirus,' Richard interrupted. 'Bugs are everywhere. It's about time people cared.'

'Well, I'm not sure if it's the same—'

'I'm serious. Welcome to the party.'

There was silence from the phone. He'd defended her advance, shut it down, but she was about to rally, he could feel it. He'd allowed Ashleigh to be his alibi. Now she had a hook in his mouth and had every intention of reeling him in.

'There's been another fire,' she said on cue. 'Donnie thinks—'

'Donnie's full of shit,' Richard snapped. 'Him and his fucking clown. That bloody cop ...'

'Did that cop bother you *again*?'

'Look, I'm busy, okay? I've got things to do.'

'Why does he keep bothering you?' Ashleigh continued. 'Is your Dad around?'

Richard hung up. They'd been friends since meeting at Blackwood High, growing close in Year 10 when they took Art and English together, becoming intimate and fucking like rabbits throughout years 11 and 12. They'd done it in her little blue hatchback outside a graduation party, a beautiful moment that was interrupted by the most awkward of situations. But then Richard had to work full-time for his dad and Ashleigh encouraged his 'airy fairy ideas', Dad said, threatened his wishes for an accountant heir.

'She's lazy, rudderless, just 30 per cent the woman you'd be able to get if you knuckled down and earned good money'.

Richard held the phone for a moment, feeling suddenly apologetic, a weak-willed jellyfish incapable of doing what was right. Ashleigh had helped him and he'd responded by treating her like shit — again — and his dad wasn't even in the country.

Richard sighed, tapped his phone irritably on the table. According to his court-appointed psychologist, Dad had a toxic power over Richard. He'd been cultivating it for years through an overtly authoritative, controlling parenting regime. It was so effective, the psychologist said, that Richard had been cognitively programmed to feel repressed even when Dad wasn't there. He did this through obsessive thoughts and, to a lesser extent, compulsions — a cerebral response agitated, perhaps, by the regular use of marijuana as an adolescent.

The psychologist further believed Richard's feelings for Ashleigh had been caught in the same piranha-infested waters. There was some truth to that, but Richard knew there was something else, something that his smug, cod-faced psychologist didn't want to hear. Richard had seen how his dad treated his mum. He'd seen how she tolerated the fish-eating megalomaniac and absorbed his slime. Richard was petrified of becoming the same monster, the same bastard caught in a web of numbers, wasting away life in a job he hated with just one thing to make it bearable — a doting partner. If they hooked up he might treat Ashleigh like a commodity, possibly create a nervous wreck of her like his dad had with his mum, and together they'd make excuses for their pointless lives by breeding and starting the cycle all over again.

Richard saved Ashleigh's new number into his phone. She'd apparently chosen *him* in high school as the guy she wanted to love and, once affection, adoration, or whatever minor version of insanity stuck in its claws, it apparently never let up — no matter how crazy its target had become. But he couldn't be thinking about Ashleigh now. He wanted another shot at Lena, one more chance to avoid becoming anything that resembled his dad, create a life with somebody who'd never tolerate idiotic things like piranhas. But he had nothing to show her yet, nothing to give, no direction, just a policeman who suspected him of arson, a fucked-up job offer, a desperate flight booked to Sydney.

Richard dropped his phone and clicked through accommodation in Glebe, in Surry Hills. He scanned punter reviews on third party websites. He read about mouldy sinks, mouldy curtains, rodent droppings, hotel corridor noise and laughing neighbours. He read about rattling windows, dripping taps, a TV too loud through the wall. He rejected them all. He needed somewhere hygienic, somewhere quiet so he could rest and look vibrant, energetic and confident, someone the galleries wanted. He couldn't have water pipes shuddering in walls, elevators banging, drunk people laughing, blokes shouting 'Oi, Darryl' at 3am, crazy people shouting on the street, always the drunk fuckers hollering, hysterical, swearing, a gaggle of manic geese fighting. He needed a quiet room. He needed peace, and there could be absolutely no motherfucking bleating, incessant, malicious, cunty little wattle birds screaming with shredded vocal chords at 5am every morning of his failed fucking life.

Richard slammed the laptop lid down and went to bed, told himself to meditate. He pictured painting his disintegrating self-portrait among the drooping pears. He'd include a white ghost in the background, a clown artist seeking revenge. His phone buzzed with a text message from where he'd put it on the bedside table. It was Ashleigh. Of course it was Ashleigh.

Hey, I get that you're stressed. It's okay. Let's just hang out when you're ready, okay? We'll get a drink xo

His alibi, his dependable friend, the gorgeous manipulator with a hook in his cheek. He lay in bed and started thinking about Ashleigh, imagined her in her T-shirt, her scent like bubble gum, like edible perfume, something more innocent from happier times and Richard wasn't meditating, Richard was wanking and it was Ashleigh's hand. It was Ashleigh's beautiful lips, her hair falling around his face, soothing, calming, and then she was on top of him, she was pulling her shirt above her head, riding him up and down, around and around, and she was coming. Not like Lena. Lena was hard work, a shirt that didn't want to be ironed, but Richard wasn't thinking about Lena. He was being fucked by Ashleigh and he was coming. He felt a rush of relaxation, a heavy feeling in his gut accompanying decreasing blood pressure, a falling heart rate. He drifted, a mess in his hand unnoticed. His mind stopped spinning, stopped ticking, allowed him to slow. Random images floated by, random cities, random impressions distorted and terrible, progressively more surreal and horrible, another symptom of his condition. A contorted mash-up of old women and the unborn lunged at him, veiled, peeling, dark eyes with murder on their mind. Richard jumped, sat upright, clutching his heart, sure he was having a cardiac arrest, gulping at air, panting, afraid. He wiped his hand on his shirt and it smelt like celery. It was filthy. He was filthy. Horrific images swirled about his mind as he went to the bathroom, cast away his T-shirt, washed his hands, brushed his teeth and came back to reality. He still hadn't booked anything. He had nowhere to go once he arrived in Sydney. He hadn't packed. He hadn't done the dishes. He went into his room and picked up his phone, ignored Ashleigh's text, checked the time. It was only 10:30pm. He had to find a hotel room, a place to fucking stay. His skin was itchy. It was covered in dust. The whole house needed dusting. He hadn't dusted it since he returned. He returned to his laptop and kept clicking through hotel listings, reviews, worked out how to get from the airport to whatever hotel he was investigating. Most of the hotels had good rooms, ensuites with balconies, plush towels, modern bathrooms with spa baths, but they were expensive. Richard could only afford the single, hopeless, damp, mouldy, loud, closed in, poky, unclean, dusty, depressing, not what it said in the brochure, not even worth three stars, cockroaches in the cupboard, broken tea mugs, a dump floating in the toilet to greet him on arrival. He could only afford rooms that nobody chose other than those passing through to do dirty things to dirty people in dirty alleyways and Richard had skin under his fingernails, skin from his neck, little shavings, and when he thought 'fuck it' and settled on a room that was quiet, like a concrete bunker, devoid of character, sound, air, life, more like a coffin than a hotel room in Sydney, with no windows, no cupboards, not even a kettle, when he was about to BOOK IT he thought again of Constable Sniles, the ogling wolf.

'Just don't you fucking go anywhere, lad. You or your *girlfriend*.'

He imagined him rocking up tomorrow morning in his shark car, rage barely concealed beneath its cartilage skin, and catching Richard on the way to the airport then asking him about the fire, why he wanted to kill people, why he had attacked the tree in the front yard, nearly burnt down his house, burnt most of the forest across the road, and did he have a good childhood? Were your parents good? Oh, they're so fucking good, Constable, Richard would say. They're so resolute I'm virtually paralysed with issues every time I step outside my fucking door and you should see me at night, he would scream at the constable in the police headquarters, little tears puddling under his eyelids, moistening his scratched, horrible cheeks, making them slippery. You should see me waking in fright ten times every fucking night, gasping, always fucking gasping, always thinking my heart just stopped, my fucking heart just stopped, Constable, but now it's started again, now I'm breathing again. It's a good thing I woke in shock, right?

'Right, Constable?' Richard shouted at his lounge room. 'Have you ever woken in shock?'

His mouse hovered on the BOOK IT tab and he knew he couldn't. If he did, it would confirm whatever guilt Constable Sniles saw in his weird, lopsided face.

Let's get a drink xo

'Get out of my head,' Richard shouted, stuck in a rut called Blackwood that had him flipping and flapping in one ridiculous swoop of its net. He swept his laptop off the desk so it clattered to the floor. He kicked the garden gnome off the windowsill so its head broke from its body. He opened the door, turning his attention to the scorched gum tree in his front yard where the fucking wattle bird was no doubt sleeping, mustering energy for the pre-dawn light so it could wake him with its teeth-shattering, brain-fucking scream.

'That's what I'll do to you,' he shouted, throwing the gnome's head at the tree. 'That's what I'll do to you when I knock you from your perch.'

He stood staring at the shadowed gum trees across the track, their gnarled branches like a company of dreadlocked trolls laughing, half expecting a flash of white to streak across the night, a clown stalking him, watching him, hating him like everyone in the district hated him.

Richard retreated inside and slammed the door, went back to his room, climbed back into bed and tried to calm down, thought again about painting, but there was no point. He wasn't good enough. It wouldn't bring him direction. Any minute his dad would come home from China and without the protection of self-made direction he'd attack Richard with numbers, push commerce down his throat, glue his arse to an office chair and give him coronavirus. Richard tried to meditate again, to focus on something completely different, just like that horrible court-appointed psychologist had taught him, the night sounds of a forest hating him, the silence of the weatherboard house smothering him, but half an hour later when his efforts were useless, when he couldn't stop hearing his heart, when he started to feel dust on his skin, dust in the air, dust settling in his nostrils, making them tingle, he was stupidly picking up his phone, re-reading Ashleigh's text, her X's and her O. He was even more stupidly texting her back, saying he went to bed early but couldn't sleep.

But sure, a drink could be good. He pressed SEND in the darkness and moments later the phone glowed dutifully with her response, lit up his face in the dust, the darkness, the weatherboard cave that no longer contained Lena and was unlikely to ever contain her again.

Awww, she wrote. *R u okay? Try to stop thinking sweetheart. It'll be okay.*

Sweetheart, she wrote, fucking sweetheart. But then of course, she was reading his mind. Ashleigh was always reading his mind. Her second text came straight away to prove she could read his mind like he'd uploaded it to her vagina.

But if u do have to think, try thinking of something nice. The best part of yesterday morning, perhaps ;)

She punctuated it with an upturned eggplant emoticon. Richard did what he was told. Five minutes later he rolled over and fell asleep.

Pyro watched the light in Ashleigh's room go out, the last light in the house to disappear. He set his backpack down on the pine needles where he was standing at the edge of Blackwood Forest, the air cool and moist on the back of his neck. It was always that way in the forest at night.

Pyro retrieved the paint tin from his backpack, pried off the lid with a screwdriver and paused, waiting for any movement in Ashleigh's house. He wanted to sneak up to her window while her light was on. He wanted to peep through her window, catch her undressing, fill his tired imagination with the real thing at last, but not tonight. Tonight he had work to do.

He stepped out of the trees and around her little blue car — a horrible, foreign-made vessel that had once contained the wrong man in her pants. He traversed the cul-de-sac lit by a single white streetlight and crept to the end of the driveway, dipping his brush into yellow paint to start working on her letterbox.

Five minutes later Pyro stepped back and surveyed his butterfly. It was amateur, but it would do. Now he had to sneak around the back of Lars' house to do something serious. No message ever mattered unless it was serious. But something caught his eye. The hatchback of Ashleigh's little blue Hyundai was open on the other side of the cul-de-sac. He was sure it had been closed only five minutes ago when he'd snuck past. A shadow emerged from next to it, a white figure that shimmered and sent Pyro's blood cold. It slid across the bitumen and towards the rectangular letterbox, apparently unaware of Pyro in the darkness.

The shape stopped and surveyed Pyro's work, the trademark symbol the clown loved to draw when they were children, back when they were imprisoned together at the childcare centre under Mother's guard, when Mother would shout at the clown along with all the other kids — not that the clown noticed. He just kept smiling, just kept painting. Perfect butterflies with one figure-eight-like movement, starting at the right wing, lifting his brush at the last moment when he returned to it so there was a gap. He did it for the better part of a year, always leaving a gap in the wing, always at its right side, and Pyro would be entranced. How could a child clown just ignore his raging mother and paint? She would shout and tell him to 'finish the thing properly if you're going to be so damned insolent'. But the only time he finished the butterfly was just before Mother tried to cook the babies. The clown child had stepped between her and the crying toddlers and presented his perfect insect. Pyro was amazed, not because he'd actually completed the wing, but because nobody ever stood up to Mother. Not even Father. Father had disappeared 'like a pussy', according to her. Mother was surprised by the completed butterfly too and actually stopped shouting for a moment. But then the clown bit her on the knee and everything went to hell.

The shadow made a warbling noise in front of Ashleigh's letterbox, a magpie awakening. It grew into a moan, a sustained howl, and a beak grew out the back of its shapeless head. It extended and the moan turned into a shriek that ruptured the night so that Lars' dog started barking from his backyard next door. A light in the house turned on. Pyro fled across the cul-de-sac towards the forest and the clown slid after him, a faceless being blurred under the streetlight. It knew every person Pyro had burnt, every animal he'd strangled, everything he'd done since Mother tried to burn the babies.

Pyro gained distance, cold air wrapping his throat like tendrils. He tripped on a log he should have known was there and Mother cackled. Mother laughed. Mother knew he was a coward being chased through the forest by a clown who'd stopped him burning the old people, the masseuse, who stopped everyone burning anything and who probably got to fuck Ashleigh in her little blue car, its little wheels squealing, its suspension groaning. Everyone got to fuck Ashleigh but Pyro. Not cowards like Pyro.

'Leave me alone,' Pyro screamed at the shape in pursuit, a figure whose presence should have been impossible after what his mother did all those years ago. He turned right onto a second path, a passage heading off the creek path and up the hill to the old manager's house, a damp refuge where he'd once camped for two weeks while living at his grandparent's house. He'd killed their cat and didn't want to shave their heads while they slept.

Pyro ran up the slope, panting, gasping for air, wishing the world behind him would burn wild and bright, cleansing, erasing, putting everything right, but the clown was no longer chasing him. The clown had stopped somewhere else. The clown was probably afraid of the old manager's house, a horrible place that had given Pyro refuge where nothing else would.

He keeled over and vomited. He wanted to go back to Ashleigh and hug her but she was protected. Everything was protected. And somewhere in the forest dark, the clown howled with frustration, with pain, with whatever message his useless vocal chords couldn't tell the world.

'Go to hell, Gerard,' Pyro screamed back at the night.

A DISTRICT BORN OF MISCHIEF

The more Sniles looked into Richard's clown, the more it seemed there was something different about the Blackwood district, something that prompted people to do stupid things. Sniles read it in SAPOL's many incident reports, online Trove newspaper articles and, after travelling to the State Library of SA at the end of his shift, archived community publications. Locals claimed it was in the air, a thin climate that excited the blood, the segregation from the city via altitude and trees. Whatever *it* was, it had arrived with the district's first settlers, three sailors who landed at the fledgling colony of Adelaide's Holdfast Bay on the *Coromandel* in 1837.

Bad weather caused a delay in *Coromandel's* offloading. The bored sailors found a large shipment of wine onboard that was supposed to be delivered to the settlement's English hierarchy. They sampled it, stole it, and decided their days as sailors were over. They jumped ship and made their way through to the unsettled, forest-covered foothills where they camped out in a cave atop an eastern ridge from where they could see the coast. The deserters didn't reveal themselves until the *Coromandel* had left, earning the right to remain as free settlers in SA — largely because the magistrate was too busy with the establishment of Adelaide to give a shit.

Fruit growers came next and cleared the scrub for orchards. Local authorities ignored the rights of the existing Indigenous and carved up the land with grants. Subdivisions for housing took off from the 1880s before a railway line was installed and the towns of Belair, Coromandel

Valley and Blackwood were established. City-slickers moved to the hills to breath the fresh air, walk the forests, commute via train to the city — a new life that was perfect, save for the fact their kids had been struck between the eyes with an urge to wreak havoc.

Old articles described how a local constable's bicycle was nicked. He found it strung to the top of a flagpole in Blackwood's centre. A minister's prized black stallion at Government Farm was found painted with white stripes so it looked like a zebra. The gates on peoples' land allotments were swapped in the night. Residents would wake to find their neighbour's gate in place where their own used to sit, and vice versa.

The flustered community blamed the climate, the thin air, the fact there was nothing to do at night and no evening train to the city 13 kilometres north. The community launched the Blackwood Boy's Club, which, as the *Blackwood Literary Magazine* printed in 1914, targeted the district's youth, because:

… the bracing effects of the climate seem to produce an extra supply of surplus energy, and the need was strongly felt of a channel where this energy could be expressed more fittingly than by the little acts of mischief of which some of us were the constant victims.

Sniles' phone vibrated in his pocket. It was a text message from Jenny. This time it was two question marks. It was 8pm and he'd finished work two hours ago.

'Shit,' he said, prompting several people in the library's open plan study space to glare. He'd lost himself in research again. Sniles messaged back to say he was winding it up.

But it wasn't just the kids causing trouble, and it wasn't just the locals. After Government Farm became Belair National Park, the land became a popular weekend destination for city folk. They arrived by train for tennis, cricket and picnics. But sport was banned on Sundays — the Lord's day of rest — so the people brought booze instead. Apparently, the 'bracing effects' of the foothills' climate inspired them to drink so much authorities had to build a small gaol in the park for unruly drunks.

From the '60s to '80s the place was carved up further for housing. Young baby boomers, besotted by fresh air and space, built homes and created gardens. Their buildings sprawled under the treetops and connected townships to become a six-suburb district in Blackwood, Coromandel Valley, Glenalta, Hawthorndene, Eden Hills and Belair. Reserves, creeks, gullies and pockets of unkempt bush were left intact to dissect the streets, providing plenty of places for kids to play, smoke cigarettes and drink alcohol.

In the 1990s, hip hop, grunge, and drug-fuelled parties swept through the region, swamping the boomers' offspring with speed, LSD, ecstasy, and copious amounts of indoor-grown, crystallised, strong-as-fuck marijuana. South Australia at the time had the most liberal marijuana laws in the country and it was being cultivated by enthusiastic green thumbs across the district. But the skunk was so powerful that some would get hooked and spend a month at Glenside psychiatric hospital near the city before returning to Blackwood pacified by pills.

There were so many delinquents crawling around Blackwood off their trolley in the 1990s that two plain-clothed police officers dubbed Jack and Jill by the kids were deployed to grab them, bust them for drugs, or to take them home to their parents. By 2001 the vandalism had calmed but a new group called the Gnome Rangers emerged. They were a band of larrikins who spent a night every few years gluing up to 200 ceramic garden gnomes to the roofs of shops, restaurants, service stations and banks. TV reporters speculated they must be firefighters with ladders but in truth they were a bunch of '90s leftovers who got incredibly drunk, climbed like monkeys, and giggled themselves silly while risking serious injury.

Sniles knew this because SAPOL had a file on them. It had never pursued the dickheads, however, because children loved the gnomes and so did the shopkeepers. They brought media attention to the district and didn't break anything.

Sniles phone started buzzing again in his pocket. Jenny was calling.

'Hey, I'm sorry,' he answered, receiving more glares from the room.

'What are you doing? You said you'd be home on time tonight.'

'I know but it's work. I'm … I'm at the library.'

Jenny clicked with frustration.

'I'm leaving now,' Sniles said.

'Thank God for that,' mumbled a man poring over spread-eagled books at his desk.

Jenny hung up without another word. Sniles threw a half-chewed pencil at the man and marched from the room. He drove home to find his wife already in bed. She didn't answer his whisper at the bedroom door so he quietly retreated, made himself another bowl of two-minute noodles, and snuck into his study to log into his computer. He started looking up accommodation for their trip to the Barossa but Blackwood's history drew him quickly back down the rabbit hole.

During the 2010s, Sniles learnt, a local cafe owner sought to capitalise on the Gnome Rangers' buzz by organising actual firefighters to place the ornaments on the roofs of selected businesses. It clearly displeased the rangers, however, because during a live cross for a television breakfast program, an original Gnome Ranger turned up to crash the party, wearing a mask and loitering behind the cafe owner in an ominous way on live TV. It was unsettling, possibly dangerous due to the anonymity of the individual involved, but it was also entertaining and people needed a laugh. The state's manufacturing base was in trouble. The Mitsubishi car factory down the road from Blackwood had closed. Local manufacturers were scaling back, moving production offshore. Markets were becoming increasingly flooded with cheaper goods made in China and other Asian countries. The rise of Sweden's Ikea was hurting Adelaide's native furniture makers. When Holden, Australia's only car brand, announced plans to shift production offshore in 2017, the state's heart was ripped out. Its proudest creation was leaving after 161 years of manufacturing, an institution that hundreds of component suppliers relied upon.

It was a sad end to a proud era and, as Sniles noticed, for the past five years there'd been no strange headlines coming from Blackwood, no more mischievous antics delighting breakfast show hosts. There were no zebra marks painted on horses, no police bicycles placed on post officers, and certainly no news reports about Richard's Blackwood Clown.

If the clown did actually exist, Sniles supposed the locals would treat him the same as they once had the Gnome Rangers. Just another kid acting stupid, another loony in a place that'd always been full of them. There was a bit about him on social media, stories about some weirdo who hid in the forests and frightened bushwalkers, but SAPOL had no information and Sniles sure as shit wasn't going to ask.

'I saw him walking down the main street. He had red hair and was covered in soot or something.'

Sniles swung about to see Jenny in her nightgown reading his laptop from over his shoulder, reciting a Facebook page Sniles had dug up that referenced the clown.

'My mate reckons he saw the clown at twilight at Frank Smith Dam,' Jenny continued, reading another post. 'His eyes lit up like red LEDs and he screamed like a pig.'

'Jenny,' Sniles began, hastily minimising his research and pulling up pages he'd found on Barossa accommodation. 'I was in the middle of looking for a place for us to stay in when—'

She turned and exited their study.

'Jenny.' Sniles picked up his laptop and walking after her. 'Look.' He clicked at the keyboard to maximise several Trip Advisor and Airbnb searches he'd made. 'There's this place in Tungkillo, see? It has a spa and we can walk to at least three wineries.'

'Did you book it?' Jenny paused in the hallway to look at the webpage, her brown, no-nonsense eyes seeming to bore a hole through the screen.

'No. I wanted to see what you thought first.'

'And then you became distracted by clowns and all this … this fire stuff you're so obsessed with.'

'Come on,' Sniles said. 'You know I like to research, and I'm the middle of an investigation.'

'You're always in the middle of an investigation.'

'They're talking about re-deploying officers for this coronavirus thing, contact tracing and the like. I've got to show progress or they'll have me tracking sick people, and ...' but Jenny's eyes were narrowing. 'How about this one?'

Sniles held up the laptop screen and clicked a button to show a bed-and-breakfast in Tanunda but accidentally re-maximised the wrong page. It was a list of every major bushfire that had impacted Blackwood since white settlement. 'Shit. Hang on.'

'Just forget it,' Jenny said, walking away. 'I'm going back to bed.'

'Jenny—'

'Just get it done.' She closed their bedroom door.

Sniles looked at it for a moment, not feeling anger — he never felt angry at Jenny; watching his arsehole father tear strips off his mother had ensured he could never cross that bridge — but he did feel unfairly treated. The Bureau of Meteorology was about to issue a 'catastrophic' fire danger rating for two days' time, its highest level of warning based on the strength and heat in the wind, the preceding weather and moisture content, the likely consequences if a fire broke out. Temperatures of up 42 degrees were forecast, along with strong and gusty northerlies of up to 80 kilometres per hour. It would be followed by a cool change that would bring strong south-westerly winds that could spread any advancing bushfire fork to its side, create a much wider front stretching back to where the fire had begun.

'There's a reason why this matters,' Sniles said through the door. 'These pyros ... they're dangerous. They could get people killed. They already have.'

'I know,' Jenny said from inside. 'Just get it done.'

'You do understand I have a job to do and—'

'I understand I've followed you to this place,' Jenny snapped, opening the door with a rush of angry air, 'where I don't know anyone. I don't have any friends. I spend my days searching for a job where nobody wants to employ anyone because of a bloody virus, and the one night my partner promised to spend with me and supposedly book this holiday in the Barossa, he's locked himself away for three hours looking at bushfires, birds and fucking clowns of all things.'

'I wasn't in there for three hours. I was at the library.'

Jenny slammed the door.

Sniles retreated to his study and booked the trip for next weekend. He only hoped he'd caught his pyromaniac by then. Otherwise, he'd probably have to give up his chance to make a difference and start investigating dead dogs — or worse — spend his days tracking some bloody son-of-a-bitch virus.

Chika chika CHEE CHAA.

Richard opened his eyes, rubbed his face, scratched his stomach. He sensed dust particles in the air, on the blankets, his pillows, clogging up his nose. A nostril started whistling. He sat up and swung his legs out of bed, felt the dust on his hands, noticed how the skin was looking slightly ashen. He scratched at it and felt dust in his armpits, his hair, the crack of his arse. He attacked his body with fingers, scratched and rubbed, blew his nose violently with tissue paper.

Chika CHEE CHAA.

Richard sprung out of bed and marched down the hallway, went outside and picked up a stick, threw it at the gum tree. He swore at the hightailing little fucker, wishing for a gun, wishing he could ask the constable for just one shot, one perfectly timed sniper attack.

Richard's phone rang from inside. The caller ID said Lars.

'What do you want?'

'He's gone,' Lars said, his voice quiet and disturbing.

'Who's gone?'

'The dog, Thompson. He's gone. The clown took him.'

'What the hell are you talking about? You left me there, you fucking idiot. You left me in that forest with that *cop*.'

'We had to scarper, man. We saw the cop and couldn't find you.'

'You didn't even look. You know my record, damn you.'

'That sucks man, but listen. Thompson's gone,' Lars said. 'The clown took him. I heard him screaming and shit from the forest all night. He must know where I live. And …' Lars lowered his voice to a whisper, the fear in his voice palpable. 'Those paintings, you know, of the butterfly?' He paused for a moment. 'There's one on Ashleigh's letterbox.'

An artery thumped in Richard's throat, once, twice … then nothing. He hit his chest.

'Call Donnie. I'm sleeping.'

'No, you're not, and I don't wanna to go in by myself.'

'In where?' A sharp pain dug into Richard's left pectoral muscle. He coughed, sure he was having a heart attack.

'Blackwood Forest. The clown's in there and I … we … I think we pissed him off … again.'

Richard hung up before Lars could say another word. He stood for a moment, waiting for another bolt of pain in his chest, feeling his pulse, gulping at air until he felt tiny pins and needles across his skin. He looked at the headless garden gnome, laughed once, twice, then kicked it against the wall with his bare foot. It hurt but not nearly enough.

*

'Why do you think he does it?' Lars said, looking at the letterbox at the end of Ashleigh's driveway. Drawn so it barely fit inside the boundaries of the metal rectangle was what was supposed to be a white butterfly. Its right wing was splotchy, more like a bitten egg than an incomplete stroke, an amateur replica of the paintings they'd stolen and burnt.

'You guys just couldn't let me go, could you?' Richard said. 'You had to bring me back here. You had to keep me involved in this shit … this ridiculous, meaningless, trivial … shit.'

'Hey, man.' Lars sounded nervous. 'We were just trying to help you, you know, Donnie said—'

'Fuck what Donnie said.' Richard stared at the butterfly, the paintwork fresh and terrible. It couldn't have been drawn by the clown. The clown's butterflies were perfect — save for their clipped wing. This was amateur rubbish. 'Donnie's the one who started this shit.'

'Dude—'

'Don't you fucking get it,' Richard snapped, turning on his friend, a man who'd smoked weed all through high school and got away with it because he had rockstar looks and a symmetrical smile. 'I found a way out of this shit, and you lot, you had your hooks in me the whole time because here we are again, and look, it's another drawing of the fucking clown picture because what? It wasn't enough that I burnt the others? I fucking paid my dues for that already.'

'Shhh,' Lars said urgently, looking across the cul-de-sac at Blackwood Forest. 'He could be listening. He's probably watching.'

'He didn't paint this shit.'

'Shhh,' Lars said again, now turning to look anxiously at Archibald Reserve next to Ashleigh's house, the scrub-filled strip that would take them to Turner's Avenue, the valley road and the old Quaker's house, a place they should never have entered on that stupid night last year.

'Listen, man.' Lars grabbed Richard's arm. 'I know you're the one who got fucked over with all this, and—'

'No shit I'm the one who got fucked over.' Richard shook off Lars' hand. 'I'm always the one who gets fucked. You and Donnie, man. You're like the plague.'

The stitching at the side of Lars' eyes suddenly drooped and he looked hurt. He pulled a joint out from behind his ear, put it in his mouth and lit it.

'Oh, great,' Richard said.

Lars sucked, coughed out smoke, exhaled a massive cloud that hung heavily in the morning air. A cloud of Lars' toxic dope crawled towards Richard's super snout so it tingled.

'I've gotta go home,' Richard said, stepping backwards.

'You think you're the only one suffering?'

Richard continued to back away as the smoke slowly reached for his face.

'You think you're different to us?'

'No, but I did work my arse off to get out of here, and you lot—'

'It doesn't matter how hard you work,' Lars said, taking another quick puff and coughing. 'None of us are going anywhere.'

Richard stopped and stared at his old friend.

'Listen.' Lars' eyes were growing glassier by the second. 'Donnie's lost his job and he's fucked 'cause he only knows how to make shit for cars and cars are done for here, right? I can't get a job that pays more than a factory packer 'cause apparently I'm not educated enough. And you, you got away but it all went wrong 'cause you're back and you've got no job, you lost your girlfriend and you look more fucked up than ever.' Lars took a bigger toke and filled his lungs to capacity, squeezing out words like an inflated pufferfish. 'Don't you get it? We're cursed, man, *all* of us.'

'It was Donnie who took those paintings,' Richard said as Lars exhaled his monstrous cloud. 'I didn't take the paintings. Donnie took the paintings.'

'It doesn't matter who took the paintings,' Lars whined, his eyes slitted and red hot. 'We were all there, and nothing's been right for any of us since.'

From the sky above came the shockwave sound of a jet. Richard looked up and saw a plane crackling with thunder, accelerating high into the sky, an airbus on its way east, probably to Sydney, probably the very flight he'd paid for but couldn't catch because he couldn't book a hotel. He swallowed, swallowed again, then turned away and walked towards the pine forest.

'Don't go in there *now*,' Lars warbled, his voice slower, deeper. 'The clown's still in there. He's got Thompson.'

'I was meant to be on that plane,' Richard said, spitting excess saliva from his mouth. He passed a mass of blackberry bushes consuming an old wire fence that hung slack.

'That fucker cursed us, *all* of us,' Lars called after him. 'And *you*, you should never, *ever*, have burnt his paintings, man. He knows it was you. He hates you the most.'

CLOWN HUNT

Richard marched into the forest, head down and furious, listening to the plane fade in the sky, a vessel filled with people who were going somewhere, who had direction, purpose, who weren't stuck in a rut called Blackwood with a bunch of useless friends.

It was Donnie who invited him out that fateful night after graduation in 2018. They sat around at Lars' house, getting drunk, listening to music, watching Lars smoke weed. At some point late in the night Donnie decided they should go for a walk. Lars agreed and jumped to his feet. Richard mumbled something about not wanting to, but then Ashleigh piped up and said she didn't want to either, probably doing her best to snare Richard alone after he'd spent half the year avoiding her. So he stuffed beers in his jacket pockets, left Ashleigh by herself and followed Donnie through Archibald Reserve towards Turners Avenue. They made their way to the winding road and ambled towards Olave Valley, spotting an old house glowing in the moonlight. Donnie said it was an old Quaker meeting house, that it was abandoned and they should go check it out. Lars didn't want to. He didn't know what a Quaker was and wanted to go back. Richard was drunk and didn't give a shit.

They crept towards the house but a big black shape attacked them from the shadows, something angry, hairy, snorting, going for Donnie, spitting at Donnie. Donnie screamed, fought with the beast, called for his mother, told whatever it was he would fucking kill it. It herded them towards the front porch of the Quakers house. Lars frantically tried the door. Donnie kicked it open. They clambered inside and slammed the door shut on the monster, heaving and gasping in the darkness.

'What the fuck? What was that? What was that thing?'

Lars sparked his cigarette lighter to reveal a room full of antique furniture, vases, silverware, old photos, mirrors, and dust, so much dust. He found a light switch but it didn't work. He found a lamp next to an old armchair facing a window but it didn't work either. He started to panic. Donnie took his lighter from him, swore because it was hot, and plummeted them all into darkness once more.

'Turn it on. Turn it back on,' Lars said. 'There's a fucking beast out there, a fucking beast.'

'It's an alpaca,' Donnie said.

Donnie lit the lighter again and he was on the other side of the room looking at a series of paintings fastened with washing line pegs to a chord strung between furniture. They were pictures of a butterfly painted in a single stroke, like a squashed figure-eight on its side, created with different colours on sheets of heavy watercolour paper, all of them uncannily symmetrical — save for the fact the artist chose to leave the right wing incomplete by leaving a gap between where he started his stroke and finished.

Donnie raised the light and more butterflies were stuck to the walls, to the un-drawn curtains. They were drawn in crayons, pencils, charcoal, in varying sizes and colours but always broken, always unfinished, a relentlessly deliberate flaw in what could have been perfection. The artist had discipline, patience, had stuck to one body of work to become a master.

Richard touched one of the hanging pictures and it left blue paint on his fingers.

'It's still wet,' Lars exclaimed.

Donnie stared at Richard's finger for a minute, eyes wide and spinning, strangely entranced. He plucked the painting from the cord and stuffed it crackling into his backpack, grabbed a handful of others and did the same.

'What are you doing?' Richard protested.

Donnie's eyes were possessed, his mouth tight. He spotted a small painting framed with glass on the mantelpiece. It was of the same symmetrical butterfly only this one was complete. Perfect. Old. Its ornate wooden frame was probably antique.

'Motherfucker,' Donnie snarled as he grabbed the framed painting and lifted it high.

That was when somebody shone a torch through the window, banged on the pane and shouted.

'Fuck!' Lars screamed. 'I told you. We're fucked.'

Donnie threw the painting to the ground so the glass shattered.

'What are you doing?' Richard screamed.

'It's him,' Donnie shouted back, eyes somehow glowing in the darkness. 'It doesn't make sense but it's *him*.'

He ran to the door and pulled it open, finding himself confronted by an old farming couple with torches.

'You kids leave this place alone.'

'Fuck off!' Donnie shouted.

He pushed the couple backwards and ran out the door. Lars and Richard followed and the couple shouted after them, an angry alpaca spat at them. They raced up the hill where they stood in the night panting, catching their breath, watching the couple's torchlight bob across the valley and back to the second house until they heard a truck engine start. A pair of headlights pointed up the hill and, to Richard's horror, a gunshot rung out.

'Shit,' Lars screamed. 'They've got a shotgun.'

The truck roared and headlights bumped up the weed-infested paddock towards them. Donnie took off down the other side of the hill. Lars followed and they ran towards an old shed that stood silver and dull in the moonlight at the centre of the paddock.

'What the hell's going on?' Richard shouted. He was afraid but he also felt guilty. He'd just entered the house of a real painter, a real artist, and watched his friend destroy their work.

They hid behind the shed seconds before headlights rose over the summit and roared down the hillside. Lars and Donnie panicked, darted across open space towards the whistling pine forest. Richard remained behind the shed. The truck pulled up next to the forest and a spotlight shone into the trees after Lars and Donnie. Voices shouted in the night. Richard ran away in the opposite direction, finding his way back to the valley road. He jogged back to civilisation, taking Archibald Reserve to Lars' house. He sat alone with Ashleigh and avoided her questions. Donnie and Lars arrived an hour later, unscathed. They didn't explain anything either. Nobody ever told Ashleigh about their crimes.

Two days later Donnie and Lars came over to show Richard a message in the local newspaper, a quarter-sized advert warning 'those who'd trespassed' on property near Olave Valley that inquiries were underway into their identities and they would be 'wise to never return to the site'.

Lars freaked out. He wanted to know who lived in the Quaker house, who they'd just made an enemy of. Donnie remained tight-lipped. Richard wanted to forget about it. He was racked with guilt, but also burning with jealousy. He'd just received his grades from the exhibition series. Teachers said his paintings were 'competent' and 'imaginative' but lacked 'discipline' and 'restraint'. He had natural talent that could be developed with the 'right direction', but he had a long way to go. The artist in the old Quaker house, however, was everything his teachers would respect — talented, dedicated, accomplished. The artist was so perfect their works could be left deliberately broken, maddingly incomplete, teasing wannabe artists like Richard who couldn't be perfect if he tried, let alone deliberately imperfect.

Lars lit a spliff. Donnie set down his backpack and pulled out the clump of paintings he'd stolen.

'What about these?'

Before he knew what he was doing, Richard had snatched the papers from Donnie's hand, grabbed Lars' lighter and set fire to the crumpled works so they crackled and snarled. Their creator had no numbers beating down their neck, no accountant father forcing them to calculate sums and formula, no reason to push harder than they should, to rush into making an immediate impact, sell a series, anything to show their dad they had direction. They only had to worry about their artwork, which was now bubbling, melting and blackening into hot little cinders. A breeze sprung from nowhere and snatched the papers from Richard's grip. Five imperfect butterflies lifted hot into the air and fluttered high over the fire track. They separated into flaming ribbons and descended upon trees in Pony Ridge Scrub on the other side of the track from Richard's house. Flames quickly sprouted and within seconds five different patches of the forest was ablaze.

Lars and Donnie backed away towards Donnie's car. They told Richard there was no hope of putting the fire out, that he should ring the CFS. They climbed into Donnie's car and disappeared down the access lane, leaving Richard to take the wrap like they always left him to take the wrap.

'I don't get it,' Dad said later while Mum scratched her neck under the red and blue police lights, the stink of bushfire smoke acrid, horrible and sharp. 'You've got everything a person needs, yet you throw it back.'

'It was an accident,' Richard said, watching Mum scratch her arms, a little moisture in her eyes, but nodding. She always nodded while Dad tightened the nooses around their necks.

'That's twice you've done this, Richard,' he said. 'Twice you've started a fire on our property. And you want to be a partner?'

'I don't want to be a partner. In fact,' he hesitated, watching CFS crews douse burning weeds in his front yard. 'I want to go to London.'

'What?' Dad leant backwards, sucking at the smoke in the air, the steam from the fire hoses. 'This is hardly the time to be talking about—'

'There's more opportunity in London—'

'But …' Dad leant forward again with blazing accountant eyes. 'Is this about art again? For Heaven's sake. You nearly burnt down our flat and you want to talk about your damned hobby?'

'Richard,' Mum pleaded, stepping forward. 'I like to paint as well, but it's not... it's not—'

'You haven't made a cent from it,' Dad interrupted, fish smoke puffing from his nostrils. Two police officers nearby smelt the brine and edged closer with opening mouths. 'And it's time you learnt about reality. Officers?'

The sharks grinned without smiling.

'I believe my son has something to tell you.'

Arrk, aaark, aaaark, aaaarrrrh.

From somewhere in Blackwood Forest a solitary raven hawked. It was the start-loud-then-fade-away call they were renowned for, a mocking, strangely lonely sound. Richard swore at the bird and marched faster into the forest, trying to outrun the memories, the fire, his failed escape with a new girlfriend in a new city, Lars' dope smoke and his missing dog.

Arrk, aaark, aaaark, aaaarrrrh.

'Shut the fuck up,' Richard shouted, turning off the path onto a track that led up the slope of the pine forest hill. The raven followed him from above, moving from tree to tree, watching, listening to Richard's mind eat itself with anxiety. The court-appointed psychologist said Richard could 're-train' his mind to respond differently to anxious thoughts, to consider his OCD symptoms a sinking plane that could be guided back to safety 'with the right lever'. But the psychologist had fish eyes, watery whites, black pupil dots that studied Richard too hard, smeared his lop-sided face with cod scum. He didn't *really* believe the Pony Ridge Scrub fire was an accident. The only thing he believed was that Richard's parents were bad for him and his friends were terrible. He said they were 'enablers' who loved to see Richard lose his shit, and he had to move one.

'But I did. I did fucking move on,' Richard shouted as the pine needles crunched underfoot. 'I found a girlfriend, dammit!'

He pulled out his phone and brought up Lena's phone number, hovering his finger over the call button before deciding to send her a text message instead.

Hi. Just thinking of you. I'm in Sydney, about to go into a meeting with Clemenger, but would love to hear from you.

Richard hit SEND and took a breath. It was better he didn't tell her about the job offer in Adelaide. She'd be far more interested if it was in Sydney. Lena would love the idea of Sydney, just like she'd loved the idea of London. From ahead came a sudden, ghoulish squeal that startled Richard. He lifted his head to see a murder of ravens squabbling on the pathway, a baby raven in their midst, squawking, cawing, begging for food from five or six jet black birds. He stepped off the path to avoid them and stumbled on a broken brick. Richard realised he'd marched all the way to another isolated building, the old manager's house. The abandoned stone structure was covered in pine needles, graffiti and the occasional burnt patch. Its yard was littered with broken glass, beer bottles, many he'd drunk himself on delinquent nights with Lars and Donnie back when they'd called it the Clown House.

The ravens screeched louder. They hopped a little closer. Richard kicked at the birds and they jumped backwards, regrouped, analysed him with side-on eyes, and started advancing again.

'Fuck off,' Richard shouted but his phone started buzzing in his hand. To his surprise it was Lena. She'd been missing him after all and wanted to hear from him. But the ravens were too loud. There were too many. If Lena heard them over the phone she'd know something wasn't right.

Richard dodged a broken wooden beam hanging over the ruined house's doorway and ducked inside. He moved up the dark hallway and stopped just as he stepped on a sheet of what must have been corrugated iron in the darkness. It crackled loudly underfoot. Richard held his breath and pushed the green ANSWER button, trying not to think about the dust swirling in his face.

'Hello?' he said, but he was too eager, too desperate. He swayed a little and there was another loud creak from the iron on the floor.

'Richard?' Lena's sensible voice said. 'Can you talk now? When does your meeting start?'

'Yeah, I can talk. I mean, I'm sitting in the waiting room, you know, it's cool.'

It's cool? The iron responded with another retort beneath his feet, a jaw of metal teeth grinding in a dark hallway. The ravens outside grew louder.

'What's that?' Lena said, concern sounding in her voice.

'Broken coffee machine,' Richard said. 'How are you?'

'Oh, yeah, I'm fine. Just ... adjusting, you know.' She breathed the last word, allowed it to exhale like a sigh.

'Yes, but are you okay?' He raised the pitch towards the end of his sentence, exuding his own concern, showing that he cared, he cared deeply. He wasn't thinking about himself, his own loss. He wanted to make sure *she* was okay.

'Oh, yeah. I'm fine. Look, I'm really glad you're in Sydney, and surprised. Wow, that's great, you know? Are you coming back?'

She was hoping he wouldn't. She was hoping he'd find his feet, and perhaps, just perhaps, she was hoping things worked out and she could join him there.

'Yeah, sure. It's going really well. I've got a few jobs lined up. But I'll be back here, I mean, in Adelaide, tomorrow, but only for a little while. I ... I might have to move here, to Sydney.'

'Oh, Richard. That's fantastic news. I'm so happy for you. You were really, I mean, you know, you were struggling, and all that stuff about, you know, your anxiety, Old Man Stanley, and all those silly adverts that caused so much trouble—'

'Hey, so I'm sorry, but I think I need to go in a second.'

'Oh right, of course.' Lena paused. 'Well, hey, I'm glad you're getting back on your feet because there's something I want to talk to you about.'

Richard switched his weight from one foot to the other. It created another screech from the iron and he froze, concentrating on the phone, concentrating so hard he almost didn't hear a whimper from further inside the cottage.

'Richard?'

He stared down the dark hallway into what was once a living room at the end of the hall but was now a ruined space with missing floorboards. A few pathetic sunbeams shone through the broken roof to light up the gaping wound in the floor.

'I'm here.' Richard closed his eyes, trying to stay focussed on Lena.

'Something unexpected has happened,' she continued as Richard heard another weak whimper. He peered through the gloom for Lars' dog, a mutt who might have injured himself, or fallen through the hole into the basement, or both. Instead, he noticed something glimmering behind the sunbeams, something yellow painted on a crumbling interior wall. 'I've met someone new.'

'Shit,' Richard said, slamming his hand over his mouth. It was another unfinished butterfly. Its shape was deformed, its head running with yellow paint, its wings squeezed from the top so they almost resembled eggs. Even the gap in its right wing was lower than usual, splotchy. It wasn't so much a statement about unfinished business or deliberate imperfection, but the mistake of a careless oaf.

'Don't be like that, Richard.'

'No, no. I wasn't swearing at you. I just… I dropped my CV and…' But what was written beneath the butterfly on the wall punched harder than Lena's words. *BURN IT ALL RICHARD*, the words said, written as badly as the symbol above, its paint having dripped through the words like blood.

'I wasn't *looking* to meet somebody,' Lena continued. 'It just… you know… kind of happened.'

'Sure sure sure,' Richard blabbered, hairs on his back sticking like needles into his T-shirt. 'Shit happens.'

'There's no need to be callous.'

'It's fine. I mean, I'm fine with that.' He retreated across the creaky iron again so it howled. 'Sorry, I've gotta go now.'

'What's that noise?'

'I'll call you back.' Richard hung up, turned around and made for daylight, bumping his head on the broken beam entrance so the ravens cackled. He kicked dirt at them and they scattered. He grabbed a broken brick to throw at them but was met with sudden and sharp pain. A masonry screw sticking out of the brick had sliced open his palm. At the same time his phone buzzed again in his pocket. Maybe it was Lena, calling to get his full attention, to twist the dagger deeper and crush him between perfect-smelling hands. He pulled his phone from his pocket but the caller ID said it was Max, the man from Cedar Door who'd pulled him in for an interview. He was about to deny the call but then ... perhaps he shouldn't. He'd lied about Sydney. If he called Lena back, he would have to have *something* to show for himself. She'd met somebody new.

'Shit.'

Richard clutched his buzzing phone and leapt through the ravens so they pecked at his feet. He sprinted away before stopping to gulp air, fill his brain with oxygen, push a green button wet with blood.

'Richard,' Max stated, his voice coarse and confident. 'Something's come up and I thought I'd see what you think. Are you available to work up a pitch?'

'Yes,' Richard panted. 'Anything.'

'Good. It's only for radio, but I want it sharp. The supermarket industry's noisy enough but it's a new client, a Chinese franchise entering the market, YingCo, and these guys have serious money. Any ideas?'

Arrk, aaark, aaaark, aaaarrrrrh. It was the solitary raven again, a fish spotter above making sure Richard didn't get away.

'Where the fuck are you, son?'

'Bushwalking.' Panting, coughing, trying to stop panting, trying to stop thinking about symbols and whimpering dogs, a raven in the sky telling the clown exactly where Richard stood. He swallowed, swallowed again, pushed his thumb into his gash and found pain, self-destruction, the present. 'Yeah, I've got an idea. Cheap. Everything's cheap.'

'Well, obviously, that's—'

'And they're Chinese so the translation for the word *cheap* probably sounds complicated to us,' Richard said, pushing a thumb into his palm so it spouted blood. 'So we get a Chinese guy talking wild, enthusiastic, a million miles an hour in Mandarin, and we get cliché Chinese music playing in the background. And after a couple seconds of this guy chattering away we get a translator translating, you know, saying one word for every 10 that the Chinese guy is saying, keeping it simple, you know, "YingCo. They sell food. It's cheap." Because the idea of the advert is to emphasise the Chinese language, you know, how complicated it sounds, and yobbos hearing it will laugh and think, yeah, those Chinese people do talk fast and their language does sound funny, but hey, that shit *is* cheap. And it *is* simple. Buy there and spend less, and so yeah, it'll piss off enough people to get attention and sure, some people might be a little offended, but for the average redneck Australian the fact the Chinese can have a laugh at our differences will make YingCo okay, you know, acceptable at a Neanderthal bigot level, you know, it'll get the typical yobbo past their casual racism and buy shit.'

Richard tried to catch his breath. He'd pushed Max, ruined a chance to get a new job and impress Lena, and somewhere, somehow, far away at the other end of one of the planes above, his dad was laughing. His dad was telling him that advertising isn't art. His dad was preparing to fry him in a pan with fish.

'Shit,' Max finally said as bright red blood welled over Richard's thumb and spilled to the pine forest floor. 'I didn't realise you were racist.'

'What?' Richard retracted his thumb. 'No. It's meant to be ironic. It's meant to play on Australia's casual disregard for—'

'What it is,' Max said, his voice rising, 'is a bunch of outdated black face shit that would cause me pain. Do you want to cause me pain?'

'No. But I thought you wanted something provocative. I thought you wanted—'

'People are about to go nuts, Richard. People are already rushing the shops to buy pasta, soup, and fucking toilet paper of all fucking things. Highlighting YingCo's Chinese, or Asian ownership, is the last thing we need right now, particularly if this coronavirus thing kicks off for real. We'll have a country of *casually racist* rednecks kicking in YingCo's doors. I thought you could—'

'Don't blame us!' It ripped out of Richard's throat before he could swallow. 'We don't sell bats and we sure as houses don't eat them. We only stock Australian meat, fruit and vegetables, all year round, no excuse. We stock it cheap too, so why pay more? It's bat crazy, just like bat soup. YingCo, Australia's freshest… no bats.'

There was silence from the phone. Above Richard the fish-spotter flapped off its branch without so much as a burp and flew quietly back towards the old manager's house.

'Got it,' Max suddenly laughed, a little too loud. 'It lets YingCo own the joke, plays up their local legacy — one we can invent — and distances them from this coronavirus shit. It's in poor enough taste to get the op-ed writers whinging too. But Richard? Some cop rang asking about you. Anything I need to know?'

'Nah,' Richard coughed, twisting inside, repulsed by the conversation, but cursing Max, cursing the constable, cursing his luck. 'It's just a case of mistaken—'

'Good,' Max said. 'See what else you can come up with. I'll call you in a few days.'

The phone went dead. Richard stood motionless for a moment, waiting for the clown to emerge from the trees, waiting for Max to call back and tell Richard he was a talentless, 'bat-crazy' accountant who didn't deserve any job. But nothing happened. He pushed his phone in his pocket and moved down the slope, turned onto the creek path, told himself to feel optimistic, to believe he'd have something to show for himself. Halfway along the creek path he'd given up trying to feel good. Lena was gone. She'd moved on, and there was a butterfly in that clown house, his name written in rotten paint and a cop who thought he was starting fires. There were bigger fish to fry and they spun and whirred so fast in Richard's mind as he marched out of the forest, past Ashleigh's little blue car and up to her porch, that he'd forgotten all about Thompson's whimpers in the gloom until he was met by Lars' worried face at the door.

Richard was focussed on the DVD case sitting on the kitchen table in front of him. It had been waiting on the porch for Richard's return from Ashleigh's, shining in the setting sun. It had a white cover and on that white cover was the clown's incomplete butterfly. It was symmetrical, drawn on a computer and printed. Richard sat at the table looking at it.

I KNOW WHO YOU ARE.

It was printed beneath the butterfly. Richard picked it up and took it into the lounge room, holding the case carefully, one hand wrapped in Ashleigh's bandage from a wound she'd attended to earlier at her house, moments after he told Lars his dog might be injured in the old manager's house and that his name was written in paint with another 'message' inside. He had offered to go back with Lars and check for the dog, but Lars hadn't wanted to. He had wanted to call the cops, a horrifying prospect considering the words written inside: *BURN IT ALL RICHARD*

'We can't,' Ashleigh had said. 'Not while someone's messing with Richard.'

Richard the suspect, Richard who 'had to be careful', she had said, because there'd been two more fires in Blackwood: a massage parlour and a house at Olave Valley. Both were completely destroyed.

'And it isn't the Blackwood Clown doing this,' Ashleigh had said.

'How do you know?' Lars had said.

'He's never bothered us.'

'Never bothered us? The guy's insane. He screams in the forest, keeps me up at night. He's got my dog.'

'You don't know that he took your dog. Thompson's very energetic and could have got out by himself. No, I think it's somebody else, some-body nasty. How could they burn down the house of that old couple in Olave Valley? They're lovely.'

Lars looked at Richard with silent horror. How did she know *them*? Ashleigh went on to explain how the old man had been on her rounds for in-home nursing care, that he and his wife were Quakers connected to the old Quaker's house they shared the valley with. She said there'd been a 'break-in' there a year or so ago and ever since then they'd wanted a nurse to help them look after the intellectually disabled guy who lived there too, 'a gentle man who can't speak'.

Lars shot Richard another look, no doubt hoping he'd maintained the secret about trespassing in the clown painter's house last year, but all Richard could think about was the shotgun fired in the night, the warning printed in the newspaper two days later, the burning paintings and the apparent 'curse' Lars believed in.

'Are you still going to visit them?' Richard asked with a tiny voice, eliciting a kind smile from Ashleigh. She probably thought he was con-cerned about the old couples' welfare.

'I don't know. It depends what they do next, if they rebuild their house or move away. I hope they rebuild. I liked going there.'

That was when she took Richard's hand, pulled him away from Lars, led him into the bathroom and talked about the Quakers' religion, the fact she thought it was interesting because they were one of the first to advocate for same sex marriage, that they believed sex before marriage was a personal choice, that they focussed less on institutionalised laws 'and more about a person's individual experience with God', and all the time she cleaned his bleeding hand, a beautiful, kind nurse fixing him, unaware his mind was rattled by burning paintings, laughing clowns, broken butterfly wings, a past that wouldn't let him go, a school of pira-nhas swimming joyously around his skull. But then she burnt his hand with alcohol that shocked him from his thoughts, rubbed the wound with alcohol-soaked bandages, covered it with cooling antiseptic cream, and drew close, allowed her scent to waft over him. She held up his hand to inspect it, lowered it, looked into Richard's eyes with green emeralds, hair shining beautiful under the bathroom fluorescent, and asked him if he was okay, if he was 'really, really okay?'

'Do you need to talk about anything, Richard?' Ashleigh asked, still lowering his hand, her breath edging closer to his nose, the rise and fall of her breasts concealed under another T-shirt, its scooped neckline encouraging him to forget his dashed hopes with Lena. 'You can talk to me, Richard. I'm not going to bite.'

His bandaged hand brushed against his pants. She held it there, staring into his eyes. He liked the smell of her breath. He liked her touch, and inside his mind the piranhas were temporarily stunned, jaws ajar so that air poppled out in bubbles. She shifted closer and his lust sniffed out her skin, pulsed, pulled, yanked him against her, her sensual, beautiful mouth opening, her chin lifting to meet his own. Somewhere inside him a painting of Lena fell into a pool of warm water and started dissolving. She *chika'ed*, she *chaa'ed*. She *CHIKA'ED*. She *CHEE'ED*.

Richard was back in his lounge room alone and the DVD player was whirring, the bird outside was hassling him. He had a DVD with a broken butterfly on its cover to watch. Richard turned on his television and pressed play. News vision of a bushfire filled the screen, cut quickly to another and then another. The edits were fast: burning houses, burning paddocks, burning trees, ambulances, water bombers, CFS trucks, footage of a CFS volunteer giving water to a koala in a burnt landscape, a kangaroo charcoaled crispy on a smouldering fence, 20-metre flames roaring over a pine forest, the sky red with smoke, amateur footage complete with occasional selfies by wide-eyed people. They were images Richard had seen recently on the television news, repeatedly re-hashed, re-played, flogged by media reporting the 'worst bushfire season in history'. Suddenly the image of a Royal Adelaide Show clown smiled at the camera, followed by the image of another clown surrounded by children and balloons, more burning houses, more burning trees, Stephen King's Pennywise, abattoir pigs squealing, a burning photo of the former Holden factory at Elizabeth, footage of people in medical masks, thermometer guns pointed at children, a woman sipping from a bowl with a bat in it and from the montage words emerged, juxtaposed over a blazing bushfire, white words super-imposed with online DVD editing freeware.

I know you like to burn Richard.

Horrible words.

I know you like to burn a lot.

Richard sat transfixed. Inside his mind an underwater gate released B-grade horror-movie piranhas to devour the squiggly flesh of his brain.

Burnt it all Richard. Burn the lot.

Richard picked up his phone with a shaking hand. He wanted to call Ashleigh. He needed cool hands, a cool bandage, her perfume blocking everything out. But then the montage stopped and amateur footage of a dog in somebody's backyard emerged. It was a German Shepherd and it suddenly squatted in the way dogs do when they're about to take shit.

'Ooooh, gross,' laughed a woman's voice as she filmed the dog doing its business.

Another video appeared, this time a little Jack Russel being walked in a city park by a man with glasses. That dog too suddenly squatted, looking at its master in the embarrassed manner of a dog taking a crap. A brown, horrible sausage came out its arse. The camera operator zoomed in so close you could see chunks of something that looked like carrot.

Richard's stomach turned.

Don't look away, Richard, the words said on-screen. *I've got a secret that will change your life.*

A labrador shat and rubbed its arse on the grass. A bull terrier finished a momentous pile and walked away to let a kelpie sniff it, piss on it, push bile into Richard's mouth. A poodle looked at the camera, looked at its filming owner, pushed soft-serve ice cream out the hole beneath its pom pom tail. A kelpie ran up to horse shit and ate it, regurgitated it, ate it once more, twisting Richard's body, making his eyes water, his tongue releasing saliva and bile rising up his throat. A huskie walked aimlessly about in a concrete backyard, surrounded by deposits of shit, then there was green shit on somebody's kitchen tiles, against the cupboards, on an owner's arm, so close to the dog's collar camera you could see arm hairs standing up through the fluorescent goop.

Gold Dog. Turning Richard green since 2019.

Richard rushed to the kitchen, vomited into the sink, once, twice, three times, splashed water onto his face, rubbed his face, scratched his face so Ashleigh's bandage on his hand became wet and unravelled. He stomped to the bathroom, kicked off his shoes, stripped and turned on the hot water, standing beneath the shower while it was still cold, icy cold wicked icicle needles digging at his skin, the smeary stench, the layer of vomit-inducing animal shit that covered his body, wet little specks he dug at while the water turned hot, scalding hot. He rotated and took it on his front, on his face, the side of his head, expunging himself of bugs, cooking like a hairless animal in a hotpot. He turned off the water and emerged red raw and stinging, blistering in areas exposed too long. He dabbed himself with a towel and started breaking apart, a lopsided face cracking down the middle, two halves of a person that didn't fit crumbling. The bathroom steam cooled and he wanted Ashleigh again, Ashleigh the nurse, the nurturer, the saint with the cool hands. He wanted her to come over and rub cream into his burnt body, soothe him, tell him it's okay and there's nothing wrong with his face or his skin or his heart or his eyes and it was just in his mind, and 'isn't it funny, Richard, that it all gets to you so much but here, here is my own skin and its beautiful and it's yours and do you feel better now Richard I love you I love you Richard I want you and I love you'.

He wanted to go back and finish the kiss in her own bathroom, her body pressed so hard up against his own, a kiss he'd broken away from when he spotted a white jacket smudged with dirt and what looked like soot in her laundry basket.

'What's that?' he'd asked, pointing to the jacket. She didn't follow his gaze but instead kept staring into his eyes, questioning, searching, licking her lips.

'It's from the fire, the old couple. I said I'd clean it.'

'The clown wears a white jacket.'

'A lot of people wear white jackets,' Ashleigh said without missing a beat.

'Why have you got the clown's jacket?' Richard said, stepping backwards, her spell broken by the clothes of a clown out to get him, a man she claimed was 'lovely'.

'You're so nervous.' Ashleigh laughed and refused to let go of his hand. 'It's just a jacket.'

'I've gotta get going. I've gotta do some work, for some agency.'

'I can help you with the cops,' she said, stepping past the white jacket lying crinkled like a dirty lie between them. 'I can be your alibi again but you've got to keep me posted on—'

'I'm meeting Lena tomorrow,' Richard blurted out, shutting Ashleigh down with the only weapon he had.

'Oh,' she said, letting go of his hand immediately. 'Tell her I said hello.'

Richard fled from her house and climbed into his dad's Mitsubishi 380. He drove fast to get away before it was too late, before the clown turned up, before the cops turned up, before he slipped into Ashleigh's cradle and any hope of salvaging a life anywhere else but here would be lost in the broth of her perfume. Once it stuck it would never come off. But she texted him as he drove, a message flying after him like a pungent, love-filled arrow.

You left your hand sanitiser in my bathroom xx

Richard stood up and collected a new towel from his cupboard, wrapped it around himself, went to his lounge room and, without looking at whatever horror the DVD was playing, without listening to whatever horrible sound was coming from the TV speakers, ejected the DVD and held it in both hands, bending it so it cracked in half. He cracked it again into quarters, then cracked it once more until the pieces were too small and too sharp to be cracked anymore.

'Fuck you motherfucker and fuck your fucking dogs!'

He threw the pieces aside, swallowed, then heard some sort of movement outside, a scuffle. He stepped quickly to the front door and threw it open. From the forest across the dirt track he sensed something unnatural among the pale greens of the native shrubs and trees, a horrible little fiend in a freshly-cleaned white jacket who shrieked at people in forests, who painted birds and laid curses, a nasty hermit who'd graduated into pyromania, animal abduction, and now DVD creation. Richard returned to his kitchen and retrieved his slingshot, his collection of ball bearings he usually aimed at the wattle bird, returned to the doorway and started shooting into the forest. Once, twice, three times, four times.

'Did I get you?' he shouted. 'Did you like that? You little fuck.'

Richard listened to the forest. Dreadlocked gum trees chuckled, a neighbour's door closed in the distance, then another. But there was no scuffling, no movement, no clown.

Chika CHEE CHAA Chika CHEE CHAA

Just the bird, of course, his relentless, hysterical fucking torturer. It was always there to keep him company, always waiting for the best moment to drill ice into his brain. Richard screamed and shot two ball bearings into his tree's foliage, then spotted the axe handle in his yard where the constable had thrown it the other day. He lurched forward, picked it up, marched to the tree and threw it spinning in the direction of the bird's guttural snark. It popped off the trunk, spun backwards, and slammed into his forehead with a *crack* so his skull rang like a mouldy bell fallen from its perch.

Richard staggered inside where broken fragments of the DVD spun in circles around him, spiralling taunts that made him nauseous, and from his forehead trickled a warm liquid that grew into a little stream that filled his eyes with blood, took the energy from his legs, and sent him crashing to the floor.

THE FUCK-UP

Sniles stared down at a dinner that, for the third night this week, was comprised of two-minute noodles. Jenny had gone to bed early, again. This time she'd left a cooked sausage out for him to add to his lonely meal, but nothing else. He wondered if she was depressed, corrected himself immediately. Of course she was depressed. He'd taken her to a place where they didn't know anybody and she couldn't land a job. He was working long hours, doing voluntary overtime, blaming it on SAPOL, leaving her alone with no connections, no one to hang out with, no one to bitch to about her absent partner.

He felt guilty about her predicament, but not guilty enough to stop. He simply *had* to take this scalp, a murderous pyromaniac who could burn people alive. Sniles knew it was all the same person. His instinct screamed it, and there was no way he was going to ignore that again, not like the time he fucked up in Victoria.

It happened on a stinking hot day in November. Sniles had decided to patrol a Mildura boat ramp where kids had been swimming illegally. He'd arrived and was horrified to find a 9-year-old dead instead. A second boy was sitting on the grass with the deceased in his lap, holding the victim's stomach together. It had been opened by a boat propeller — the precise reason swimming was banned there in the first place. Entrails led across grass to the water's edge. The surviving kid rose his hand as Constable Sniles approached and pointed a trembling finger upstream.

'The speedboat went that way,' he said, his lips blue. 'Black.'

Sniles followed the boy's finger but sensed something wrong. Upstream looked bland, featureless, dulled by the smoke that had been choking the atmosphere for months due to raging bushfires in the west. Downstream looked electric, the Murray River a light mud colour that shimmered with messages.

'You sure he didn't go that way?'

The boy shook his head. Tears reddened his devastated eyes.

Sniles hesitated. He only had one patrol boat at his disposal and instinct told him to send it downstream. Even now, the brown waters lapped and splashed with golden sunlight fragments, promising the skull pieces of a kid-killer should Sniles listen. But the boy was adamant and the longer Sniles waited, the further the killer could travel. He swore and sent the patrol boat upstream, deployed patrol cars in the same direction. Surely the kid saw it right. But they didn't find anyone. No one upstream had even seen a black speedboat. After half an hour Sniles rushed the patrol cars downstream instead, commissioned a fisherman's boat and went out on the water himself. But it was too late. He'd listened to a boy in shock rather than his own instinct and a kid-killer escaped.

The people of Mildura were grief-stricken at first. The death of a child in such tragic circumstances was heartbreaking. But as the week wore on and the police failed to uncover a single lead, their grief turned to anger. The woman at the newsagency stopped saying hello when Sniles bought a paper in the mornings. Farmers gave him a hard look when they crossed paths on the street. One local almond grower spat on the street in front of Sniles and called him a 'useless prick'.

'How many speeding fines did you pigs give out while that killer got away?'

Rattled and angry, Sniles returned to the boat ramp, hoping beyond logic there might be something he'd missed, evidence overlooked. When he arrived, he spotted two teenagers swimming in the river, blatantly ignoring the police tape.

'What the hell are you doing?' Sniles shouted from the shore.

One of the bobbing heads turned, a cheeky redhead who spouted water from his mouth.

'Having a swim, officer,' he said. 'It's 40 bloody degrees.'

'What it is, is a crime scene.' Sniles recognised the little shit. His father was an unsuccessful farmer who grew whatever crop was in favour, ripping it up and planting varieties with the latest fashion. The kid had been in trouble before — thieving, vandalising — and even now, his freckly forehead shone wet with guilt. 'Get out of there.'

'Give it up, mate,' the ranga continued. 'You ain't gonna catch the killer. You pigs only know how to give out speeding fines.'

'It's an offence to trespass on a crime scene,' Sniles said, stretching his neck.

'We're not on your crime scene. We're swimming in the river.'

'Then you won't mind if I get rid of this rubbish.' Sniles picked up the kids' clothes and bags from the riverbank. 'It's clearly not yours.'

'Oi,' the ranga shouted as Sniles threw the lot into the water. The teenager swam fast towards a backpack that for the moment floated on the surface. 'My phone's in there, you pig.'

Sniles retrieved his baton as the teenager reached his bag.

'Fuck you,' the kid shouted, standing in the waist-high water, holding his bag aloft as water poured from its corners. 'You useless bloody copper. Get a real job.'

Sniles grabbed the teenager by his red hair, yanked him out of the water and onto the grass where the 9-year-old had died the previous week. The ranga screamed, flailed and kicked, his skinny body wet and white. Sniles let go of him but the brat spat at his legs, threw his soaking backpack at Sniles' face. Something hard in the bag struck him on his cheekbone.

'Maz,' the other kid in the water pleaded, hovering offshore. Sniles looked at him for a moment, his underdeveloped face crinkling with fear. 'I'm sorry, officer.'

'Get out of here, son,' Sniles said, flicking his baton so it extended, turning his attention to the red-headed fucker at his feet. He swished the baton through the air and split the teenager's cheek. He swung it again and hit the back of his soggy head, a cabbage cracked open. He hit him again, tension of the week unleashed, a flurry of blows that at one point crunched the fingers of an outstretched hand trying to protect its host.

Eventually screams from the other kid penetrated the invisible sludge that encased Sniles' rage and he stepped back, his baton dripping, an unconscious teenager bubbling blood onto the grass. He knelt down to feel for a pulse, but the skin was too swollen, too tight, too purple.

Sniles pulled the mess from the grassy riverbank and bundled him into the car, suddenly worried, suddenly fearful. The fuzziness had subsided and, while he still saw the kid instinctively as a criminal, he knew this time he'd gone too far. This time, Sniles was going to cop it.

At hospital the doctor brought the teenager back to consciousness, but not before the intake nurse took photos of his busted face. Her images appeared in the *Sunraysia Daily*, hounding Constable Sniles out of town with sarcastic headlines quoting angry locals.

Officer 'acts the hero' in horrific teenager beating
Mildura boy bashed for 'swimming in the river'

Local biddies travelled all the way to Melbourne to watch Sniles burn in court, this 'hero' from Swan Hill with a terrible temper. The boy's lawyer listed Sniles past moments of rage to the courtroom. He'd knocked a drunk unconscious in 2015 when they tried to drive home from the Mildura tavern and crashed into a parked car. He'd forced a 21-year-old caught stealing a carton of diet soda in 2017 to drink the lot until they shat and pissed their pants and cried. He'd stormed a meth lab in 2018 and pulled the occupant by his ear into the front yard so violently that it needed to be stitched back on. And then, of course, he'd nearly beat a 16-year-old to death in November 2019 for swimming in the river.

To the horror of the Mildura community, not to mention regional media who wanted the hero's head, Sniles was cleared. The ranga might have sustained three broken fingers, a fractured cheekbone, concussion, cuts and gashes that required 20 stitches to stop bleeding, but he'd also broken into every sporting club in Mildura. It all came out in court when his mate blabbered. When it emerged that the redhead also broke into the local RSL and stole war medals, Victoria Police saw their opportunity and pounced. They laid multiple charges of trespassing, burglary and vandalism, then offered to drop them just as quickly if the redhead withdrew his allegations against Sniles.

The brat didn't hesitate. The community might be out for Sniles' head, but the ranga's own cranium wasn't that safe either. Stealing war medals and vandalising sport clubs was a good way to lose it in a country like Australia. He withdrew his allegations and nicked off to the Northern Territory faster than the papers could write 'un-Australian'.

Sniles decided right there and then that he would never ignore his instincts again, no matter how far they flew in the face of logic. The redhead's thievery was proof his instincts never lied, even if Sniles went too far. He also promised Jenny that he would deal with his temper, that he would get help if necessary, or maybe even allow her to counsel him herself.

That was when Jenny punched him in the chest. Short yet strong, she was made of country stock and her blow had power.

'Don't fuck with me, Rory. You either fix your shit, or you get lost.'

'I mean it,' Sniles said, grabbing her hands and squeezing them tight. 'I want to be better than this.'

'You son of a bitch.' Every secret in town went through Mildura's best psychologist at some stage, and persistent rumours about her partner's aggression had proved true. Jenny shook her head but squeezed him back regardless. 'I didn't shack up with some violent bastard from Swan Hill just to prove every gossiping biddie in this place right.'

Victoria Police were less forgiving. They might have cleared Rory Sniles' name to salvage their own reputation but his days in the field were over. They wanted him on restricted duties in Melbourne. Sniles considered asking for a transfer to Queensland but Jenny would hate the tropical weather — if she'd even agree to leave Mildura. New South

Wales was a possibility but it was covered in smoke thanks to the relentless bushfires that had been raging since July. Then there was Adelaide, South Australia, a place with its own bushfire problems, but which seemed better equipped to deal with them after more than a century of experience. It was also relatively isolated, both geographically and in the media. Where better than an oversized town sleeping quietly at the bottom of the world to wait out bad publicity?

When he suggested an Adelaide transfer to his superiors, they secured him a place within 10 minutes. Jenny was less excited, but Mildura's rejection of her partner was insurmountable. He couldn't leave his house without somebody spitting in his general direction. To his relief, and the surprise of the Mildura community — who must have considered her crazier than her patients — Jenny agreed to go with him.

Five months later, mashing a single sausage into cheap noodles, Sniles wondered if this case would be the final straw, rather than his saving grace. Folklore, clowns, historical names and head cases, it was fast becoming more than he'd bargained for, and his relationship with Jenny was on the brink. Failure here in South Australia would spell the end, Sniles was sure of it, but if he caught this motherfucking arsonist, whoever it was, things would be better, he knew that too.

His fork clinked against the bowl, a tiny echo exuding solitude from the otherwise silent kitchen. From down the hallway he heard a door softly closing.

A month ago Pyro had come to Ashleigh's house for reassurance, some kind of hope. General Motors had just announced it was ending the Holden brand for good and whatever light was left in Pyro's gut had gone out. But the first thing Ashleigh told him was their friend was coming back from the UK. She'd heard it from Lars: Richard would be home in a matter of weeks. Pyro's gut hardened and turned black. He was suddenly out of time. He had to make a move on her. He had to deploy the best card he had: sympathy.

'I ... just miss my father a bit,' he'd told Ashleigh as they stood outside her house. 'I haven't seen him since I was five.'

He had no phone number, no address, not even a photograph, just the ashes of one taken during the sunniest week of Pyro's life, back before the childcare fire, when Mother was forcing him to tell her how much he 'loved her', forcing him to sleep in her bed at night. He wasn't allowed to have his own room anymore because he 'might grow up too fast' and leave Mother 'like your father did'.

He told Ashleigh how the photo showed his younger self beaming back at the camera as he stood alongside his father. His mother had gone interstate to battle for the inheritance of a dying relative and Pyro was allowed a rare stay with Father at his grandparents' house.

Father took the week off from his job at the Holden factory, gave Pyro his own room, read him books, tucked him in at night, took him to the football where people shouted, swore, were allowed to get excited about something other than Mother. Father had a beard at the time and

Pyro collected trimmings from his electric razor. He had the idea to stick some to his face with paper glue, spending a full hour in the bathroom before announcing himself in the kitchen to his grandparents and Father.

'Look at the little boy trying to look like his father,' Grandmother had crooned. 'Shall we take you outside for a photograph?'

Mother had smiled at the polaroid photo for benefit of his naïve grandparents when she picked Pyro up. But when she took him home she ripped the photo into three pieces and chided Pyro for putting glue on his face. She washed his face with acetone, cursed his father, called him a pussy for leaving before she'd arrived to pick up their son. She took the photo pieces out back and set fire to them, a dirty, licking blue flame that curled the print, erased the memories, burnt her fingers. She flung the pieces away to curl and writhe on the ground, her face contorting as she swore. But when she went inside Pyro scooped up the ashes of the picture and put them in his jar with Father's stubble, a secret stash of memories Mother would never find.

'That's so sad,' Ashleigh said, hugging Pyro, smothering him with perfume. She withdrew and Pyro felt stunned. 'Have you ever tried to find him? ... Your father?'

'He disappeared a few months after that, just before the fire,' Pyro said, wanting another hug.

'The childcare centre?' Ashleigh asked, cautiously.

Pyro nodded.

'He said he was going to Queensland, that he'd come back but... even after the fire, and I had to live at my grandparent's house, he never did.'

He watched her closely, hoping she wouldn't ask if he believed Mother had killed Father. The cops thought she had and so had everyone else. Pyro hadn't known what was worse: his mother killing his father, or the idea that his father could leave him and stay away forever.

But instead Ashleigh moved in for another hug, held him for a good 30 seconds, 30 seconds that suggested softness, kindness, infinite perfume and the end of loneliness.

'Hey,' Ashleigh said, brightening up. 'You wanna know a secret?'

'I don't know,' Pyro said, wanting to push his face into her hair.

'You know that guy, that guy you lot call the clown?'

Pyro blinked.

'I kissed him,' Ashleigh said, standing back with a triumphant look on her face. 'You should have seen his face. I don't think he'd ever been kissed by a woman in his life.'

'Wha ... where ... how?'

'I met him. I'm his new nurse.' She laughed again. 'Isn't it nuts? His name's Gerard Brummer and he's on my round.'

Then she drew in close, conspiratorially, sending her beautiful perfume over Pyro's head again.

'Don't tell anyone but ... he lives at the old Quaker's house, you know, at Olave Valley? There's an old couple next door who used to look after him but there was a break-in and they're getting too old to deal with everything so they organised Home Stay Assistance for me to look after him. What are the odds?'

Pyro's stomach disappeared. He'd been stunned when they broke into the old Quaker's house a year ago to find fresh paintings of the butterfly, evidence Gerard was still alive. But now Ashleigh was saying he was the clown as well? A weird freak who ran about the forests screaming and who, apparently thanks to Pyro's *own* stupidity, had landed Ashleigh for his private nurse? If it wasn't bad enough that her dirty friend was coming home to get in the way, now the little fucker responsible for Mother's death was, in fact, the Blackwood Clown, a weirdo who'd somehow managed to be kissed by the very woman Pyro had pined over for years.

'Are you okay?' Ashleigh asked, her face troubled.

'I'm fine,' Pyro said. 'I just wasn't ... expecting that ... you know. You *kissed* him?' Her blonde hair in his clown-face teeth, red lips on his clown-face cheeks, hands that had never gotten close to Pyro. Everyone had gotten close to Ashleigh except Pyro, even Gerard had gotten close to Ashleigh, Gerard the motherfucking clown fucking psycho.

'Hey,' she said. 'What's the matter? It was just a bit of fun. It was just—'

'How did it happen?'

She flinched at his demanding tone but explained how she'd been working for Stay Home Assistance and visited patients in their homes. Gerard Brummer was a 30-something hermit, a brand-new client who needed support because he couldn't talk. He could only make 'bird noises'.

On her first visit to the 'dilapidated house', Ashleigh said she met a red-headed, child-faced man in a 'smelly white suit'. He made his strange noises, constantly smiled, and towards the end stood up and disappeared altogether. While looking for him Ashleigh came across the butterflies.

'They're amazing,' she said, frowning as Pyro grimaced. 'So perfect, yet so weird.'

She couldn't find Gerard and, being at the end of her shift, gave up looking for him and left. When she arrived home she heard a bump and turned around, just in time to see the boot of her parked hatchback close — she said she never opened it — and a flash of white disappear into Blackwood Forest. Gerard had apparently crawled into the boot of her hatchback and hitched a ride.

Ashleigh continued visiting the old Quaker's house where she developed what she called a 'friendship with the strangely beautiful' man. At the same time Brummer kept visiting Blackwood Forest. She knew this because she heard him 'shrieking like a galah' from inside the forest. After a while she put two and two together and realised Brummer was, in fact, the Blackwood Clown that everyone talked about. But then she said something that made Pyro want to grab her head and squeeze it.

One day at the Quaker's house Gerard apparently leant forward and held her hand, turned it over and traced her palm gently for five minutes without a sound. She said it was 'strangely intimate', a mood accentuated by the candles Gerard used for light because the hermit didn't have electricity. There was a candle on the kitchen table where they sat and, lost in the moment, she accidentally brushed her arm close enough to burn her skin. In that instant Gerard let loose a little whistle 'like a baby bird, and no joke, the flame disappeared in a puff of smoke, as if he'd killed it with his voice'.

'It was the weirdest thing, and Gerard didn't even look at the candle. He just kept tracing my hand and it started to feel … I don't know, kind of nice …' Ashleigh trailed off, leaving a black hole in Pyro's heart, a circling chasm that spun faster and faster, vacuuming up whatever hope he had left to win her.

'So that's it?' he asked as she stared into space, tracing a finger over her hand in a way that made him sick. 'You kissed him? What about the rest?'

'What?' She said it too quickly, her supple mouth opening with fraudulent confusion. 'What are you talking about?

'The clown.' He imagined Ashleigh's hair burning, the perfume in her aura igniting, flames melting her luscious fucking face.

'I don't know what you're—'

'Bullshit.'

Ashleigh frowned again and that little scar emerged above her eyebrow. Pyro wanted suddenly to bite it, cut it out.

'I gotta go,' he stammered. Ashleigh's hair was at his fingertips. He wanted to grab it, wanted to pull, shred and burn. 'I've got shit to do.'

'Burn the hussy,' Mother laughed inside his head as he walked to his car. 'Burn the clown-fucking bitch.'

'I'm not burning Ashleigh, *Mother*,' he hissed back.

*

A month later Pyro stood in Richard's yard painting his tree in the mid-morning light, slapping on the yellow, doing a better job at the clown's butterfly than any of the others he'd painted. But he couldn't spend too long on it. He didn't know where Richard was, or when he was coming home, and there were neighbours about even if the front yard was slightly private. They hated the occupant of this property. They didn't trust the little shit arsonist and now there was a real pyro on the block, a more effective pyro, a motherfucking clown-hating psycho with one more trick to send her dirty lover mad.

Pyro finished what was meant to be the clown's butterfly — streaks of yellow paint running over the black bark. It was wobbly and resembled nothing of the perfect insects the clown could reproduce, but Pyro didn't care. It was all about the message. Her dirty lover would see this tree and feel hunted, targeted by a screaming freak in a white suit who should have been dead.

He took the brush and can back to his car, placing it in a plastic bag beside two cans of petrol into the boot. There were memories waiting inside each of the cans, Mother's hair, Thompson's hair, Ashleigh's hair, Father's beard. He always liked to include a bit of Father's beard. His disappearance was the worst memory of the lot.

Pyro was about to close the boot when a familiar shriek rose from Pony Ridge Scrub. Pyro's bones went rigid and he peered into the trees across the road, the rustling foliage, the scraggly, intertwined black limbs that had re-sprouted after Richard's fire last year. There was another shriek and it was getting louder, angrier, as if the act of replicating his butterfly had summoned the clown back from death.

'You were dead,' Pyro shouted back, his voice weak and afraid. 'Your name's Gerard and you are meant to be dead.'

The responding cry smashed through his ear canal, slicing at his brain.

'You shouldn't be here,' Pyro shouted back, holding his ears and stepping nervously towards Pony Ridge Scrub. He stepped off the road and hid in the trees. The shrieking stopped and a relative silence returned. From a neighbour's property he heard a door slam. What if somebody called the police? What if her dirty lover came back to find Pyro here with the fake butterfly on the tree? What if the clown suddenly attacked and Pyro went missing like his father?

'Coward,' Mother spat.

Pyro lingered uncomfortably in the scrub for moment, staring into the trees, seeing nothing, fearing an ambush. He could stand it no longer and ran back to his car, expecting a clown to fly out of the forest and slam itself against the window, shrieking like a bird, squashing itself against the windscreen. He reversed out of the driveway, looking for neighbours, and nearly lost control of the car as he skidded across the dirt track.

'You fucking pussy,' Mother screamed.

Pyro tore out of there so quickly he didn't notice that the boot of his Commodore had been closed.

COMPLICIT

Sniles sat in an Adelaide hospital, watching Ashleigh dote on the mad bastard in his hospital bed. She pushed hair back from Richard's bandaged-wrapped brow and Sniles felt a twinge of jealousy. Jenny had once looked at him like that, back when they'd hooked up after a local football final, moved in together just six months later. She'd fallen for him despite the stories about his temper but beating up the teenager and fleeing the state was too great a stretch and she hadn't looked at him the same since. Ashleigh, on the other hand, appeared ready to marry Richard on the spot. But there was a sense of complicity between them, an invisible scent among the disinfectant, the pine germ-killers, the surrounding hospital sickness. Something about Ashleigh's flushed face screamed with secrets, some kind of mystery that pissed Sniles off.

'Take me through it again,' he said. 'How were you feeling, right before you brained yourself with an axe handle?'

Richard sighed with agitation. His eyes were hazy and doped, his left bloodshot from the head trauma he'd sustained.

'Why do you keep bothering him?' Ashleigh said, leaning back into her bedside chair. 'He's already told you everything about his accident.'

'They're questions, Miss. I'm a police officer and I ask questions.'

'We need to talk about the Blackwood Clown,' Richard drooled.

Sniles ground his teeth. If Dawksted found out that his best lead was blaming everything on a vengeful, screaming clown, Sniles would never hear the end of it.

'Look. I checked it out, stupidly. Other than a few bullshit stories on social media, there's no record of any Blackwood Clown. I've certainly never heard of it and neither have—'

'But you're not from here, are you, Constable?' The ice in the girl's tongue was acute. She saw him flinch and smiled, brightening as if she'd never shot an arrow at all. 'Otherwise you would have heard of him.'

'What makes you think I'm not from here?' Sniles wanted to arrest her.

'I don't know,' Ashleigh said breezily. 'Just a feeling.'

'But you should have heard of him, shouldn't you?' Richard said. 'You're a *police* officer, aren't you? You're meant to know about all the crazies, not just fuck-ups like me. I guess it's easier to just pin it all on me.

'Pin *what* on you?' Sniles asked, feeling his backbone extend, his torso rising over Richard's inert form.

'The bushfire man, the fucking firebug. That's why you're here, isn't it?'

'And the rest, Richard.'

'The what?'

'The fucking rest,' Sniles shouted, raising his fist.

'Anger management,' the blonde protested, standing upright between Richard and Sniles. Her green eyes were fearless. She reminded Sniles of Mildura's best, the local biddies who'd travelled to Melbourne to see Sniles squirm under lights, hoping he'd get castrated by the judge over the redhead. 'I think you need to calm down. There's enough going on in the world right now without having to worry about policemen losing their tempers.'

'Don't worry yourself about me,' Sniles said, smiling hot. 'I only dish up what's deserved. Why didn't you want us to call your parents, Richard?'

Richard shook his head and again, Ashleigh swept the hair from his forehead.

'Because, Richard,' Sniles continued, desperate to break the girl's control of the situation. 'You're bothering me. In fact, you're bothering *a lot* of authorities.'

Richard's mouth started to tremble. For a moment he looked like he wanted to break open, a river gush from his soul, but the blonde stroked his chin, leant into his ear, breathed secret thoughts.

'Son? I think it's in your best interests if we speak privately for a moment.'

'I'll get a coffee,' Ashleigh suddenly declared, gliding towards the door, throttling Sniles with perfume as she passed. 'Would you like one, officer?'

'No.' He waited for her to leave and sat alongside Richard. 'It was no accident you gave yourself four stitches and concussion, was it?' The eyes of his prey flittered. 'You were racked in guilt, right? For your horrible deeds?'

'What? No,' Richard protested, drool stretching between his lips. 'It was that bloody bird. I told you—'

'Oh, yes, a wattle bird that has it in for you, a… what did you call it? A relentless "cunty little fucker". Son, I sit here and look at you, the scratches on your face, your head injury, and feel partly responsible. Do you know why? You've got all this ridiculous shit swimming around your brain and frankly, I should never have let you go.'

'But—'

'Here you are, on the verge of being committed to stop the self-harm—'

'I didn't—'

'Telling stories about evil birds and clowns, and all this could have been prevented, couldn't it? If I'd just taken you in from the start.'

'He's real.' Richard's voice cracked. 'It's the clown and he's been hassling me since I got back.'

'Do you like massage, Richard?'

'Wha … what?'

'Massage. Happy endings?'

'I don't know what you're talking about.'

'Do you feel so dirty you have to burn them to death, cover your tracks?' Sniles tapped a finger against Richard's bandaged forehead so he jerked. 'Just how fucked up are you, son?'

'Richard, you silly duffer.'

Sniles swung around to see Ashleigh standing at the foot of the bed. 'You left this at my house.'

Perfume punched Sniles as she stepped around him and placed a clear tube of antibacterial gel wash on the side table.

'I wanted to give it back before I forgot. People are starting to hoard this stuff, you know, because of coronavirus.' She walked briskly back to the door, pausing to give Sniles a smile. 'I know you'll need it.'

Sniles couldn't stand it. He wanted to grab her shoulders and shake but she left the room again.

'Listen, you little shit,' he said, knocking over the gel and leaning in close to Richard. 'You either help me out, you and your bloody girl-friend, or I'll have you locked up with every infected son-of-a-bitch we can find. Got it?'

'I *told* you. It's the clown. The fucking Blackwood Clown. He's got it in for me, and Lars, and Donnie. Donnie fucking hates him. Donnie started it all. You should talk to Donnie.'

'Where is this Donnie, huh? Or Lars? Have they seen this clown?'

'I don't bloody know,' Richard shouted. 'I just want to get away from this place, from Dad's numbers and fires and missing dogs—'

'What dog?' Sniles interrupted. Richard's hair suddenly seemed more real than it should, more curly, a high resolution photograph in a grey hospital ward.

'Lars' dog. I think he's trapped in that basement at the old manager's house but it's got paint on the wall as well and says my name but I've got nothing to do with anything.'

'What kind of dog?' Sniles pictured the stolen dog found strangled behind the old railway water tower on Saturday — the day of the first fire at Olave Valley.

'A red heeler,' Richard continued. 'The guy's fucking nuts, man. He painted one of his butterflies inside the house. I'm telling you. He's got it in for me.'

'What butterfly?' The words bolted through Sniles mind. An aura was lighting up the edges of Richard's face.

'He wants you to think I'm the one whose burning shit but I'm not. I just want direction. I should have gone to Sydney.'

'As in a butterfly with a gap in its wing, in yellow paint?'

'Yeah, it's his thing, his painting. It's what we burned—'

'Like the one on your tree.'

'No, in the old manager's house, and in the forest, it's there and he put my name on it, but I've got nothing to do with anything, I swear. And there's a butterfly on Ashleigh's letterbox as well.'

'There's one painted on your tree too, Richard, the tree you tried to burn down, in your front yard. I've just came from there.'

Sniles watched the man's eyes widen and turn inwards. For a moment he imagined he saw the fish Richard spoke of swimming across his retina, shadows darting beneath overcast waters. Then he saw Richard's fear, real fear.

'He's painted a butterfly ... on my tree?'

Sniles nodded. Richard scratched his cheeks so hard the little scabs broke away. He rubbed his broken hands together, rubbed his wrists, rubbed the bandage on his head.

'What does he want with me? What does he want?'

'Somebody's fucking with you, Richard.' Sniles said, leaning closer. 'It's somebody you know and somebody real sick, sicker than you even. And I'm not looking for some dickhead who dresses up as a clown and chases people through the trees.' Sniles chuckled. 'I'm looking for someone dangerous.'

'The clown's harmless.' Ashleigh was standing inside the door again with a takeaway cup of coffee. 'He's just an intellectually disabled guy who wouldn't hurt a fly. He's been hanging around for years and I've never heard of him chasing anyone or burning anything. Why would he start now?'

Her eyes flickered as Sniles stared at her

150

'A good question. The only person I know around here who likes to burn things is Richard.'

'I don't want to burn anything,' Richard hollered. 'I just want to get on with my fucking life. Mind my own fucking business. I've got a chance with Cedar Desk, an advertising job I could have if I want it but I don't know 'cause it's fucking corrupt and I haven't been able to think about anything other than you and your clown and his fucking vid—'

'Shhh,' Ashleigh said, glaring at Sniles. She pushed past to stroke the nutter's face. 'Calm down. He's just stirring you because he's frustrated. We're all frustrated, officer, but don't you think Richard's had enough?'

'*I've* had enough of this shit.' Sniles stood up, carefully edging around Ashleigh without touching her. She sat immediately in his chair and swept Richard's hair from his face again. 'There's strong winds coming tomorrow, real bad conditions for bushfires, and if I don't …' Sniles stopped as the aroma of coffee smacked him in the face and washed him in a wave of tiredness.

'How bad's it going to be?' Ashleigh asked as globules of fresh blood welled from her boyfriend's scarred cheeks.

'Real bad,' Sniles said. 'And I'll be out and checking on everyone, even you.'

She didn't flinch.

'And you'd better hope it is just some harmless, *intellectually disabled* person drawing those things, and not some murderous pyromaniac. Because if it is the latter, then you should be worried. He's got both of you in his sights.'

Ashleigh's face remained impassive, one hand rubbing Richard's chest a little as she held the constable's gaze.

'Apparently, there's a painting on my tree, Ashleigh,' Richard explained to her. She turned to regard him for a moment, his head bandage, his face scratches, the blood on his pillow. She sighed, letting down her guard for a moment, revealing the first true emotion Sniles had seen on her face. Sadness. She turned to look back at Sniles, resetting her cheeks, her wicked, emerald, don't fuck-with-me eyes.

'Then I hope you catch him soon,' she said softly.

Sniles left to find coffee and to find out about Lars' missing dog. It would be just his luck if the dog strangled on Saturday, the crime he'd refused to investigate, turned out to be his best lead yet. Dawksted would never let him forget *that*.

INCENDIARY

The party grew fast as the sun sighed into the horizon. Carload after carload pulled onto the lawn. Beers *clinked* as groups of guys alighted. Some were already drunk. They shouted and swore, edged around a growing lot of mostly foreign-made SUVs and hatchbacks, Subaru Foresters, Volkswagen Golfs, Mazda 3s, four or five giant Toyota Hilux utes driven by cashed up tradies. Somewhere among them Pyro's own maroon Holden VT waited with a petrol can in the boot, sparklers in the glove box, his memories waiting to be distributed, set free, cleansed.

'Hey, man,' said a drunk guy with a cap on sideways. He leant against a 1970s Celica, a badly maintained relic that needed wrecking.

'What's up?' Pyro edged through the vehicles, a used car lot of smooth, foreign-made future fuckers.

'You seen Chris? That cunt's gotta … gotta move his car.' The man hiccupped, jerked on legs that would bubble, roast, and melt in Pyro's fire. He pointed at the collection of modern cars on the front lawn that boxed in his beaten-up Celica. 'Can't get out, you see?'

'Nah, man,' Pyro said, trying to step past. 'Haven't seen him.'

The guy flicked a cigarette lighter, sucked weed from a pipe. Pyro imagined sparks vacuuming into his lungs, igniting something inside and expanding. The guy would swell and glow, his lungs a lampshade fashioned from stretched skin. Instead Pyro plucked a clump of hair from the back of the man's head.

'Ow, fuck.' The man pushed off the car, holding his head. 'What the fuck, man?'

'Sorry,' Pyro said, stuffing the hair in his jacket pocket. 'My jacket zipper got caught in your hair.'

Pyro walked onwards towards his car and tried ringing Ashleigh.

'Hey, man,' the guy drawled, stumbling after him. 'Why'd you pull my hair, man?'

He got her message bank again. Why wasn't Ashleigh answering her phone?

'Dude. You pulled my hair.'

'What are you, a pervert?' Pyro said, unzipping and standing by the boot of his car. 'I'm taking a slash. Fuck off.'

Pyro watched the guy stumble back to the house, mumbling about getting more beer. He zipped up and rubbed his face, thinking again of Ashleigh, wondering what she was doing. It was at a party like this where he'd seen her little blue car bouncing up and down after graduation. He'd stepped closer and seen her legs sticking up inside, then her dirty friend's back, Richard fucking the only girl he ever imagined he'd love. He remembered wanting to burn her little blue car, watch the whole scene go up in flames, just like he wanted to open the petrol caps of all the fuck-wit cars in this party's front yard right now, force a petrol-soaked rag inside the Toyotas, the Volkswagens, the Mazdas, turn them into foreign-made bombs, turn their overseas parts into shrapnel that would slice people's legs in half. Then he would throw petrol over the house, splash it on every wall, light it up and watch drunk fuck-ers run from the house, not knowing which way to go. The cars would explode, *kaboom*, and create more fire, more smoke. Somebody would die. Another would lose half their face. Hair would burn, crackling, disappearing, beautiful. He'd wash clean in the smoke then jump into his local-made, job-creating Holden and make tracks. Tomorrow was the big day. Northerlies coming like a freight train. *Catastrophic danger*, the papers were saying. *Inferno warning: the 'worst conditions since Ash Wednesday'*. Winds that would send his fire charging through people's hair, her hair, her car, her little blue bouncing fucking car.

Pyro ran his fingers over the boot's smooth metal, picturing the contents inside, the paint, petrol cans, the memories needing to burn. He pushed the key into the boot, a clump of the drunk fucker's hair oily and flammable in his pocket. For a second he thought he heard a rustle, but then he was blinded by floodlights. Somebody's pimped up ute, a Ford Ranger, like all the rich fuckers were driving these days, complete with four spotlights mounted on the roof, was growling towards him, pulling into the front yard. He retrieved his key and shrunk away from the light as another set of lights appeared further down the road. Wait, he told himself. You need to be patient.

Richard gazed out the window as Ashleigh drove him from the hospital in her car.

'That guy's a real bastard, isn't he?'

The little Getz engine whined and caused Richard's seatbelt to rattle at the anchor next to his head. He wiggled it to try and stop the racket and noticed the grab handle above it was still missing. They'd broken it all those years ago shagging on this seat.

'It's like he *wants* you to freak out.'

'Ashleigh, I don't…' Richard turned about and saw that the top button of her blouse was undone. It was as if she'd heard his thoughts, recalled the same memory. 'I don't want to talk about the cop, okay?'

'Okay,' she said softly, soaking in his gaze without blushing. She slowed to negotiate the Blackwood roundabout, almost drawing to a stop despite the road being clear.

'But drive faster, yeah? Richard said. 'I'm not that fragile.'

She smiled and accelerated, the engine whining happily as if it approved. Richard focussed on her neck, the wisps of blonde hair hanging over her clear skin, a thin curtain that had escaped from her ponytail. He couldn't be thinking about the cop and his shark snout. She was taking him home with her blouse unbuttoned and his piranhas were hungry. They were desperate for Richard to lose focus so they could attack him, some of them had acquired clown faces, others constable faces, still others had numbers painted on their sides. If Ashleigh took him to bed after that there'd be nothing but jellyfish between his legs.

He had to stay centred. He had to keep staring at Ashleigh.

'Thanks again,' he said as a piranha bit his eyes and made him blink, 'for taking me to hospital.'

He reached for Ashleigh's hand on the gear stick, gripped it tight. Little bones and veins shifted beneath her skin. He focussed on her perfume. The gaseous distraction filled the cabin, choked the fish. He squeezed Ashleigh's hand tighter, crushed it onto the gear stick. She smiled again as the world passed by, her profile beautiful and sweet.

'Seriously,' Richard continued. 'I think I needed someone to … I think I needed …'

A fish flapped about on the backseat.

'I think I need you,' Richard blurted out, water trickling from beneath his seat to pool at his feet.

'How's your head, Richard?' Ashleigh asked, blushing under his gaze, although Richard had wondered if she ever lost control of her autonomous functions.

'It's fine,' he said. 'I can't even feel it, but let's get home, yeah? Let's drive this car a little fucking faster, yeah?'

A fish nibbled at his heel. He lifted Ashleigh's hand from the gearstick to push it against his face, trying to feel something other than the ugly, needle-sharp teeth that were about to shred his ankle, shred his mind, destroy everything that mattered. They only ever attacked the things that mattered. Ashleigh pulled over and put her other hand on his other cheek, cool hands, dry hands, lathering him with perfume. She drew her face closer to his, emerald eyes that stared into his own, broke through the amassing school of fish so they scattered. She held him for a moment and his heart slowed. Sensible reality returned. They were in a car parked on the side of Main Road while others whizzed past and she was kissing him on the lips.

She took him back to his house where they ignored the broken butterfly on his burnt tree, a splotchy, asymmetrical mess like her letterbox. She made no mention of the axe wounds in the tree, the barbed wire, the garden gnome's head in the yard. She made no mention of the smashed-up DVD player in the lounge room, the DVD in pieces. She turned on his stereo, blue-toothed her phone, put on some chilled-out trip hop. She took Richard's hand and led him to the bedroom, to his bed, laid down and caressed him. She put a hand under his shirt and touched his stomach, his chest. She pulled away from his heart when she felt him flinch. It caused his heartbeat to race so she pulled in close to the side of his face, smelt his face, bed sheets gushing with movement. Richard wanted briefly to think about the dust in his bedroom's air, to rub the dust off his nose, to think about not thinking about dust. But Ashleigh climbed on top of him. Ashleigh stared into his eyes and pulled him back from the pond's edge. She pulled her hair loose so a curtain fell over her shoulders. She swooped down and pushed her lips onto his own, kissing him, biting him, drawing pain, demanding attention, until finally, thankfully, Richard could feel her, sense her, the heat from her sex, the weight of her breasts hovering before him. He was alive. He was touching her skin beneath her blouse and it was soft, ridiculously soft. He lifted the fabric, ran hands up her spine, pulled at the remaining buttons so her top opened easily. She sat up and pushed down upon him, their denim jeans grinding. He had to get to her flesh, throw her blouse to the side, expose shoulders beneath waterfall hair, release the swell inside her black bra. His hands fumbled with the strap, twisting and pulling at the clasp so it came loose as she pushed against him, sucking the air from his throat, swallowing his tongue like he swallowed hers. The bra fell away and Richard wished he could have a scratch-and-sniff picture made of that moment in time. Her beautiful, peach-like breasts were staring back at him like two cyclops. He took them in his hands, smelling their fragrance, sitting up so she could pull off his own shirt. She pushed him back down and together they squirmed like freshly made dough.

But then Richard had to stop and get a condom.

He reached over to his bedside table where he felt a layer of dust on the drawer handle, on the contents inside. A piranha bit his hand. Another

wriggled under the sheets and nibbled his ankles. He retrieved the condom box, scratched at its lid hurriedly so dust lifted into the air, entered
his lungs, but he couldn't open the box and piranhas were moving up
his legs, wiggling across his skin, threatening to ruin the moment. He
deployed every technique the psychologist taught him. He tried breathing, embracing disaster, smiling in the face of a plane crash. He tried to
maintain focus on naked Ashleigh in his bed, a woman he'd fantasised
over at least five times in the past week, who once upon a time fucked
him senseless in her little blue car, long before Lena, long before fires
and clowns who could paint. He finally retrieved a condom from the
box but his heart beat thick and loud in his ears. *Wham wham wham,
bang bang bang, we're going to die now. Burn it all, Richard, you fucking
little shit.* He pulled the latex free and tried to enclose a blowfish that
was already deflating, but it might be enough. It might be just enough
to get it in, consummate and all would begin. The piranhas usually gave
up once he was in. But the condom was wrong. He'd tried putting it
on the wrong way and now it was contaminated. It had fish juice on its
outside and if they fucked they'd be risking baby piranhas, instant pun-
ishment for all things sweet and peaceful. He could never take chances
with Ashleigh. He couldn't be trapped, not here, not now, not like this
and not without direction.

'Fuck it,' he said and Ashleigh stopped kissing him, leant back and
observed him, knowing something was wrong.

'What's wrong, Richard?' she said, putting her hand where she
shouldn't, feeling it loose, floppy and hopeless, nowhere to go, no man-
hood, nothing to give, to shake off the dust and be present.

Richard leapt out of bed. He ran to the bathroom and punched the
mirror, once, so it broke, twice, so cracked glass fragments flew from
the cabinet, a third time, so he really felt the pain, pushed glass into his
knuckles, made holes in the useless flesh of his manless self.

'Richard. Please, Richard,' Ashleigh shouted from the bathroom door,
naked, her glorious breasts perfect but powerless. There was nothing

here for her, just a man stuck in a swirling world of fish, a man sitting on the bath, feeling the porcelain cold on his naked arse, blood dripping from his hand onto dull blue tiles, broken bits of mirror glass, a moment as erotic as a dead bird hanging from a painted tree and a constable with inquiring eyes.

Richard hung his head and listened to the pain in his hand. It was strong. It was sharp. He'd cut himself deep while a beautiful, naked, important girl who'd been expecting sex watched on, shocked, but not horrified, crying, but not afraid.

'Sorry for ruining the moment,' he said.

'I don't care about that,' she said, sincerely, perfectly Ashleigh. She moved into the bathroom, stepped around the glass fragments and sat down on the bath beside him. She picked up his wrist to look at his hand. Blood pattered into a pool on the tiles. She tested it for broken bones, grimaced when he grimaced. She lowered his wrist and looked up at him from her blonde mass, a mischievous look in her eye, humour, and something else Richard would never understand.

'Guess we'd better go back to hospital then,' she said, her eyes glimmering. She patted his leg. 'Better make it a different one though, hey? Otherwise they'll think you're fucking nuts.'

The butterfly painting looked pathetic in the torchlight, a poor, splotchy mess on a crumbling wall inside the old manager's house at Blackwood Forest. But what Constable Sniles found beneath it was far more interesting.

BURN IT ALL RICHARD, the words said.

They were scrawled in fresh yellow paint over the walls of what was once a lounge room, each letter about half a metre high. It was the same paint used to create the butterfly on the letterbox at Ashleigh's house, probably Richard's tree.

BURN IT ALL RICHARD

A slight breeze descended through the holes of the old manager's house. A warm breeze. Rows of dust swirled in Sniles' torchlight, sank into the massive hole that nearly covered the room's floorboards. Its edges were jagged, rotten. They'd clearly been stamped in, probably by the same kids who'd ripped down beams, smashed beer bottles and scrawled graffiti. Sniles guided his torch beam into the exposed basement below, a dirt floor littered with rubble, beer bottles, burnt pieces of wood, an old pair of blunt scissors. There was something else, something light blue sitting in the dirt. He couldn't tell what it was but it shined with importance, demanded his attention like a key object in a computer game.

Sniles edged around the hole to an old wooden ladder in the far corner. He climbed carefully into the hole, testing the strength of the rungs as he descended. In the dirt basement he shone his torch around and noticed several pieces of corrugated iron. He lifted one of the pieces with his torch. There was nothing but dirt beneath it. He progressed to the basement's centre where the blue object glowed. He drew closer and sucked in a breath of musky air. It was a disposable razor, clean, as if it had been discarded recently. He didn't dare touch it but looked around for footprints in the dirt, saw nothing readily discernible but another sheet of corrugated iron, one end buried in dirt, the other covered in obscenities written with old yellow paint.

'… blue fucking car … wanka'.

He used his torch to poke underneath the iron, prise it upwards so air sucked underneath and billowed out again, throwing with it a horrible stench, rotting meat, a carcass, the creative smell of decomposing life.

Not again, Sniles thought, sagging inside. Not another death.

The iron let loose a horrible shriek as it bent higher. Sniles' heart whacked in his throat. Images of past horrors, the 9-year-old, the beaten ranga, the dozen or so fatal crashes he'd attended on Australia's brutal highways. He crouched to peer underneath and spotted fur. Matted fur. Old fur. Different coloured fur. Little claws, little paws, a tail or three, a cluster of dead animals. Sniles breathed a sigh of relief, dropped the edge of iron so it snapped back to the ground with a *crack*. He retrieved a broken floorboard and used it to bend the stubborn piece upwards again, wedging the iron ajar so he could get a better look with his torch.

The bodies belonged to a possum, a cat, a bird, possibly another cat, lined up in a row. The fur had been hacked from the possum and cat in places and pink skin showed through. They were fresh kills. The bird behind them was a caramelised sheen of black, rotted skin pulled taught over a featherless frame. The fourth thing at the rear of the crypt was barely more than a yellowed skeleton.

Sniles shone his torch back on the possum. There was something about it, something familiar. He had a missing dog, a strangled and shaved dog, a pile of dead, shaven animals, people burned to death or nearly burned to death, serial killer shit, but there was something else too, something about the possum. He retrieved his phone and took photos of the animals, the corrugated iron and its obscenities, back-tracked his steps across the basement. He took photos of the razor, climbed the ladder, crept around the broken loungeroom floor and made his way to a doorway on the far side where stars shone through large holes in the roof.

Even before he pointed his torch inside he knew what he was about to find. He could smell the fear, the sweat and piss. His light revealed it lying on its side, its tongue swollen and sticking out the side of its snout.

'You must be Thompson,' he said.

The dog's torso had been crudely hacked free of hair, much like the dog he'd found under the old railway water tower by the station. There was no blood. Sniles guessed the animal had been strangled like the railway dog. He was about to step inside when he saw scuff marks in the dust, the dog's paws scratching at the floorboards in its final moments. There were also footprints in the dust, several of them clear and detailed.

He didn't need to be a forensic specialist to see they were the same as those they'd found in the valley, the same son of a bitch who lit the first fire, who'd slipped away to come back two days later to try and kill the old couple who witnessed it.

'Motherfucker,' Sniles said. He took photos with his phone, framed it so the footprints were clearly visible with the dead dog. He wrote a text message and prepared to send it back to his superintendent with his best picture.

The latest is I've just found a second shaved dog, in Blackwood, not more than 1km from the farmhouse fires. Footprints appear to match those found at the Olave Valley fire.

He was about to press send when his phone started ringing. It was Jenny. She wanted to know if he'd heard anything about the 'lockdown everyone's talking about'. She said the Prime Minister was apparently going to close everything because of coronavirus. She wanted to know when Sniles was coming home. He told her there was no lockdown at this stage, that the government was just advising against gatherings of more than 500 people, a precautionary measure as it ordered all internationals flying into the country to self-isolate. Then he told her about the graffiti and the animals he found, that it was a breakthrough of sorts, but there was something else, something he couldn't quite grasp, something to do with the animals.

'What the hell?' Jenny said, irritation showing in her voice. 'You have a woman who's worried to death about a virus the ABC says could infect 80,000 Australians by the end of the month, a *partner* you haven't managed to come home and have dinner with in days, but all you want to talk about is dead animals. When are you going to stop worrying about dogs, pyromaniacs and possums and—'

'That's it,' Sniles shouted into the phone, edging around the hole in the floorboards and down the hallway. 'There *was* a fucking possum.' On the porch of a different old house where nobody ever answered the door, across the valley from a couple that were nearly burnt to death in their beds two days later. Hair had been hacked from its body. Sniles thought it had been attacked by an animal at the time, a feral cat, a fox, perhaps a dog that didn't like the taste. But it was the fucking pyromaniac. He had to find out who lived there. Perhaps the pyro had been under his nose from the start.

'I have to go.'

He stepped through the hallway where a piece of corrugated iron wailed at him from the floor.

'Don't you hang up on me, Rory.'

He ducked outside and started jogging down the hill, his torchlight bouncing over the dried pine needles and pine cones. There was heat coming tomorrow, fan-forced heat. Sniles had an opportunity to stop the darn inferno before it was lit. He had a lead, the old Quaker's house, but he had something else too, connections. If the pyro was the masseuse burner *and* the dog strangler, then chances were he'd been caught on CCTV last week, back when he stole a dog from the Foodland carpark, a crime Sniles never followed up because he didn't think it was worth it.

'I'm sorry, darling. It'll all be okay, I promise. But I've really got to check on something — before Dawksted stumbles across it first.'

Sniles pocketed his phone and ran to his car.

'Why do we have to see Donnie?' Richard asked inside Ashleigh's car, stinking of insecurity and a limp dick. He clenched his broken hand inside its freshly set cast. It was still numb from the anaesthetic the nurse had administered.

'Maybe he knows something,' Ashleigh said. 'About the painting on your tree, about what's going on. Maybe he can help.'

'How is Donnie going to help me?' Richard said. 'He's the one who started this shit in the first place. He's the one who took me and Lars to the ....'

But he stopped. He was about to tell Ashleigh about their trespassing at the old Quaker's house last year, something they'd said they'd never do. But maybe she *should* know about it. Maybe she could help make sense of it all. Ashleigh didn't prod him to continue, however, and Richard sensed her respect for him had wavered. Being an eccentric germaphobe with an asymmetrical face was one thing. It may even be appealing to people like Ashleigh. But being unable to fuck when expected, was not so cool. That was lame. You could be odd, but you couldn't be lame.

'Stop sulking,' Ashleigh said without taking her eyes from the road. 'Just stop it, okay? Forget about what happened.'

But Richard didn't want to swing past some 'coronavirus party' organised by dickheads who believed Australia was about to go into lockdown, who believed tonight was the last they'd have to party before the Prime Minister isolated everyone in their homes. He wanted to take Ashleigh home, satisfy her, get back on top with a girl he never should have let go. Then they could talk about that night last year that seemed to have started so much trouble.

'Let's just go in and have a drink,' she said. 'I could do with a little air.'

They pulled up at the house where nearly two dozen cars covered the front lawn like spilled toys. A few people were standing about drinking, smoking, cigarette lighters flashing in the night. She stepped out the car, managed a smile and, before Richard had even removed her seatbelt, walked quickly towards the front door. Richard climbed out the car reluctantly, watched by a few drunk people in hoods and baseball caps. Ashleigh skipped onto the porch and his chest tightened as she disappeared through the door without him.

From inside the house the stereo blared Jimi Hendrix — funky, groovy, bass heavy. One of the hoods hanging outside the door flicked a lighter and sucked at a weed pipe, its red glow illuminating a gaunt face.

'Hey,' the hood drawled as Richard stepped onto the porch. 'This dude looks *fucked up* man, like he's been in some kind of *car crash*, man.'

Richard stepped inside, pushing the door against a couple of lads standing directly inside. They stared at him with glassy eyes. Dope smoke filled the house. Floorboards trembled with cap-wearing hoods in flannelette shirts, beanies, a few dreadlocked goons, multiple sets of speakers blasting music from all over the house. A couple of pissed people pretended to cough over each other then gripped their throats with asphyxiation before giggling stupidly. A dreadlocked surfer gritted wine-stained teeth into a wobbly smile as Richard squeezed past. He made it to the lounge room where people stood about shouting over the music, shouting in each other's ears. Ashleigh wasn't in sight. The hoods stared at Richard's bandaged head, his bandaged hand, the cast on his other hand, the scratches on his face, and he could feel their dope smoke sticking to his skin, infiltrating blood cells at his surface. He held his breath but the dope pushed into his lungs, inflated alveoli pockets, and a warm wave swelled over his skin.

'You okay, Richard?' a guy with curly-blonde hair asked. He looked familiar, a face slightly lopsided like his own. Richard guessed he knew him from high school, or one of many school parties he'd gone to back in the day. 'What have you done to yourself, man?'

'It's nothing. You got a beer?'

Party fumes pushed into Richard's lungs. In response the wave grew warmer, wound down his muscles, washed away his tension, shifted his thoughts to the music, the juice in the snare drum, the wooden *crunch* of Hendrix playing percussion on his guitar, a ghost telling the world he'll live his life the way he wants to.

'Play on.'

'Fuck, I'm getting stoned just standing here,' Richard said to the guy, who smiled. Hendrix's music was a flower slapping him in the face, a soft plant pushing down his throat, heating his stomach.

'I need a fucking beer to chill me out.' But he wasn't losing it. He wasn't panicking. He felt good. The guy's smile made him smile, even if he was wearing what looked like office clothes, a grey shirt, black pants, office shoes. 'Fuck, are you an accountant?'

'Nah, man,' the guy said, smiling wider, eliciting a smile from Richard. 'I'm a journalist these days, unfortunately, just came from work. What have you done, man? You look kinda messed up.'

'I got attacked by a bird, man. It threw an axe handle at me.'

The guy frowned and his smile turned crooked.

'What … what?'

Richard laughed. He couldn't help it.

'It's true, man.' His smile vibrated his jawbone, manipulated his face so it stretched uncontrollably. 'It got me right in the head.'

The guy followed Richard's smile, copied it, experimented with it. Footstep drums from another world thumped about them.

'I threw it at the bird,' Richard giggled as silk scarves swirled through the air, over their heads, in and around every Hendrix-loving, cap-wearing, motherfucking stoner in the room. 'And the bastard threw it back.'

'But ... what ... how?' the guy's face was a beetroot, his mouth a useless slit cut into it.

'Got me right in the head,' Richard said, clenching his teeth, trying to get a grip, people staring, Hendrix singing about a Golden Rose, the man's office shoes shining, his untucked office shirt sweating, an accountant's uniform that was as absurd as the virus they were apparently celebrating.

'I need a fucking beer,' Richard said, his eyes tearing with laughter, his mouth clenching, muscles tightening, drums, guitars and bass bashing the floorboards, gyrating hoods who were stoned like Richard was stoned. *Bam bam bam.* His heart started racing, pounding in his throat. *Bam bam bam*, over the music, over Hendrix, over the floorboards, over their sweaty, coronavirus faces.

'I've gotta get a fucking beer,' he said to the man, at the others in the room, his heart swelling, whatever peace he'd felt accelerating up the runway, preparing to take off.

The music switched to hip hop and another guy sidled up to Richard, moved his head in time to the beats. He handed Richard a beer with cool pragmatism, a hip hop reality slap that did nothing to stop the ocean rushing through his ears. Richard sucked on the beer and pushed into the kitchen, his head stuck in a sea shell filled with stingers. *Bam bam bam.* Panic. Fear. Imminent cardiac arrest. *Bam bam bam.* People watching, staring, Ashleigh nowhere, speakers and hip hop beats everywhere. *Bam bam bam.* Pain in his chest. He bumped into somebody, ignored somebody else, escaped outside through a screen door and slid down the side of the house to find darkness and bent over, vomiting beer, vomiting air, breathing, concentrating on breathing, trying to think about anything but his racing heart, the noise, the rush, the take-off, the plane trying to crash. He tried to find the flight stick and ease it back, pull it back and land that relentlessly decrepit terrorising fucking plane.

He collapsed back into the dark concrete, back against the wall of the house and sucked at his beer, swallowed, thought about swallowing, the sound it made, the dryness of his throat, realised he'd been thinking about swallowing, that a piranha had slipped in unnoticed. Another one opened and closed its mouth in the puddle of Richard's vomit, but at least he wasn't dying. At least he wasn't having a heart attack. The act of vomiting had settled him down. But he had to blink. His eyes were raw and he needed to blink. Surely he wouldn't start thinking about blinking now. *Blink blink blink.* He stood up and lunged from the darkness, marched into the backyard where about 20 hoods stood about two chiminea fires, garbling loudly over the hip hop. Richard scanned their faces, blinking, trying to focus on their clothes, swallowing, dope smoke erupting from their lungs. Some of the hoods looked familiar, like the guy inside, acquaintances at parties, high school students, accomplices to late night drunken conversations.

'Don't,' Ashleigh's voice cried from further out back, an urgent tone breaking through the noise. Richard pushed through the hoods to the edge of paving where a few bushes fenced a lawn behind them. 'You've done enough.'

Richard spotted Ashleigh with her back to him, standing before Donnie. His grin was disconnected from his face, eyes blacker than the night about them. Ashleigh hit Donnie in the arm, a weak hit, a beaten hit, followed by a sob.

'Clown fucker,' he said, smiling back, his arms poised at his sides.

'Stop it,' Ashleigh said, hitting him again. 'Look what you've done to Richard.'

Her face turned for a second and Richard saw that it was covered in tears. He'd never seen Ashleigh cry before.

Richard stepped from the bush.

'Richard,' Donnie said, a massive grin splitting his sweaty clean face. 'We were just talking about … Hey, I heard you were in hospital. What happened? Somebody breathe on you?'

'Wattle bird,' he said, putting his bandaged arm around Ashleigh, pulling her away, rattled by her wet eyes that for the first time didn't look in control.

'What's Donnie done to me?' Richard asked her.

Ashleigh buried her head into his shoulder, the warmth of her breath wet on his neck. Richard looked over her at Donnie who lowered his gaze from the bandage on Richard's head to Ashleigh in his arms.

'Well, isn't this sweet?' Donnie said, his voice somehow deeper and distorted. He turned to pick up a longneck beer bottle from a table and spat into the night. 'Fuck, Richard. You didn't waste time getting back into her pants, did you?'

'Shut up, Donnie,' Ashleigh wailed.

'What the fuck are you doing to me?' Richard asked Donnie.

Ashleigh extracted herself from Richard's arms, took his good hand, the one wrapped in bandages rather than a cast, and tugged it weakly back towards the party.

'Dammit, I wanna know what's going on.'

Donnie took a gulp of beer and regarded Richard. His actions were calm, but his face was a firestorm, black holes for eyes, black mouth, wet lips, shiny wet cheeks.

'You should ask Ashleigh,' he said. 'Ask her about the clown.'

'C'mon, Richard,' Ashleigh said, pulling his hand weakly, unconvincingly.

'She *loves* the clown,' Donnie said. 'You know what I mean, Richard?' Donnie flicked his tongue, a serpent with a black mouth.

'What the fuck is wrong with you?'

'You're what's wrong,' Donnie barked. 'You should never have come back. Why'd you have to come back?' The venom was strong. Old. 'You've just gotta have it all, don't ya. Back two weeks and you're already in her pants.'

'What the hell are you—'

'Look at you,' Donnie snapped. 'You're all fucked up, aren't you? Sympathy, hey? It works wonders.'

Ashleigh found her strength and yanked Richard's bandaged hand, pulled him away towards the party so they weaved through the blokes, the drunks, the infected stoners standing around chiminea fires nodding their heads to hip hop. Ashleigh opened the screen door.

'I'm not going back in there,' Richard said, pulling away.

He stomped to the side of the house and she followed him down the dark laneway, stepped over the piranha suffocating in his puke. They emerged from the side of the house and made their way through the cars. Ashleigh's weight at the end of his hand was lifeless, purposeless. She was a dead fish but she owed him an explanation. They made it to Ashleigh's Getz and Richard saw with dismay that another car, a Subaru Forester, had parked behind it and cut off their escape.

'Son of a bitch,' he said, turning and pulling Ashleigh's hand towards a group of hoods across the yard. There was a thumping sound coming from within their circle.

'Richard,' Ashleigh said. 'I need to explain—'

'In a minute,' Richard said. 'I just want to get the fuck out of here, okay?'

He led her to the group of hoods. The thumping seemed to come from inside a car at their centre.

'Hey,' Richard shouted. 'Who's driving that wagon? That Subaru over there?'

One of the shadows, a bloke wearing a cap, looked briefly at Richard before turning back to his group. The thumping stopped and there was a sudden scream from inside the car, a muffled, blood-curdling shriek.

'Oh my god,' Ashleigh exclaimed quietly.

'What?' Richard said.

'It's him. It's Ger …,' She stopped and swallowed her word. 'He shrieks like that from the forest, when he … when I'm …' Ashleigh tried to pull Richard away from the hoods.

Richard pushed through the hip hoppers to find them circling the dark car's closed boot, weed and cigarette smoke oozing from their clothes. Another thump came from inside it. Richard lunged through the hoods and hit the lid with his bandaged hand.

'Hey, man,' the black cap said in the darkness. 'Chill out. Some dude's stuck in there.'

'I know who it is.' Richard pounded the boot again, hard. One of the hip hoppers tried to shove him away but Richard pushed back, shouted at the boot, brought his fist down again. Its occupant shrieked once more from inside, loud, a giant cat stuck in a paper shredder.

Another hip hopper pushed Richard and he fell over. His jaw hit the ground first and blood filled his mouth, wet, metallic, tart with dope, a passive hell that could only affect someone as susceptible as Richard, someone who over the past week had been all but destroyed by a shriek-ing, laughing, howling fucking clown who was right there with them, hiding in a car. He got to his knees and realised it wasn't just any car.

'That's Donnie's fucking car,' Richard shouted, wiping the blood from his lip, hostile hip hoppers ready for an offensive. 'The fucking Black-wood Clown's in Donnie's fucking boot!'

'This guy's tripping,' one of them said.

'He's always tripping,' came a discordant voice from behind them. Richard turned to see the hulk of Donnie blocking what pitiful light came from the house's open front door. Hip hoppers backed out his way as he rolled up to the car. The clown stopped hollering.

'How the fuck did he get in there?' Donnie growled, his voice pinch-ing so it squeaked a little. He turned to Richard. 'Wanna get him out?'

'Donnie.' Ashleigh's voice was weaker than ever.

Donnie reached into his pocket and produced keys. They rattled in his hand as he pushed one into the keyhole and released the boot, jumping back as if he was expecting a clown-in-a-box to leap out, but nothing happened. The interior of the boot was dark and silent. The guy in the black cap produced a mobile phone and turned on its light. The rest of them leant forward for a better look. Inside the boot a per-son lay in foetal position, eyes shut. His face was childlike and smooth, a kid-faced adult with scraggly, shoulder-length red hair pretending to be asleep. His brown boots were dirty. His white jacket was clean but he stank of body odour. There was another smell too. Petrol. Black Cap moved the light and directed it to where two 10-litre cans of petrol were sitting next to a plastic bag.

'Motherfucker,' Richard said.

'What did I tell you?' Donnie said, his voice breaking. 'It's the pyro and he's got petrol and he's in my boot.'

'This is too freaked for me,' one of the hip hoppers said as he backed away towards the house. He was followed by the others, leaving only Black Cap and his mobile phone light.

'Is he asleep?' Black Cap said.

'I don't know,' Donnie snapped.

'He can't be,' Richard said. 'He was just screaming.'

He pushed the clown's shoulder with his good hand. He didn't move and his eyes remained closed.

'He looks so young,' Richard said, pushing the man's shoulders again.

'He doesn't look like a clown,' Black Cap said.

'He's got petrol in my fucking car,' Donnie whinnied. 'This motherfucker was gonna burn this house down while you were all inside.'

'Hey,' Richard said, shaking the man's shoulder. 'Get up.'

'It's the *pyro*, Richard,' Donnie said. 'And the cops think it's *you*.'

'C'mon, you fuck,' Richard said, shaking harder. 'Stop messing about.' He hit the clown's shoulder with his bandaged hand, slapped his cheek, the baby skin too underdeveloped to grow stubble. He slapped him harder. 'Wake up.'

'Don't,' Ashleigh said.

The clown's eyes shot open, looked past everyone and straight at Ashleigh, recognising her and smiling. His eyes darted to Richard, darted to Donnie, then back to Richard again. He suddenly lunged forward and clamped his jaw over Richard's fingers, shook his head like a dog and tugged, ripped at the flesh. Richard screamed and hit the clown with his cast, tore free his fingers so a fountain of blood sprayed through the torchlight. He clutched them to his chest, staring down at a cornered animal exposed in Black Cap's phone light. It panted and gnashed with blood on his chin. The clown stretched his lips flat against his skull, smiled at them, one after the other, then threw back his head and shrieked. It was loud. It dug into Richard's ear canal and pecked out his brains. Richard flung out his bleeding hand and punched the source of the terror. The clown's voice faltered as his head ricocheted against the far side of the boot.

'Stop it,' Ashleigh shouted.

'Fuck'n get him, Richard,' Donnie yelled.

The clown recovered and smiled with squinting eyes. He lunged forward and Richard punched his jaw, his child-like, horrible, blood-dripping teeth. The clown collapsed into the boot and curled into a protective ball. Richard raised his second arm, his broken hand set in plaster.

'Stop it,' Ashleigh screamed. 'You've got to stop.'

Through the clown's protective fingers he could see the smile expanding, even as blood poured from his skull. His thin wrists were covered in white downy hair, piddly artist arms protecting his head. Ashleigh wrestled Richard back and shouted in his ear.

'It wasn't him. It wasn't him.'

Donnie laughed. The clown whimpered like a wretched bird, one child-like eye staring at them from between blood-covered fingers — but still his gaping mouth continued to smile.

'Then why's he smiling?' Richard said through tears that filled his own eyes. 'Why's the fucker just keep smiling?'

''Cause he's different to us,' Ashleigh sobbed. 'Can't you see that?'

She pushed Richard away from the car. The freak-in-the-box gripped the edge of the boot with two bloodied hands and pulled himself to his knees. Donnie prepared to slam the boot lid on him.

'Don't.' Ashleigh lurched forward and punched Donnie's face. He staggered away, shocked, clutching his cheek. The rest of them watched as the clown lifted himself up and over the lid of the boot, falling to the ground. Bubbling sounds emerged from his throat as he climbed to his feet and pushed off Donnie's car to topple against the next. He found support from another car, then another, limping away through bodies of metal dim-lit by surrounding streetlights.

'I'm sorry,' Ashleigh called after the clown. 'I'm so sorry.'

'*You're* sorry,' Donnie said. 'He was in my boot. In my *boot.*'

'You brought him here,' Ashleigh snarled, moving to stand between Donnie and the clown, her blonde hair seeming to rise like hackles. 'You did this.'

Donnie slammed his boot closed.

'You gotta watch out for that clown fucker, Richard,' he said, walking backwards towards the house, his eyes on the clown. 'She ain't what she seems. Ask her what I'm talking about.'

The clown continued to hobble out of the car lot. He reached the skeletal branches of a gum tree at the edge of the property, a troll whose shadows couldn't be penetrated by the white streetlight above. It slinked forward and swallowed him.

'Ashleigh?' Richard said after the clown vanished into the night. His broken hand was aching, terribly. His finger too was an emerging terror, pulsing blood through every bite in his skin.

'Yes?' Her voice sounded sad and exhausted.

'I've gotta go back to hospital.'

ORANGE RESPITE

According to Richard's court-appointed psychologist, OCD was caused by a mixture of genetic and environmental factors, as well as personality traits and distressing events. There was also a potential biological factor — possible links to unnatural levels of serotonin — that suggested chemical abnormalities in the brain were a factor.

Sufferers like Richard typically felt ashamed or embarrassed by their symptoms. They did not like people knowing about it. They did not like talking about it. Whenever their symptoms were mentioned, they could see how ridiculous they were, see them for the nonsense they truly were. But the piranhas came back regardless of how silly they were, over and over and over again, and all the embarrassment in the world didn't stop a thing.

The problem with being officially diagnosed while facing trial for arson, however, was that it left the condition on Richard's medical record for all to see. He saw it in doctors' faces when they treated him for a virus, for a cold that wouldn't go away, or when he came in with a fresh cast on one hand, shredded fingers on the other, and blamed a stray dog for the latter. They would give Richard a little glance, take in his lopsided face, the scratches on it, and ask him 'how he was doing?', no doubt assuming that whatever treatment he sought was somehow connected to his busted brain.

The Indian doctor attending to Richard's latest effort was no exception. He stitched Richard's finger, bandaged it, told to him stay away from stray dogs, then gave him a brochure on 'living with depression'.

Richard offered Ashleigh a strained smile, but she was in no mood for humour. She was winning him back after years of rejection but there'd been little to celebrate. This was the third hospital they'd visited in less than 24 hours. When they left the southern suburbs hospital her face was depressed, flattened by the orange streetlights whizzing above them that covered them in a dull wash that obscured every other colour.

'If I never see another doctor again I'll be … I'll be …,' but Richard didn't bother to finish. Ashleigh wasn't interested. She was focussed on an Adelaide road they had to themselves at 1:30am on a Thursday morning. He decided to cut to the chase.

'What did Donnie do to me?'

'Hmmm?' Ashleigh asked distantly.

'Back at the party, when you were crying out back with Donnie, you said to him, 'Look what you've done to Richard'.'

To either side of the orange road was darkness, black hills, nothingness they would soon join for more mystery, more dreadlocked trees.

'What did that mean?' Richard prodded.

'It didn't mean anything.'

'The way the clown looked at you when he heard your voice. And how you shouted at Donnie when—'

'Richard,' Ashleigh said, finally looking at him, orange light sucking the life from her eyes. 'He's the guy in the old Quaker's house I told you about. I've been contracted to visit him ever since you lot stole his paintings.' She shrugged. 'Yeah, I know all about that night.'

'Did you know that he's been hassling me, trying to send me mad? And why was he in Donnie's boot, Ashleigh. His fucking *boot*?'

Ashleigh pushed her car a little faster. Overhanging streetlights *shooped* as they passed beneath, their passage blurred in a freeway glow.

'Ashleigh, you've got to tell me—'

'I will,' she said, suddenly angry. 'But not now, okay? I just want to get home, okay? I want to sleep.'

'And me?'

'I'm sleeping with you.'

Richard held his tongue. There was so much to be extracted from her orange-washed face, so many secrets he had to uncover, but she was giving him another chance. Lena would never have given him another chance. He tried to stop thinking about the clown and focus on the car's engine, Ashleigh's little blue Hyundai, the bitumen whining beneath them. He focused on the little movements of her throat, her beautiful neck, the pain in his freshly stitched fingers.

They turned from the freeway. The streetlights turned white and released their hold over their washed-out lives. She looked so young in the white light, so sad, so perfect, and he'd never done anything but hurt her. He reached his bandaged hand out to touch her hair. Blood pumped thick in his bitten finger. He gave up and dropped his hand back in his lap. Ashleigh allowed him a little smile. She put a hand on his leg and let it sit there for the next three kilometres until the lights turned orange again and she had to change gears.

When they arrived at Richard's house she followed him to the door, took his keys from his pocket because his hands were useless. She led the way inside and, like last time, said nothing about the broken pieces of Richard's life covering the lounge room floor. She said nothing about the broken mirror and the blood on the bathroom tiles. She walked straight into Richard's bedroom, took off her clothes and slipped under the covers. Richard stepped towards the bed, sat on the bed and kicked off his shoes. Ashleigh helped him take off his belt. He crawled under the covers and she slid into him. They laid like that for some time, smothered in secrets, until her slim hand started making tiny movements on his chest, bringing with it an unprecedented wave of peace. The lateness of the hour, the aftermath of anxiety and pain, alcohol, marijuana, hospital drugs, it all contributed to a calmness he hadn't known for years. After a time, she crawled over and laid on top of him, slowly moving her hips. Richard, in a wave of Ashleigh and nothing more, responded in kind. It was smooth. It was easy. It was right in a world gone nuts. When he mentioned the need for a condom she pushed him back onto the bed.

'You don't need it with me … right now,' she whispered.

'Are you sure?'

'I promise.'

They fell into an ocean where there were no fish, everyone could breathe, and the only thing that mattered was holding onto a mermaid that took him all the way down.

Sleep brought with it dreams and smoke, lots of it. It filled Richard's house, crept silently inside through the open door backlit by fractured yellow sunbeams. Richard crept through his kitchen, wading through a gushing sound that was somehow Ashleigh breathing. A man appeared in his doorway, a furious bushfire sunset behind him. He held a crippled arm and his back was slightly bent. He crept inside a few paces and stopped. Richard felt sorrow, shame, guilt. He approached the clown, his red, shoulder-length hair, eyes that were wet, green, beautiful, a little blood dripping from his ear where Richard had hit him with his cast.

'I'm sorry,' Richard tried to say, his mouth filled with smoke. The clown's red lips widened, but they didn't smile. Instead they drooped and slanted to the left. His left cheekbone was lopsided too.

'I'm sorry,' Richard tried to say again to the child with Ashleigh's eyes, a lounge room world of hissing air.

'*CHAA*,' the clown said, raising his arms to either side of his body, his dirty white suit. '*CHAA*.' The clown flapped his hands and rose into the air, a clown-bird with Ashleigh's sad, sad eyes.

He burst into flames and Richard woke with a start to the pre-dawn glow poking around his bedroom blind. Ashleigh breathed near his ear, her head in the same place it had come to rest last night. There was a little drool from her mouth on his armpit, a numbness in Richard's arm.

Chika CHEE CHAA chika CHAA

Ashleigh stirred, sucked in a lungful of air. She lifted her head from Richard's arm and looked at the blinds.

'What is *that*?' she murmured, half asleep, rolling back onto Richard without waiting for his answer.

'The wattle bird,' Richard growled.

'You poor thing,' she said, sleepily, dismissing the wattle bird's nuisance call and nestling back into his arm. Richard wanted to press his head into her hair and let it go, let everything go, fall back to sleep like Ashleigh.

Chika CHEE CHAA chika CHAA

'Put your earplugs in, Richard.' Ashleigh whispered as his body tensed. She leant over him to find his earplugs in his bedroom drawer, her naked breasts and hair tickling his face. She found what she needed and curled back into his neck, resettling before she softly, sweetly, rolled the little foam plugs into compressed cylinders and pushed them carefully into his ears, her slim fingers making little tapping sounds as if she was adjusting seashells. Butterflies fluttered in Richard's heart. He'd never experienced anything so intimate. A minute or so later the plugs expanded and the wattle bird's call was partially culled — not completely, nothing could ever cull it completely — but muted enough, her hair soft and perfect enough, her breath on his neck and her arm warm enough, to be momentarily shifted outside along with everything else.

They fell back to sleep.

It was still dark the first time Sniles woke gasping.

'What the hell is wrong with you people?' he shouted into the uncertain space between dreams and consciousness.

Jenny ordered him to lay back down. 'You can't do anything about it now,' she said. 'Get some sleep.'

The second time he woke it was dawn.

'Ashleigh,' he cried, sitting upright, eyes wide-open. The faint glow of dawn illuminated the backside of their blinds. Jenny slapped his back while he stared at the blinds, the outside world silent save the sound of a warbling magpie.

'There's no Ashleigh here,' she said, yanking him back down.

'Sorry, darling,' Sniles said. 'It's just some girl who's involved. They're all bloody involved.'

'Well, she can bloody well stay out of my bedroom.'

Sniles looked at the clock radio, 6:00am. He'd been asleep only five hours after working at the office until midnight, connecting dots, putting his convictions in an email for the superintendent.

'You finally got the CCTV footage,' Officer Dawksted had said before knocking off earlier in the evening. 'Anything in it?'

'I need passwords to access it,' Sniles lied, minimising the desktop window as Dawksted slithered around his desk to look at the screen. 'I'm waiting on the supermarket manager.'

Dawksted looked at Sniles' screen suspiciously. The Foodland manager had emailed him links and access to Dropbox files of CCTV footage of the car park. Sniles had been looking at the footage from the camera closest to the bank from where the dog was stolen on Sunday — before it was found dead near Blackwood Railway Station. But they were from the wrong angle. A fourth was downloading.

'Who's this?' Dawsted pointed to another file on Sniles' screen. 'Gerard Brummer?

'He owns the second house in the valley, next door to the farmhouse that burnt down,' Sniles said, scrolling through the SAPOL file he'd found under his name. 'But check this out.'

Gerard Brummer was one of the 13 children present in 1986 when arsonist and attempted multiple murderer Helen Lawson burnt down the Parade Childcare Centre in Blackwood. On the morning of October 21, Lawson had arrived at the centre where she hit a staff member, a woman named Eliza Murray, over the head with a frying pan, knocked her unconscious and tied her up inside an office. She then poured petrol all over the structure, locked the doors and lit it up with herself and 13 children inside.

'Fucking hell,' Dawksted said.

'Any of this ring a bell?' Sniles asked.

'Well, yeah, but—'

But the four-year-old Gerard Brummer hit Lawson over the head with the same frying pan and knocked her out. He then managed to break a window in the play area and herded 12 children out the window, getting the biggest kids to pass the babies to each other. He woke the unconscious Eliza Murray, untied her, and tugged her towards the broken window as parts of the burning roof started falling in. Lawson was left inside to burn to death. Murray survived, but from there the file became corrupted. It wasn't clear if the kid came out unscathed, or not.

'Alright, so Brummer's a *hero*. So what?'

Sniles ignored the bait, feeling heat in his teeth as he stared into Dawksted's skull.

'You have a kid involved in a serious arson attack, who apparently lives next door to a farmhouse burnt down with two people inside, and … there's more.'

Three weeks before the fire, Lawson had made a complaint to the childcare centre's management about Brummer, claiming he 'bit her' on the leg. But a number of parents questioned her behaviour leading up to the incident. Management launched an internal investigation and a week later chose to terminate Lawson's employment, citing inadequate training and aggressive behaviour. A few days later she returned with petrol.

'But whoever digitised these files fucked it up, see?' Sniles pointed to the screen where parts of the scanned pages were distorted and blurred. 'There's nothing about whether Brummer was injured, or any of the kids. I can't see anything past here.'

'Well, at least that Eliza woman came through okay,' Dawksted said after squinting at the screen. 'There's a bit you can read here that says she was pregnant. Apparently she didn't even know until she went to hospital with that head injury from the fire. Imagine that.'

'But what happened to Brummer?'

'Hey don't ask me,' Dawksted said. 'I was getting my dick sucked at high school during 1986.'

'But it was your district.'

'Like I said,' Dawksted continued, removing his squinting eyes from the screen. 'I was getting my dick sucked.'

Sniles swore and looked for Brummer's birthdate and natural family. The only data he could find was a listing under guardianship to a John Shepherd — in *1960*.

'What the fuck?' Sniles said aloud. 'How can he be a child in 1986 *and* a child in 1960? What the fuck is wrong with your files?'

'Sniles,' Dawksted said, resignedly. 'It's late. Go home to your partner—'

'Leave Jenny out of it,' Sniles snapped.

'Bloody hell.' Dawksted's mouth opened in a little circle, a black hole into stupidity. 'Just can't win with you, can I?' He wobbled away down the corridor. 'Hero.'

Sniles threw a half-chewed pencil at Dawkted's fat arse and looked up John Shepherd instead, a school science teacher who was injured in the Ash Wednesday bushfire of 1983. He apparently retired after that and moved to Queensland where he died just over a decade later — leaving the house at Olave Valley in Brummer's name. The only other thing that stood out was the religion listed on Shepherd's death certificate, Quaker, whatever a Quaker was.

'This is useless,' Sniles said aloud at the same time as his computer emitted a *ping*. The Dropbox file had finished downloading and CCTV footage opened on his screen. Sniles made sure Dawksted was out of sight and scrolled to about ten minutes before 12:45pm, which was when the dog owner noticed his white Maltese had been stolen from outside the bank.

The footage was uneventful for a few minutes until Sniles spotted the owner walking his dog through the Foodland carpark. He passed a maroon-coloured car from where Sniles noticed a flash from the car's interior, then another one, both from the driver's seat. It flashed one more time as the man walked out of shot. Sniles guessed it was a cigarette lighter. The door of the car opened and a large heavy-set man with a shaved head got out, pulled on his hood, slammed his door and walked in the direction the man had taken. Sniles recognised his frame immediately as being that of the pyro he'd chased at the first valley fire. He had the same physique, the same hood, the same scalp waiting to be taken, and his car's number plate was clearly visible. A gush of air entered his stomach. Sniles punched the registration number into the police database.

A surname popped up immediately, a familiar family name that made Sniles sit back in his chair, exhaling the air he'd been holding, looking around frantically to make sure Dawksted wasn't watching. Lawson, Donald Lawson. Son of arsonist and attempted child murderer Helen Lawson.

'Bloody hell,' he said aloud. He punched Donald's name into the database. It brought up more details about his mother, in particular a note about her husband, David. The man had disappeared a month before the fire, leaving a note for his parents, for Donald, saying he couldn't bear the strain of a split family anymore, that one day he'd come back for Donald. A detective at the time suspected homicide, that Helen had knocked him off, but there was no trace, no lead, absolutely nothing to base a case on other than Helen's psychotic state before she died in the childcare centre fire.

Sniles scrolled through Donald's wrap-sheet, his underage drinking while growing up at his grandparents' house after the fire, vandalism, broken school windows, smashed school computers, breaking and entering — and nearly fell off his chair. He'd been caught stealing cigarettes with a Lars Tonkin. Sniles knew that name as well. He flipped through his notebook back to the entry he took from Richard and Ashleigh when he first visited her house. She'd called him *Donnie*, not Donald, and he was a friend of Lars, of Richard, son of psychopath Helen Lawson, probably a murderous pyromaniac, and apparently a dog killer as well.

Sniles wrote a midnight email to his superintendent with his findings, complete with the pictures of the dead animals at the old manager's house, the footprints, his theory, everything he needed to extract a warrant and arrest Donnie as soon as possible. He suggested somebody look into Gerard Brummer, find the original files that were scanned into the system, find his birthplace and age, his parents' records if possible, his whereabouts and if he still lived in the old Quaker's house or not. He thought briefly about mentioning reports of a clown but decided against it. He'd been ridiculed enough.

Sniles took note of Donnie's address and decided to pay him a visit on his way home from the station. He lived in a nondescript unit in a block of five off Blackwood's main street. Sniles knocked on the door but there was nobody home, no car and units were attached to it either side so Sniles couldn't peer into the backyard. He went home, tired, needing sleep, knowing he had his scalp, one big enough to shut up the likes of

Dawksted once and for all. All he had to do was find him.

'Go on, get up,' Jenny hissed in the dawn glow. The clock radio said 6:15am. He'd been laying in their bed mulling over everything for 15 minutes and didn't even know it. 'I'm sick of hearing you think.'

Sniles turned over and rested a hand on her shoulders beneath the bed covers.

'What the hell's wrong with these people, Jenny?'

She left his question sitting on the bed for a moment. Her snub threatened to overwhelm him, bring him to tears, a final insult to reinforce the tatters of their relationship. But then she turned over and whispered into his ear.

'Maybe if people were less focussed on other people's problems, and more focussed on overcoming their own, there'd be less shit for the rest of us to shovel.'

'What are you saying?'

'I'm telling you to get out there, do what you have to do, but do it quickly. I didn't leave my life behind to be the partner of a man who screams the names of other women in his sleep.'

Sniles wanted to get up and smash the clues together so hard they split into new pieces, died and rained.

'I'm sorry, Jenny. I'm just so … I'll do this and things will change. I promise. And we'll go on that holiday, to the Barossa.'

Ten minutes later Sniles sat in his backyard, sipping instant coffee, feeling heat in the air already. The Bureau of Meteorology had issued its 'catastrophic' fire danger warning, a term he struggled to get his head around. Shouting Armageddon every time a hot windy day was forecast in the driest state in the driest country must surely be like crying wolf to such a fire-weary population. He also believed in bold newspaper print it served as a call to arms for every would-be arsonist who hadn't seen the weather forecast. Sniles only hoped the bureau's other prediction would eventuate. A cool change was due to arrive in the afternoon, bringing with it possible rain. With any luck, it would fall in the hills.

His phone buzzed in his pocket. It was his superintendent with a text message.

Good work Sniles. Units are on the way to Lawson's address with an arrest warrant. We're searching archives for original hard copies on Gerard Brummer. Preliminary findings are he receives weekly visits from a contracted nursing agency. Dawksted will make contact with Stay Home Assistance, Adelaide Hills branch, for further information and we'll send a patrol to the Olave Valley address.

Stay Home Assistance. Sniles' eye lingered on the name. Leaves shook and rippled as a blast of hot air hit his face, dried his skin, scattered dead leaves on the paving about him. If the Bureau of Meteorology was correct, the north-easterlies would hit 25 knots in less than an hour.

'Shit,' Sniles said, standing up as a gumnut plopped into his coffee. Stay Home Assistance. He flicked his notepad pages back to find the entry from Ashleigh for the second time, the name of the nursing agency she worked for. She didn't just know *about* the clown, she was his *nurse*, Gerard Brummer's nurse. Ashleigh was connected to Richard, Donnie *and* the clown. It was a four-way cluster fuck.

Sniles threw out the rest of his coffee and went inside to get changed.

An irregular *thwok* drew Richard from slumber. He pulled out his remaining ear plug; the other had fallen out while he slept.

Thwok

Ashleigh sighed, dumped a hefty dose of morning breath in his face.

'Morning,' she said. 'Did you end up sleeping okay?' Richard lifted his chin and tried to rise above her breath's shooting range.

'I did actually,' he said, wriggling away from her hand that had started clawing up his thigh. 'What's that noise?'

'Don't think about it,' Ashleigh crooned, throttling him with foul air, a full onslaught this time.

'I've gotta find out.' Richard swung his legs out of bed and his hands shouted in pain, particularly his broken hand. He went to the window and looked behind the blind, saw his metal cat blowing about in the tree.

Thwok

'It's never done that before.'

'Somebody's full of beans this morning.'

Actually his body was heavy. His hands were angry and his thighs ached. He wanted nothing more than to collapse back into bed, a log falling heavy, cut down by the first proper night's sleep in weeks. But there was an annoying sound outside and Ashleigh's breath stank.

'Come back to bed,' she said, shifting a little and letting the covers slip down her cleavage. But he was on top with Ashleigh, at least for the moment, and he didn't want to risk another flop. Not now.

'I'm hungry, babe,' he said, the word 'babe' rolling off his tongue too fast to be stopped, regretting it immediately. He pulled on his tracksuit pants. 'You need to tell me about Donnie. You need to tell me what you two were talking about, and what's going on with the clown.'

Richard left her alone with his little snip and shuffled from the room. He sat down at his kitchen table, heavy, groggy. He couldn't remember the last time he'd slept so soundly. He flicked on the radio and listened to news reports about people panic-buying and stripping the shops of food and supplies. The Prime Minister was calling it 'ridiculous', 'un-Australian'. He said supermarkets were not closing and everyone needed to calm down and act normal.

Ashleigh emerged from the bedroom, wearing Richard's T-shirt from yesterday. Her usually vibrant face was waxen under her blonde mass of bed hair. She glided across the kitchen's linoleum floor and sat down before him, black mascara smudges beneath her beautiful green eyes.

'I guess,' she sighed, striking Richard once more with her breath. 'It's kind of—'

'Wait.' Richard turned off the radio and held up his bandaged hand. He took a pear from the bowl and handed it to her.

'No thanks.' Ashleigh waved it away. 'Richard you should know—'

'Have some.' Her mouth needed to be neutralised with pears. 'Fruit first, then we talk, yeah?'

She didn't take the pear.

'I'll cut it up.' Richard retrieved a knife from the sink and returned to the table, holding the pear upright with his cast-covered hand, cutting it awkwardly. Her emerald eyes assessed him as she put the slice in her mouth. Richard started cutting a second slice but the fruit slid in its own juice. He squashed it immobile with his cast and managed to cut a second slice awkwardly, pushing it into her hand, not giving up until she took it reluctantly, watching him thoughtfully, the glass louvres in the window next to them rattling in the wind.

'I don't want any more pear,' she said when Richard started trying to cut a third slice. 'And there's nothing between me and Donnie.'

'He wishes there was.' It came out wrong, as if she hadn't just spent the last 24 hours in and out of hospitals with him, caring for him, fucking him. 'I mean, you know, he's always had a thing for you, right? Remember that time he watched us in your car?'

'He was never watching,' Ashleigh said.

'He was watching alright.' While everyone else was inside, drinking, talking, having fun, Donnie was peeping on them in Ashleigh's car, that first night at the party, the beautiful, fateful night at the end of high school. 'He was there and he was—'

'It doesn't matter he was there, Richard. He wasn't watching.'

The window slats next to their heads shook again. Richard cut more pear. The wet fruit slipped beneath his cast and fell to the ground with a splat.

'Forget the damned pear, Richard.'

'What is it then? You said it last night. What has Donnie been doing to me?'

'I think ….' Ashleigh crossed her arms as if it was cold. But the wisps of air slithering through the glass louvres were warm, very warm, even though it was still early and, as Richard suddenly realised, no wattle bird had been screeching from its tree.

Thwok

'I think he's been messing with you, Richard. The orchard, the painting on your tree … It isn't the clown. Gerard wouldn't do that sort of thing.'

'His name's Gerard?'

Ashleigh lowered her arms onto the table, palms up, one of them landing in pear juice so Richard wanted to get a sponge.

'I *told* you. That old couple pay for his care. Gerard Brummer's an orphan and—'

'A fucking pyromaniac.' Richard stood up, hitting his back against the wall behind him. 'And you washed his jacket. You were fucking washing his jacket. I saw it.'

'So what if I clean his clothes? Who else is gonna do it now that his neighbours' house burnt down. Sit down, Richard. Please?'

Outside the leaves shook in the air, laughing in the wind, and the wattle bird was silent. The wattle bird was gone. Richard sat down. It wasn't right that the wattle bird was silent.

'Okay, fine. I'll tell you something, but don't tell Lars.' Ashleigh lowered her voice. 'I think Gerard comes to the pine forest across the road, and does his thing in the forest … yells and stuff … because of me. He likes me.'

Richard watched beads of water pool in Ashleigh's eyes, slide down her cheeks, drip onto the table.

'He's been doing it all year, and he can't talk, you know, he can only scream.'

'Like a bird.'

'What?' Ashleigh said.

'We burnt his paintings. I burnt his paintings. He's gonna finish me off. Eat me with fish. Fish and chips.'

'Richard,' Ashleigh said, suddenly giggling, each spasm shaking her hair. 'Gerard doesn't know who stole his paintings. The old couple told me all about that night. They were really mad but they don't know who it was. I do, because you lot left me alone, remember? It's funny how these things work out. But Gerard wouldn't have a clue.'

'He sent me videos of dogs shitting.'

'What?' Ashleigh let slip another little giggle. She stifled it with her hand and air moisture congealed and beaded on the table. 'What video?'

'A DVD of dogs shitting, hundreds of them. It made me puke. It made me …' Richard waved his hand at the debris in the lounge room, the pieces of DVD, the headless garden gnome, moisture congealing on the table and running to the floor. 'He did it 'cause I escaped to London. It was fucking disgusting and it made me puke.'

He stood up, moved to the sink and looked down into the drain, seeing the clown's face in the darkness, white and bleeding under the torchlight in Donnie's boot, smiling, no matter how many times Richard hit it, and Donnie just watching, Donnie just standing there enjoying the whole thing, always watching but never acting, letting Richard do it all.

'Richard, Gerard wouldn't even know how to turn on a TV, let alone make a stupid DVD.'

'What were you and Donnie talking about?' he said, still staring into the drain. 'What's Donnie done?'

'He hates Gerard,' Ashleigh said. 'It's something to do with his mother and that childcare centre fire, back when he was a kid. You know about that?'

'Everyone knows about that.'

'He still thinks his dad's alive.'

'She killed him. Everyone knows that too.'

'Donnie doesn't. He still believes he ran away. Donnie's all messed up about it and … I think he's trying to fuck with you because of me. He's fucking with both of you. He's jealous … of you, and Gerard too, I think.'

'What about the fires, hey? Did he try and kill the old couple?'

'I don't know,' Ashleigh said. The glass slats next to her head now rattled so hard they threatened to break. 'Richard?'

He turned around and she looked worried. Emerald water was spilling from her eyes in a torrent, down her cheeks and over her shoulders, a waterfall supplying a swimming pool at her feet. Despite the resistance he'd felt this morning, he started to feel pity for her, the same affection he felt last night.

'I don't know what he's going to do.'

'I fucking hate this place,' Richard sighed, sitting down with a squelch. It was all so typically wet, typically sticky, typically Blackwood.

'It's not the place, Richard,' she said, her eyes flashing with defiance despite her tears. 'It's the company you keep.'

'You keep it too.'

'I keep it for you.'

Richard swallowed. At that moment his mobile phone rang. He snatched it from the table and answered without looking at the caller ID. He was worried it would be Max from Cedar Desk asking about his rotten YingCo advert.

'Hello?'

'Richard,' Sniles said. 'What are you doing right now?'

'I'm eating pears, Constable,' Richard said, emphasising the name of the law to Ashleigh. 'And the clown does exist. His name is Gerard—'

'Brummer. Gerard Brummer,' Sniles said.

'You know?'

'Of course I do, but I'm more interested in Donnie. Donald Lawson. Have you seen him?'

'Donnie?' Richard said, throwing the name back at Ashleigh, but getting lost in her eyes, sucked away as green water continued to pour from her face. 'Yeah, last night. Want his number?' He pulled away and retrieved Donnie's number, spoke it into the phone, lifted it back to his ear. 'Did you get that?'

'I got it. Is Ashleigh with you, Richard?'

A gust of wind shook the front door. From outside came the sound of a massive crack, a tree shedding a limb. The storm had arrived, a hot storm, just like the constable had said, but there was still no wattle bird. Not even a cackle.

'No.'

'She's his nurse, Richard. The clown's nurse. Did you know that?'

A whirlpool formed in the kitchen pool, tipped Richard on his side, tugged at his legs, tried to suck him spiralling down.

'You need to be careful with her, Richard. She's not everything she seems.'

'Sorry?' Richard heard himself say, trying to swim, stay afloat. 'I can't hear you.' He saw one of his hands reach out and open the louvres, pulling the plug on the pool, water gushing out as hot air gushed in, filling the kitchen with bits and pieces of trees, dust, heat, lots of heat.

'She knows more about all of this than she lets on.'

'You're breaking up, Constable.' He watched the heat grab hold of Ashleigh's hair, flap it about her smooth face. 'I'll have to call you back.'

Richard hung up the phone and put it down on a table covered with mud, wet gum nuts, a few flapping fish. Ashleigh sat impassive before him, her hands still on the table, her hair blowing over the top of her head, one flushed cheek exposed to the storm.

'You need to go,' Richard said. 'You need to get dressed and you need to go.'

'What did he say?'

Richard closed the windowpane, cutting off the air, letting Ashleigh's hair drop back to her shoulders.

'You know what he said. You hear everything.'

He returned to his bedroom and pulled on his jeans. It was a struggle, a stitched finger, a cut up palm and a broken hand. He had to leave his belt unbuckled. He pulled on a T-shirt, found some socks, kicked his shoes out into the hallway to see Ashleigh still sitting at the kitchen table. He kicked his shoes down the hallway towards her and sat at the kitchen table.

'You know I love you, don't you?' she said, stabbing Richard in the heart. 'Even when you went out with Lena, said you were going overseas. I was okay with it. I mean, you two had nothing in common, but I was just glad you were finally standing up to your dad.'

She waited momentarily for him to say something.

'But you were gone a long time. I needed ...'

'What?'

'I have needs too, you know.'

'What does that mean?'

Ashleigh stepped around the table, touched his face and her hands were cool and clean. He'd been touched by her all night, all morning, and not one little piranha had taken a bite. Not one piranha had leapt from her whirlpool eyes.

'It means I need to be loved too. But everything's become so complicated. Gerard and Donnie, the cop, you, none of it was—'

'And so what? Did you fuck Donnie?'

'No.'

'Then who? The *clown?*'

She stepped back, her mouth opening, her tongue preparing to unleash new piranhas.

'Of course not. But I might have … led him on, that's all. It was nice going there. Those butterflies of his are amazing.'

Richard's phone rang again. It was the same number. It was the constable. He picked it up and pushed it into Ashleigh's hands, not wanting to hear his voice. He shuffled away to the lounge room as she answered it, turned the front door handle. The door blew inwards, heavy with dust, with dirt from the outside world.

Thwok

He looked for his metal cat in the tree, a useless bird-scarer being blown about in the wind, but that's when he saw it.

The painting on his tree was no longer a splotchy reproduction of a warped insect with a broken edge. The mess had been covered over with black paint and the picture repainted. It was a symmetrical butterfly, its right wing fully completed, fully joined, utterly perfect. It had been painted in red like the eyes of a clown he'd beaten up in a mad pyromaniac's car.

'Oh fuck,' Richard said.

Thwok

The clown was standing next to the tree, his white jacket stained with red paint, his face swollen with a black eye, hitting a paint brush against a tin of red paint in his other hand. *Thwok.* The clown met Richard's stare and smiled, his jaw opening wide, teeth disappearing, nose protruding, a smile that split across the middle and arched backwards so his head seemed to topple apart, and from the opening came a horrible shriek, broken glass in a banshee's throat, a shark launching from the surface of a piranha infested sea. It flew through the air, opened its jaws, and swallowed Richard's head.

THE ARCHIBALD BUSHFIRE

Donnie lit the sparkler and stood back. He had planned to watch the petrol-drenched leaves beneath the sparkler explode and ignite a petrol trail all the way to the childcare centre 30 metres away. Instead he ran down a scrub-covered slope leading to the train station, turned onto a side street and jumped into his parked car.

He drove around the block and doubled back, coasting slowly along the main road with all the other cars. Traffic was busier than usual with coronavirus panic-buyers in foreign-made, oversized SUVs creating a bottleneck in and out of the Woolworths and Foodland carparks. Their daft cars murmured and growled at each other, idle, frustrated, loaded fat with groceries or empty and desperate to be packed. Dozens of people skirted about them, rushing into stores, afraid of missing out, afraid of a world collapsing on their heads. Donnie wanted to throw Molotov cocktails at them all, a bunch of useless morons who'd apparently responded to the first pandemic in 100 years by hoarding toilet paper. Instead he continued back to his first target, the childcare centre Mother had failed to destroy all those years ago.

Black smoke from it was already billowing over the road, encouraged by an ever-increasing wind. The procession of cars stopped and Donnie opened his door, standing up and craning his head for a better view. There was screaming, shouting, two people running as the smoke grew thicker and blacker by the second, a brooding, cancerous tumour bulging and popping with the occasional red flame in its midst. Donnie realised with surprise that a car covered in black smoke on the road had caught alight too. The beast had swallowed the childcare centre and was already moving.

'Holy shit,' a male driver standing next to the car behind him exclaimed. 'It was closed today, right?'

'Yeah,' Donnie said. 'Always closed on catastrophic fire danger days.'

'Pussy,' Donnie's mother hissed in his ears. 'There was no one there.'

'Shut the fuck up,' Donnie growled as he climbed back into his Holden and performed a three-point turn back towards Coromandel Valley. 'I wouldn't burn babies like you, *Mother*.'

He lifted the towel covering a box on the passenger seat to reveal two Molotov cocktails.

'I'm just making it clean. I'm making all of it clean.'

Donnie's phone rang and he pulled it from his pocket, saw a phone number he'd never seen before. He rejected the call. He had a blue car to burn, a foreign piece of shit that would never use parts from an out-of-work fitter and turner like Donnie. The little blue car had housed his friends fucking, back when they'd finished high school, back when he'd imagined himself together with Ashleigh, married, children, a steady job making parts for Holden, no fires, no mothers, only to step outside a party to see her car bouncing up and down. It hurt so much he'd let slip a moan of his own and Richard had heard it. Richard had turned his head and seen Donnie running away, a coward, a pervert, a dirty man watching from the bushes. They'd never spoken about it but it was there. It was always there.

He arrived in Coromandel Valley and accelerated against the wind towards Blackwood Forest. The pines looked hot already, a lighter green than usual, waiting for him to light them up, waiting to explode and erase themselves along with the old manager's house within.

He pulled into Ashleigh and Lars' cul-de-sac, slowed as he approached their houses. The street was empty. Only panic-buyers and pyros wanted to be outside on a bitching hot day like this, when gum trees dropped their branches and hot air caked the sweat on your face, dried your lips, and primed everything for ignition.

He slammed his foot on the brakes. Out the front of Ashleigh's house was a police car, the last of the Holdens, a disgusting front-wheel drive made in Germany after the company fucked off overseas, a sick joke laughing at out-of-work fuckers like Donnie. It was the only car there and a shadow lurked in the driver's seat. Donnie indicated and casually turned right down a side street, a section of his grand plan foiled by another fucking cop.

'Useless,' Mother spat. 'You useless cunt.'

Donnie manoeuvred through the streets back to Turners Avenue, swearing, hitting the steering wheel until his phone rang again in his pocket, the same unknown number, hassling him, wanting him.

'What?'

'Donald Lawson?'

'Yeah. Who's this?' He negotiated a chicane with one hand on the steering wheel, a stronger gust of air battering his car with dust, leaves and grass.

'This is Senior Constable Rory Sniles. Where are you today, Donnie?'

'I've been at home. Why?'

'No, you haven't. We've been at your unit. It's empty.'

'Well, I'm not there now, am I? Dickhead!'

He'd been fingered, probably by Richard. He'd do the clown's house, then check in at Richard's. Ashleigh was there; he was sure of it. He'd burn her horrible little fucking Hyundai there, burn everything there.

'We've met before, Donnie,' the constable growled. 'You nearly killed me six days ago at Olave Valley, you little bastard.'

Donnie turned up the dirt track and accelerated. Two Molotov cocktails full of hair clinked alongside him. Two cans of petrol in the boot waited silently to be spilled.

'You went back and tried to kill that old couple, didn't you? You sick little fuck.'

Two jars full of hair bristled inside his glove box, memories he wanted cleaned, erased, forgotten, his screaming mother, his coward father, his coward self who stole animals, punched their scared little faces, little brown eyes and wet little noses, shaved them, then buried them in the old manager's house.

'And the masseuses, you dirty shit. Why the masseuses?'

Because they were the only women who ever saw him, the only women who ever touched him. Not like Ashleigh. He could never get close to Ashleigh. Everyone else got to fuck Ashleigh, but not cowards like Donnie, cowards who couldn't even get it up for a whore.

'I'm talking to you, Donnie.'

The clown's valley was in sight, the acrid smell of past bushfires strong in the wind. He would block all exits from the shitty old Quaker's house, just in case the freak was home, just in case he tried to come out biting. Then he'd throw a cocktail, pour petrol, set the fucker alight.

'Motherfucker,' Donnie shouted, slamming on the brakes and dropping the phone.

From the valley road he could see another police car parked in the clown's front yard, waiting.

'Just leave me alone. Mind your own fucking business and leave me alone.'

He turned the car around and tore back down the hill towards Turner's Avenue, the constable laughing down the phone line from the floor.

'I got you pegged, mate,' Constable Sniles said. 'Why don't you come into the station. It'll be better for you.'

Donnie hung up and retrieved Ashleigh's phone number, dialled the number. She had to be at Richard's house. They were probably fucking in her little blue car in front of his painted fucking tree. But he had to find out if the cops were there as well. There was only one way in via Richard's access lane, one way out, and if they spotted him, he'd be caught.

'Donnie?' Ashleigh said over the phone, her voice loud, urgent and crackling with wind.

'Are you at Richards?' he said. 'I want to say sorry … for last night …

to both of you.'

'Richard's gone crazy,' Ashleigh wailed, her voice broken, wet and crunchy. 'Gerard was here. He painted Richard's tree—'

'*I* painted Richard's tree.'

'No. Gerard came back and made it better and now Richard's gone crazy.'

They were all there — Richard, Ashleigh, a clown who was 'better', who'd had the nerve to taste Ashleigh, who'd climbed into Donnie's boot with baby eyes and white clown teeth. They were probably all about to fuck in her little blue car right now.

'Richard's got a weapon,' Ashleigh shouted. 'An axe handle or something and he's gonna hurt Gerard again.'

'Are the cops there?' Donnie snarled.

'No, but they rang for you. They wanted your number.' She stopped blabbering and for a moment all Donnie could hear was the sound of wind blowing over the mouthpiece. 'It's you, isn't it? The arsonist. The old couple. You're sick, Donnie. You nearly killed people. You need—'

'Oh, and Richard's just dandy, is he? He's not fucking crazy at all. And you, you've gotta be the sickest one of the lot. You fucked a clown.'

'I didn't fuck him, you prick!'

The phone went dead. Within a second it rang again. It was the constable. Donnie ignored it, pulled over, picked up a Molotov cocktail and lit the rag. He leant out the window and threw it into native bushes shouldering the road. It bordered a suburb of houses, a population of thousands stretching over the foothills. The bushes fronted Archibald Reserve, a no-man's land of grassy fire fuel that stretched in a corridor behind homes towards Blackwood Forest. If he was lucky, his fire would burn all the way through to Lars and Ashleigh's house, then the pines.

Bushes flared quickly into flames, fanned by winds that angled licking spears towards the dried grasses and fallen bark of the reserve. Embers and leaves rose burning into the air. They were caught by the wind and whisked away to light new fires elsewhere. A different fire spear entered a neighbour's front yard, found more dried grass and headed towards their front door. The door opened and a child stared out. He was quickly pulled inside and replaced by a man who slammed the door on the advancing flames. Donnie hit the accelerator and pointed his car towards Richard's.

*

Richard stood holding the axe handle on the dirt track leading into the quarry. It was the only way out and the clown had cornered himself, closed in on all three sides by the sandstone pit, an amphitheatre cut into the slope of Pony Ridge Scrub. The smell of fire was in the sky and the clown stood panting, smiling in his stupid white suit, red hair and eyes that looked like a fucking child's, one of them swollen and half closed.

'Why?' Richard tried to say but hot air blasted his face. A swirl of angry air descended into the gully, bringing with it a spiral of smoke, dust, and, as both the clown and Richard watched, embers from a nearby fire. The burning leaves fell from the sky in a rain of vengeance.

'No,' Richard wailed. 'Not here. Not again!'

They zeroed in on clumps of dried grass to either side of the track, sparking little spot fires as more wind swirled into the quarry, fanning the newborn flames so they consumed the grass and crawled across dried leaves, banksia bushes, the legs of gumtree trolls.

'They're gonna blame me for this,' Richard cried.

The clown stepped forward, his mouth opening wide, a giant smile breaking his face in two, and from the chasm erupted a mighty shriek that blasted the spot fires so they seemed to shake and retreat. Richard covered his ears. The clown bolted past and leapt into the bushes, leaving the flames to recoil and writhe in his wake. They recovered, finding more grass to feed on, and reared upwards to come again for Pony Ridge Scrub, for convicted arsonist Richard Caruso.

'Shit.'

Richard turned, leapt over the flames and lunged into the scrub after the clown, ducking and dodging the branches, hearing the clown crash ahead, seeing glimpses of red hair in the smoke now coming from behind him. He hoped the fucker would turn and run down the slope. There was nowhere to go at the bottom, just a dried creek, impenetrable black-berry bushes. But a spark flew past Richard's face. Embers jumped from bush to bush. Dreadlocked trolls shook and snarled and there was some-thing else, another shape running in the forest. A gust of wind lifted the broth and he saw Donnie, big Donnie, running down the forest slope towards the clown, coming to head him off.

The clown saw Donnie coming, turned about and ran back towards Richard.

'Hold him, Richard,' Donnie shouted from across the forest. 'Don't let him get away.'

A swarm of sparks blew against Richard's back as the clown flapped towards him, sweating, covered in soot, a few scratches bright red against his white swollen face, opening his smile, his biting smile, a wild look in his black eye, clown hands coming at Richard, outstretched, long spindly fingers that hit his neck like bird talons. He bowled Richard over, knocked the axe handle from his hand, and there was a red beak opening over Richard's eyes, clasping the bridge of his nose, biting, a squawk like a hungry baby bird, a sweaty, thrashing, spindly-clawed freak crushing his body. Richard could feel the clown's bird-heart beating at a million miles an hour through his chest, his own heart stuttering in response, his nose crushed by sharp piranha-bird teeth, the taste of salt in his mouth from the clown's drool. Somewhere outside the nightmare Donnie shouted, big Donnie, the son-of-a-bitch who'd been messing with Richard from the start. Wind roared in the trees, applauding the clown's attack, braying for Richard's arsonist blood. Noise erupted from Richard's throat, a cry for mercy that sounded louder and more desper-ate than the burning world about them. The piranha let go of his nose. The sucking, heart-beating, sweaty bird-child pushed off Richard and looked at him with a bruised and swollen face. Anger receded in those eyes, was replaced with compassion, sadness, loneliness — and then the face was gone. The clown jumped over him and ran up the hill. Seconds later Donnie appeared. He crouched next to Richard and shouted.

'Fucking hell, Richard. You let him get away.'

And then, inexplicably, he yanked a piece of Richard's hair out his temple.

'Ow.'

Donnie's great shape thumped way up the slope and through the forest, his heaving lungs fading into the smoke. But Richard's heart was thumping too fast and there was clown drool in his mouth, crackling in the distance, a branch falling to the ground. He heard screaming, the kind of screaming you heard at night in big cities in bad districts on TV, and he realised it was Ashleigh. She screamed again, more desperate, more anguished. Richard leapt to his feet and ran up the slope towards his house.

'Stop,' Ashleigh shouted from within the smoke. Glass smashed.

'Ashleigh,' Richard called, ducking beneath a branch and coughing. The smoke was thicker here, a whipping cloud that stung his eyes, and what would his parents say if he got blamed for this one? They'd have him locked in a psych ward, quarantined with his piranhas, ordered back to work in Dad's accounting firm.

'Only numbers will keep you stable,' Dad would say.

Richard stumbled through branches and over a lip of gravel — the access track to his house. It was covered in dark smoke and it smelt plastic, toxic. Tears streamed from his eyes and he glimpsed through the heat a fire-spiked monster where Ashleigh's blue car had been parked. It groaned, melted, no longer blue but something orange, black and alive.

'Ashleigh,' Richard shouted but she was gone. Donnie was gone. He ran to his front yard, found his garden hose, turned on the water and tried to douse the car, but there was little water pressure. His neighbours must be pouring water onto their roofs. He stuffed the hose into his mouth to wash out the clown's drool — infectious crud that could make a person shriek.

Richard heard a noise to his side. A shadow emerged from the smoke, limping, panting, smiling, always the clown was smiling, but there was something different now. There was recognition, acknowledgment. Blood dribbled from the clown's chin.

'Where's Ashleigh?' Richard asked, bracing himself defensively, readying the hose to whip him. The clown stopped and pointed down the road.

'With Donnie?'

The clown gurgled, his non-swollen eye unbearably wide. He stepped forward and spat a globule of blood onto the concrete. Richard turned the hose on it. The blood washed away to reveal something flesh-like and solid in its wake, Donnie's finger.

'Fuck me,' Richard said, as sirens wailed in the air.

Fire crawled to the other side of the access track, licked the edges, tested its chances. The clown shrieked and it was louder than Ashleigh's distress, louder than the wind above, the shaking trees, the dirty flames eating her car. The fire reared backwards in response and, rather than push across the gravel towards them, moved onwards through the forest. The clown took another step towards Richard, his smile bigger, broader, his eyes urgent and pleading. He pointed at Donnie's finger on the ground, a little piece of bone jutting from its end. Richard, who was still holding his ears after the clown's fire-controlling scream, nodded and dropped his hands.

'Yeah. *He's* the one who stole your paintings. I never stole a thing.'

From the distance Richard heard shouting, his name being cursed, a neighbour hollering about the flames laying waste to Pony Ridge Scrub.

He dropped the hose and took out his phone, dialled Constable Sniles.

'Richard?' Sniles shouted. It was noisy at his end. People were shouting among sirens. 'Where are you right now? Right fucking now? There's at least three fronts burning across the district, you crazy son-of-a-bitch, and Donnie couldn't have lit them all.'

Flashing red lights streaked through the smoke. It was a CFS truck crawling along Richard's access track, a crew of firefighters in yellow suits and white helmets on its back. They hosed water onto the forest, kept the road wet, maintained the firebreak.

'I'm at home but I know where he is,' Richard shouted.

The constable barked orders at the other end, told people to slow down, drive in the other direction. He yelled at some guy called Dawksted and told him to sort out a bottleneck or there was 'gonna be hell to pay'.

'He's not finished,' Richard said. 'He's got Ashleigh. He's kidnapped her.'

The clown stood watching from barely a metre away, smiling with his swollen cheeks. He seemed frozen, empty, as if he were a dog waiting for a ball to be thrown. Richard realised suddenly the clown wasn't blinking.

'Fucking blink, will you?'

'Where is he, Richard?' Sniles said over the phone. 'Where's Donnie?'

'The pine forest.'

'How do you know?'

'I just know, okay? He's gonna … I don't know, fucking burn her, burn himself. He's all fucked up, like a car with a bad brain, you know? Haywire.'

The CFS truck pulled into Richard's yard. Firefighters jumped out and drenched the flames still eating Ashleigh's car. Hissing steam and smoke threw up over their faces.

'There's a fire here too, and he set Ashleigh's car on fire, and I didn't do any of it, thank you very much. Hey,' Richard shouted at the clown. 'Stop smiling, and start blinking, for fuck's sake.'

'Hey,' Sniles shouted at somebody on the other end again. 'Quit filming and get the hell out of here or I'll shove that phone right up your fucking arse'.

'And the Blackwood Clown's here,' Richard shouted into the phone. 'He bit Donnie's finger off.'

There was more shouting on the other end, a crowd of excited people, swearing, car horns beeping.

'As in Gerard Brummer?' the constable asked, sounding closer to the
phone than he had for the entire conversation.

'Yes.'

'Right.' There was the thud of a door closing, sounds of panic at
the constable's end suddenly muted. 'Just don't go anywhere, lad. I'm
coming to get you both.'

TRAFFIC JAM

'You'd better be straight with me about all this,' Sniles said to Richard, swerving the car to avoid a couple running across the road with suitcases. He swerved again, this time avoiding a fleeing dog with its tail between its legs. 'I don't trust that girlfriend of yours. For all I know she's in on this shit.'

They roared along Upper Sturt Road, wild bushland of Belair National Park to their left, the homes of Glenalta to their right. Billowing smoke filled the sky. Sniles prayed the north-easterlies didn't switch to south-westerlies as forecast, send the fire behind them over peoples' properties. The business strip was ablaze on the main road and a third bushfire was moving fast at Turner's Avenue. People who'd been panicking over coronavirus and stocking up on groceries were now evacuating right across the district in a flurry of activity, grabbing their precious hand sanitiser, pasta, flour bags, toilet papers and soaps, shoving them in boxes, stuffing them in bags, wrapping valuables in bed sheets and throwing bundles into cars. But it seemed impossible that Donnie could set three fires in three different locations so quickly.

'That's *three* fires, Richard, one on the main road in Blackwood, one at Turners Avenue, and the fire back at yours. I'll ask you one more time. Did you light that fire back there?'

'I told you I didn't,' Richard said from the backseat, a dirty plaster cast covering one hand, unravelling bandages on the other. 'But move it, will you? You've gotta go faster.'

'What about him?' Sniles asked thrusting his thumb behind them.

Gerard had refused to sit inside the car. Instead he'd shouted and banged on the boot until Sniles opened it and let him inside before closing it again.

'How should I know? Apparently he likes to ride in the boot.'

'The fire. Did he start the fire? You told me in hospital he was the pyro.'

'That was before I knew Donnie was the pyro. But this guy?' Richard stuck his tongue out and scraped it between his teeth as if he had a bad taste in his mouth. 'This guy's something else altogether.'

The CB radio crackled. A dispatch officer unleashed a tirade of police codes and called for back-up on Main Road and Coromandel Parade in Blackwood, back at Fourth Avenue from where they'd just come.

'This is chaos,' Sniles said, accelerating. 'Your friend hit the childcare centre in Blackwood and the fire took off, stretched right over the main road. It's taken five cars and three businesses and it's still moving. CFS can't get a hold of anything in this wind.' Sniles hit the steering wheel. 'I told them. I fucking told them.'

'He's not my friend,' Richard said. 'He's a lunatic.'

Sniles turned on his red and blue lights, swerved into the oncoming lane to overtake eight cars driving in a slow convoy.

Richard twisted his head and started licking the chair headrest.

'What are you doing?'

'I've got clown drool in my mouth.'

'Calm the hell—'

'It's in my blood like an infected piranha and my ...' Richard stopped himself, sat on his bandaged hand and looked steadfast out the window for a moment. He suddenly turned and glared at Sniles. 'Shoot my wattle bird.'

'What?'

'The fucking wattle bird in my tree. You cops are supposed to help, aren't you?' Richard leant forward and shouted. 'Shoot it.'

'Cut it out.' Sniles let loose a sharp elbow that sent Richard backwards into his seat. 'Somebody other than Donnie must have started that fire back there, and if you're not gonna tell me—'

'I did tell you. It came from the sky, ashes from Donnie's fire. *He's* the pyro. And if you hadn't spent so much time hassling *me*, getting agro with *me*, you might have caught him by now. Shoot my fucking wattle bird, *officer.*'

Sniles slammed on the brakes. He leapt out the car and walked around to the bonnet where he smashed his forearms upon it three times, staring hot into Richard's face through the windscreen. He marched around to Richard's door, ready to pull the mad fucker from the car, hit him, pummel him, make him bleed. But from the back of the boot came a shriek. It was horrible, the sound of a teenager watching his friend getting beaten by a policeman on a riverbank.

'Officer?' A man's voice asked from behind him. The shrieking stopped. Sniles swung around and saw a worried man in a suit standing beside the open door of his SUV. It was stuffed with groceries and camping equipment. Behind him were several other cars in a row, people inside looking at him expectantly. It was a minor traffic jam, a queue of evacuating cars banked up at a Turner's Avenue chicane. 'Can the virus travel in smoke?'

'What the fuck?'

Cars from both ends were trying to push through the single lane chicane simultaneously, followed by more cars at their rear. Some arsehole started honking his horn, followed by another. A potentially deadly scenario was unfolding and there were more chicanes to come, installed by some bright spark in complete ignorance to the fact this was a bushfire zone people might need to evacuate, fast. Coronavirus, and what it could or couldn't do, was the last thing this man should be worrying about.

'Get back in your car and get out of here,' Sniles told the man before climbing into his own car. 'Now.'

'If you shoot my wattle bird I'll forget you hit me,' Richard said from the back seat.

'Done.' Sniles picked up the CB transmitter. 'Dawksted?'

'Done,' Richard repeated, erupting into joyful laughter.

'Where are you, Sniles?' Dawksted shouted back after a few seconds. 'I need help back here. I'm trying to evacuate these idiots but … oi!' Dawksted shouted off the mouthpiece. 'Break that shit up, right now.'

'Dawksted,' Sniles said into the phone. 'You've gotta send somebody down here. There's a traffic jam on Turner's Avenue north. Thirty cars already.'

'Traffic jam? The whole place is jammed. I just stopped two dickheads fighting over a trolley of toilet paper. A major fire is about to total the district and people are shopping like lunatics.'

'I've got eyes on the arsonist. I know where he is right now. I've got Richard Caruso in the car and he says—'

'Richard Caruso? *That's* who your arsonist is? Everybody knows Richard *Caruso*.'

'Dammit, Dawksted. There's no time for this. Can you send someone down here or not?'

'Caruso's no killer. He's an arsehole arsonist, a total fucktard who set his own tree alight, but he's no killer … oi!' Dawksted shouted off the mouthpiece again. 'Cut that shit out or I'll arrest you both.'

'I know he's not the killer but he knows where Donnie is. I've got a potential kidnapping. The fucker's running riot and I've got Gerard Brummer in my boot.'

'Gerard Brummer?'

'Yes. Gerard Brummer.'

'There is no Gerard Brummer.'

'What the fuck are you talking about Dawksted?'

'We found the original file in archives, the hard copy on the 1986 childcare fire. Brummer *died* in the childcare fire 28 years ago, along with Helen Lawson. It was kept from the public because there's no records of the kid, no birth certificate. He shouldn't have been there in the first place. It was a real fuck-up and somebody somewhere wanted it kept quiet. You're chasing ghosts and right now, you need to think about real people, because Sniles, the wind is shifting.'

Sniles looked at the sky. Dirty yellow ghost streams swirled and sank, heavy with soot. The wind was stuttering, a sign it was about to swing, and Gerard, the guy in his boot, the shrieking freak, was meant to be dead.

'What about the body?' Sniles said. 'You can't hide a body.'

'He was burnt to smithereens, incinerated, I don't fucking know. Brummer's body was never found.'

'What about the woman injured in the childcare centre fire, Eliza Murray?' Sniles continued. 'The file said she was pregnant after the fire. What did she name her kid? Maybe she named it after the kid that saved her life. Maybe Gerard was *her* kid.'

'Sniles,' Dawksted barked. 'It's fucking chaos up here. There's cars and people everywhere, all jammed up, all going nuts. The biggest front's to the south of Turners Ave, moving south-west. Eight houses are gone already and if the wind shifts, Sniles, if that happens, then I don't need to tell you what's gonna happen around here, do I? Forget thirty cars, mate. Think thousands.'

Dawksted was right. The only double-lane mass exit from the area was Shepherd's Hill Road that headed west from Blackwood roundabout, but that was only useful if people could get to the main road in the first place. They had kilometres of winding roads to negotiate, roads tunnelled by gum trees, chicanes, potential bottlenecks for thousands of people trying to evacuate the district at once. They could take Upper Sturt Road, but that headed west where a wind change would drive the fire. The only other exit was down old and new Belair roads, but the former was close to Pony Ridge Scrub and could already be in flames. It was a cluster fuck that had been brewing for years, no doubt paid lip service to by politicians who never wanted to spend money and update road infrastructure. Right now, however, he had a ghost in his boot. A kidnapping to foil. Everything he'd been chasing was within reach.

'Sniles,' Dawksted prodded. 'You there?'

The man in a suit was approaching his window, one of the gridlocked baby boomers who were multiplying by the minute. He was wearing a facemask and his hair flapped about. The wind was starting up again. Sniles switched off the CB and wound down his window.

'Forget about the damned virus, for God's sake,' he said to the man. 'Head east. The fire's gonna swing any minute.'

Sniles turned on his siren and drowned out his protests, drove up and onto the footpath and through somebody's garden, hitting his horn as the smoke became darker, more dense. They made it pass the mini traffic jam and returned to the road. In his rear view mirror he saw other cars following his lead, driving onto peoples' gardens.

'The clown's not dead,' Richard said from the back. 'He's a hermit, that's all. He's off the grid in that old house, painting all the time. He doesn't have to work or anything. *That's* why he's so good at it.'

Sniles negotiated another chicane, forcing an urban four-wheel-drive to drive onto somebody's front garden as he pushed through. Another car at the other end reversed to let him back on the road.

'Hey clown.' Richard thumped the back of his seat. 'Shriek for the constable so he knows you're real. Show him how you can make the fire—'

'Shut up or I'll fucking hit you again.'

'Don't forget your promise,' Richard said curtly, sitting back, out of range from Sniles' elbow.

They passed blackened bush skeletons on the side of the road, burnt grass leading to a smoking house. A CFS truck in the driveway poured water on the carnage. Behind the house they could see a volcano of smoke billowing away to the west. The fire was pushing through Archibald Reserve. It led all the way past Lars and Ashleigh's houses to Blackwood Forest.

Sniles swung the car onto their street, drove parallel to the pine forest. Its canopy was sucking hungrily at the smoke. Ahead of them a maroon Holden was parked on the side of the cul-de-sac, its passenger door left open.

'That's Donnie's car, right there,' Richard said.

The suspect's car looked empty. The parked patrol car Sniles had negotiated to stay there had already gone, no doubt to help untangle the district's deadly bottlenecks. He pulled in behind the maroon car and turned off the engine.

'Well then,' Sniles said, popping the boot. 'Let's get out your clown and see what he does.'

The car wobbled as Gerard clambered from the boot. Before they could even get out the car, he emitted a ear-piercing shriek, streaked past their windows, and plunged into the forest.

Richard leapt from the car and, without waiting for the Constable, sprinted to Lars' front door, tried to open it then pounded against it.

'Lars,' he shouted. 'Open the fucking door.'

He ran through the carport and found the side door unlocked. He went inside and turned on the kitchen tap, lowered his mouth to the water, splashed it inside and over his face. He picked up dishwater detergent, sucked the green fluid from its nozzle. It tasted sharp, full of chemicals. Soap always tasted horrible but it was better than clown slime.

'What're you doing?' Lars asked, emerging from the dim-lit lounge room. There was a pipe in his hand.

'The clown drooled in my mouth,' Richard gurgled, spitting bubbles from his mouth, coughing so the soap got up his nose and made his eyes water. 'Donnie's got Ashleigh.'

'What do you mean?' Lars wobbled.

'How long have you known about Ashleigh and Donnie?' Richard said, marching into the lounge room so Lars backed away. 'And Gerard?'

'You mean—'

'The *clown*, Lars. The ghost. He's out there 'cause of Ashleigh, 'cause of Donnie, 'cause of *me*.'

'He's a ... he's a ghost?'

'You were in on this shit.' He knocked the pipe from Lars' hand and pushed him backwards. 'You and Donnie were fucking with me from the start.'

Richard's fist flew into Lars' stomach so residual smoke puffed from his nostrils. He keeled over, coughed, held his breath on the floor. Richard wanted to kick him.

'Do you ever think about breathing, Lars? Do you ever think about blinking? Blink blink blink, about swallowing, your beating heart? Do you ever think about thinking? Do you ever think about the shit you and Donnie pulled and what it might do to a thinking fuck like me? Do you? Do you?'

'It was Donnie's idea,' Lars spluttered, tears welling in his blood-shot eyes. '*He* painted your name on that tree.'

'No shit it was Donnie's idea. That doesn't make it okay. It's not okay to sit around telling stories that make people want to scratch their faces off.'

'Wh … what?' Lars said, turning over, sitting up.

Richard pushed him with his foot so he fell back down. The constable started thumping at the front door.

'Donnie was freaked about you coming home,' Lars spluttered. ''Cause of Ashleigh. You're right. He's sweet on her. He thought it would be funny to pretend the clown was after you at the valley that day. It was just a joke, and we got you, right? Until that cop turned up and we had to get out of there. I'd never even heard the name Gerard 'til Ashleigh said it the other—'

'You were fucking with me this whole time. You're a fucking accomplice.'

'No,' Lars said.

'You made a video of dogs shitting.'

'What?' Lars laughed a little despite himself.

'Fucking dogs shitting, Lars, sick mother-fucking shit. And those old people nearly *died* in that fire. Donnie's a fucking psycho and you're an accessory.'

'No,' Lars shouted. 'It's the clown, man. He's real, and you're right. We shouldn't have gone back there. We made him mad. We made the clown real fucking mad, and he's got my dog.'

'Don't be stupid,' Richard said, reaching down to grab Lars' collar. 'Donnie took your dog.'

The constable thumped the door again, sharp, aggressive, as if he was punching it.

'Caruso, you little fucker. Open up.'

'Who's that?' Lars said.

'A cop,' Richard said.

'Shit. I've got weed.'

'That's the least of your problems,' Richard said, stepping over Lars to open the front door. 'This guy's a real bastard.'

*

Sniles lifted his elbow as Richard pushed past him out the door, copping him in the jaw.

'What the fuck are you doing, running off without me like that, locking me outside?'

Richard stumbled and, bizarrely, spat soap suds onto the porch. Sniles wanted to follow up with a little kick but was hit with the smell of dope. He looked through the door and saw the man called Lars splayed on the floor, bug-eyed, a brass pipe sitting on grey carpet stained by parties and age.

'Wait there,' Sniles said to Richard, stepping inside, his eyes on the greasy-haired stoner. 'This won't take a minute.'

He closed the door, swamped in a mixture of dope and bushfire smoke, a stoner's den made dingier by old curtains the colour of shit.

'I found your dog,' Sniles said.

'You ... you did?' the man called Lars sniffed, red eyes flickering between Sniles and the pipe. A water chopper thumped overhead, flying low up the reserve towards a fire front that was drawing closer with every second.

'He's dead, shaved, dumped in that cottage up there, with all the others. Your pyro friend killed him, like he killed that masseuse, like he's

218

gonna try and kill your friend.'

Lars stood up, his mouth trembling, a loser getting high while the district burned about him and his dog lay dead. Sniles pushed Lars hard in the chest so he fell backwards over a coffee table cluttered with plates and plastic drink bottles.

'Hey,' Lars stammered, cowering a little and trying to regain his footing. 'I don't know anything about any of that. That clown, he's—'

'Shut up,' Sniles said, flicking his baton so it extended. 'This is what's going to happen. I'm going to hit you once, okay? Just enough to shove that stupid dope-smoking grin down your throat, okay?'

'But …' The man's bottom lipped quivered, specks of dry white saliva on his cheeks. He was stoned, so recklessly stoned. 'You don't even know me.'

'Yeah I do. You're just like all the other deadbeats who never learn a thing.'

'But I am. I'm learning Chinese.'

Sniles whipped Lars across the cheeks with his baton. The greasy twat knocked over a stereo speaker and fell into an armchair. Sniles put a knee in Lar's chest and raised his baton again.

'But you said you'd only hit me once,' the ponce pleaded, bracing for impact.

Sniles hit him across the other cheek, a slapping sound that wasn't satisfying enough. He wanted to hit him again. He always wanted to hit them again, despite what he'd told his psychologist girlfriend, but there was a sudden crash from the back of the house. Sniles swung around and got a face full of hot smoke. Flames flicked over the edge of the broken window, the curtains already alight.

'Shit,' he said, pulling Lars to his feet and opening the door. 'C'mon. Move it.'

He pushed the fucker outside and onto the porch where streams of smoke billowed from behind the house. Richard was gone. There was crackling behind the house and behind the smoke, a hungry roar. The wind had dropped a little but blackberry bushes across the cul-de-sac were already burning, spot fires advancing into the pines. In minutes the first of the trees would go up.

Sniles covered his mouth and pulled Lars towards his car parked in the cul-de-sac, their backs searing in the heat.

'Take my car and drive around to the other side of the forest,' he said, throwing his car keys at Lars, who dropped and picked them up in slow motion. 'I'm gonna go in there and get my scalp, get your friends out of there. We're gonna come out the other side of the forest where you'll be waiting for us there, okay?'

Lars picked up the keys, coughing from the smoke, a red line on either cheek where Sniles' baton had struck him.

'And if you're not there, if you fuck with me, son, I'm gonna come back and we'll pick up where we left off.' He tapped his baton. 'Got it?'

*

Ashleigh's sobs haunted Donnie from the basement, little sobs from the woman he'd loved, needed, had wanted for so long but had never so much as kissed. They'd shared their most intimate moment five minutes ago when he'd hacked the blonde hair from her head. It lay on the floorboards at his feet. Now he had his mother's hair, his dead father's hair, the clown's hair, Richard's hair, hair from all the animals he'd killed, and the hair of the lover he'd never won.

He scooped up the shredded mess up and returned to the edge of the hole in the floorboards. She lay in her jeans and bra looking up at him from the basement dirt below, her head bleeding where he'd hacked too close to her scalp, her mouth gagged, the fear in her face mixed with pain. The rope remained tight around her ankles, linked to the rope holding her arms behind her back. Her back was arched, her cleavage wet with sweat. He was pretty sure she'd broken her foot when he pushed her into the hole. He regretted that but he was close now, close to erasing everything he'd ever regretted. But he wondered, as he stared down at the flesh in her bra, if he should go one step further and try and take what he'd always wanted but had never won. It would be bad, but he could erase it afterwards. He was about to erase everything.

He dropped the bundle of her hair into the hole so it landed on Lars' horrible mutt and the pile of animal carcasses beside her — a pyre covered with petrol and the contents of his memory jars. Her hair was the brightest contribution to the pile, glistening with blood under a few smoky sunbeams clawing through holes in the roof. Most of it had come from Donnie's severed finger, an injury that hurt like hell and which he'd wrapped in the shirt ripped from Ashleigh's back, Richard's shirt. But some of it had come from his nose after Ashleigh socked him one, a powerful punch that had taken him by surprise and hurt him in more ways than one.

Ashleigh whimpered again, shook her head, pleaded with her eyes, her wet, green, powerful eyes, the eyes that everyone doted on, fell in love with, became obsessed with. Tears mixed with the sweat on her breasts and something stirred in Donnie's crotch, something that couldn't rise in the massage parlours. *This* is what it wanted. *This* is what Donnie needed.

'Burn the hussy,' his mother said. 'Burn her like I burned your father.'

'Shut up, Mother, you bitch,' Donnie snarled as he started towards the basement ladder. 'And close your fucking eyes.'

The corrugated iron in the hallway behind him creaked. Donnie swung around. Too late. A flash of white flew through the smoke, slammed into his chest and sent him backwards into the hole, and onto Ashleigh then onto his pile of bones, petrol and hair. A white shape landed on his body. A thrashing thing, an animal thing, punched the air from his lungs, cracked a rib, its terrible fingers went at his eyes, and his throat. A wail, a scream, then searing pain on his nose, a clown attacking his face with its teeth. He gripped its head, wrestled it from his face, felt half his nose tear away.

'Motherfucker,' he cried. 'It was Mother who killed you. *Mother.*'

The clown shrieked, punched, bit, possessed by all the animals Donnie had ever killed, a ferocious whirlwind with claws. Somewhere in the flurry he heard Ashleigh screaming, another voice swearing, a male. It was Richard.

'Richard! Help me,' Donnie wailed. 'It's the clown, the fucking clown.'

He wrestled with his assailant, pushed it into the carcass of a dog he'd killed three months ago, the possum he'd killed last week, a cat skeleton's brittle ribcage. Their twisting bodies knocked over the petrol cans, rolled in wet petrol hair so it stuck to their arms and stung their eyes. He managed to punch the snapping creature so it fell off his face, gave him space, allowed him to see Ashleigh climbing the ladder with Richard climbing after her. Her dirty lover looked back at Donnie, wide-eyed and focussed — the cunt was never focussed — prodding Ashleigh onwards and upwards, stealing her like he always stole her, taking her away to fuck in her little blue car.

'I burnt your Korean piece of shit Hyundai,' Donnie screamed, moments before he was struck across the face with a plank of wood.

*

The clown stood over Donnie's collapsed frame, blood covering his chin, a piece of hard black wood in one hand, or was it a talon? Richard didn't know. Ashleigh paused on the ladder above him and stared into the hole. Tufts of blonde hair flopped sadly over her bleeding scalp. Her eyes were wet with gratitude for this strange ally in the basement, a clown who opened and closed his bloodied jaw, gobbing as if he were trying to talk, his eyes seeming to grow smaller as he stared back at Ashleigh.

'Maarm,' the clown gurgled, raising his head so his Adam's apple stuck into the air while his legs sunk into the pile of dead animals and hair in front of Donnie's inert form.

'Maarm,' he warbled again, and Ashleigh's eyes filled with love. Her lips — bruised and swollen —pursed and her love poured towards the gurgling clown, whose face seemed to be disappearing, a smudge with an Adam's apple moving up and down, a nose protruding from the blank space that used to be his face, a face Richard himself had hit over and over again.

'Gerard,' Ashleigh sighed, as the clown's nose extended further and hardened, splitting across its middle so its lower half drooped open, closed again, a long beak opening and closing, a bird cooling itself in hot air, two talons brushing bits of hair from the feathers of its white suit, a crest shining white, a contented bird breathing and sighing on top of a pyre.

Something bright fell from the sky. A piece of ash encased in a dull orange flame that had found its way through a hole in the roof. It headed slowly towards Ashleigh, then swirled away at the last moment to land on the crushed animals at the clown's feet, a warped mass of hair drenched with petrol. *Fwooomph.* Fire flared over Donnie's horizontal body. He jolted awake, twisted with agony. *Fwooomph.* Fire found the clown, grabbed its tail feathers, leapt up its crest, took its talons, its beak and filled its face with flames. It exploded into flaming red wings that flared and engulfed the pyre, extended and flapped, lifted the clown from the earth. Ashleigh screamed and climbed the rest of the ladder. Richard followed. Black smoke erupted. Dirty, featureless monsters in a dark basement rose and screeched.

A strong arm yanked Richard up the last rung, pushed him down the hallway towards the light outside. Ashleigh ran ahead as the corrugated iron croaked underfoot. Both of them escaped outside to leave the constable inside with two bodies burning and thrashing about, one of them a shrieking eagle, the other screaming unholy. Their combined noise was the iron structures of a world collapsing, mass ripped to pieces by opposing forces of gravity, logic's carpet yanked from beneath them and turned to smoke.

*

Sniles saw that the flaming hell in the basement was comprised of two parts, one human shape writhing in the dirt — a black core encased in flames — the second a fireball hovering a metre off the ground. At its centre was something the size of man but where its face should have been there was a beak. It squealed, and it had wings, flaming wings. They spread. They flapped. They beat the burning air and threw plumes of petrol smoke about but as much as they tried the fireball couldn't rise. It could only hover and scream the cries of a thousand hungry birds.

Sniles aimed his gun at Donald Lawson's heart, fired twice *bang bang* and claimed his scalp.

Outside in the distance a car horn honked over and over. A pitter patter of rain came from the broken corrugated roof above. It was tentative, unwilling to pour on the burning shape flapping below, a victim who'd somehow made the worst friends in the world. It directed its faceless pain at Sniles and exploded into a rage of sparks that rose from the basement and orbited the room. They bunched before Sniles, rotating at high revs into a figure-eight pattern, an infinity symbol, a butterfly. It grazed his cheeks without heat. With a final howl, the ball of sparks shot down the hallway, encircled Ashleigh at the entrance, then disappeared with a *crack*.

Sniles watched Ashleigh from where he sat on Richard's steps, enjoying the fresh scent of rain's aftermath. It had only stopped last night, after constantly pouring for the two days since the clown had died. Ashleigh, her head shaven and made neat by a hairdresser despite the plasters, placed a bouquet slowly against the tree's red butterfly, a crutch under one arm to support her broken foot.

'So have we got a deal?' Sniles said to Richard sitting alongside him on the porch. 'Don't mess with me, son. All I have to say is you were right there at the ignition point inside Pony Ridge Scrub and every cop in the district's gonna come knocking on your door.'

'Yeah, we've got a deal,' Richard said.

'And if that mate of yours says I so much as flicked him, you'll tell them—'

'That he's full of shit.' Richard sipped from a bottle of mouthwash for the tenth time, swishing it around and spitting it out. 'And that's fine with me. Lars has always been full of shit.'

Ashleigh flattened her palm on the oversized butterfly on the tree trunk, a red pattern resembling the screaming sparks that were seared into Sniles' mind like a hot, moving scar. She turned away.

'So what was he?' Richard said, eyes stuck on his girlfriend. 'A ghost? Some kind of phoenix? Was he Eliza Murray's kid, the woman your mate mentioned on the phone?'

Sniles sighed. He didn't like the fact he had to trust Richard to keep his mouth shut about the clown. He'd found respect at SAPOL for the first time. He'd been praised for his work connecting the dots, finding Donald Lawson, honing in on a kidnapping situation and saving Ashleigh's life. Even Dawksted had begrudgingly congratulated him. It would have been different if the rain hadn't arrived and put out the fires. He'd probably have been strung up for failing to sort out traffic bottlenecks and castigated for the deaths that almost certainly would have occurred. But he was rolling with it, feeling good about South Australia for the first time. The problem was when the smoke cleared they'd only found one human body among the carnage, Donnie's. Apart from the remains of an estimated 16 animals, forensics had found no second body in the basement, no Gerard Brummer. Sniles had to change the story he'd told Dawksted, put his 'confusion about Gerard Brummer' down to the smoke, flames, and a case of mistaken identity for Lars Weber — a stoner who'd survived the fire just fine, albeit with two bruises on his face from Sniles' baton.

'I think we need to put it behind us, Richard.'

SAPOL were keen to appoint Sniles to a new taskforce for reviewing the area's response to a major bushfire, a police-led campaign that would hopefully force the politicians to improve road infrastructure for a growing population. SAPOL called it Taskforce Spearhead. It loved its daft operational names. But first there was coronavirus to deal with. Non-essential gatherings of more than 100 people had been banned, aged care facilities had been cut off from the rest of society, community sport had stopped and they were planning to cancel Anzac Day celebrations as well. Even Sniles' and Jenny's Barossa Valley booking had been cancelled, much to Jenny's wry amusement. The last thing SAPOL wanted to hear was stories about ghosts or screaming butterfly sparks. Any talk about 'phoenixes' or 'reincarnated children' and their fledgling appreciation of Sniles could easily deteriorate.

Ashleigh limped back from the tree, her eyes a little wet. Despite her grief, the slight smile she wore when Sniles first met her was still apparent. Even now, he couldn't shake the feeling she was hiding something.

She always seemed to be hiding something.

'Richard?' Sniles said. 'I'm gonna do you a favour.' He pulled Jenny's card from his wallet and handed it to him. 'This is my partner, Jenny. She's a psychologist and she's bloody good at what she does. I mean, if it wasn't for her, I would have cracked your head open on several occasions, believe me.'

'I don't need another psychologist,' Richard said, taking the card suspiciously.

'Are you kidding me?' Sniles said. 'Son, you need a lobotomy. But that's only half the point I'm making. When Jenny and I hooked up, I could be angrier than sin. My dad was a bastard and it rubbed off on me. But she stuck with me, no matter how much people hated her for it, and now I've controlled that anger, to an extent, or I can at least keep it contained … most of the time.'

'Are you kidding *me*?' Richard said, setting down his mouthwash bottle. 'You hit me. You hit Lars. You smashed your bonnet and you—'

'I could have done much worse, son, much much worse.'

'So what do you want me to do? Call your girlfriend?'

A gentle breeze swept in, replacing the scent of rain with scorched earth and burnt eucalyptus.

'That's exactly what I want you to do,' Sniles said as Richard gurgled more mouthwash. He sure as hell didn't want him talking to anyone else. 'But make no mistake. If I ever so much as hear about you being near another bushfire, for whatever fucking reason, clown, ghosts, psychopathic friends or whatever, I'm going to come down on you like a shit-ton of motherfucking bricks. Got it?'

Ashleigh stopped and watched a bird fly overhead, smiling happily to herself, two hands on her lower stomach, looking radiant as ever despite her injuries, healthier than she should, at peace, almost as if she was …

'Fuck me,' Sniles said, dropping his wallet and standing up. '*That's* what it is.'

'What?' Richard said, spitting out his mouthwash in fright.

'Of course.' Sniles laughed. He looked down at the pitiful Richard Caruso. His eyes were showing fear again, his mouth trembled at the lip of his mouthwash bottle. 'Holy shit.'

'What?' Richard said, putting down the bottle, pulling at the collar of his shirt and licking it.

'Stop that,' Sniles said.

'I can't,' Richard said, his eyes growing wet and hopeless. 'I've got clown drool all through my body, some kind of ghost drool. My friend turned out to be a raving fucking lunatic ready to kill everyone and anyone. Cedar Desk are hassling me to develop a concept so bad it'll probably work, *again*, and if I don't do it I'll have no job before Dad comes home, no excuse not to work for him, no direction. I'll have to become an accountant again, chew his numbers in an office stinking of fish, and now you're talking about some new horror, some new ... *thing* ... to fuck with my head, and you're talking about your girlfriend like she's *special*, like she's gonna be able to tell me something I haven't heard before, and—'

Slap

The retort was loud enough to grab Ashleigh's attention. She started hobbling faster towards them as Sniles grabbed Richard by his collar and pulled him close.

'You're damned right she's special. And you forget about Gerard Brummer. He didn't exist. Got it? You never talk about him again, or any ghosts, or phoenixes, or any of that shit. What you do, is you get your shit together. You call Jenny. You do whatever she says, and you start opening your eyes to get a real good look at everything you've got.'

'Everything okay?' Ashleigh said, approaching the stairs, her cheeks flushed, her eyes hardening at Sniles.

'Your promise,' Richard whispered at Sniles. 'In the car. You promised.'

Sniles let him go, turned and looked at Richard's tree. He looked up and down Richard's street at the neighbours' properties a least 50 metres away. Richard's street was no more than an access lane after all, a fire break with a scorched forest on the other side. It was isolated enough.

'Fine,' he said. 'I'll do it. But only if *you* call Jenny and take responsibility for *yourself*. Understand?'

Richard nodded. Sniles stepped down the porch and smiled at Ashleigh. She frowned coldly back at him.

'And for God's sake, man. Help this young lady up the stairs.'

DEAD PIRANHA

Chika CHEE CHAA chika CHEE CHAA

Richard woke to a cold dawn, the slightest grey around the curtains. He wanted to bury himself into Ashleigh's hair but it was gone, shaved. He burrowed into her neck instead, smelling one of her plasters.

Chika CHEE CHAA chika CHAA

His mind swirled and locked onto the night before, when they'd tried to make love but failed. He'd been distracted by his father's phone call. He'd heard there'd been fires. 'Was everything okay?' And there was insinuation in Dad's voice. Silence when he told him it was Donnie. Perfect, sensible Donnie, a man who didn't have his 'head in the clouds', who was, in fact, an unemployed psychopath who'd been shot dead trying to burn Ashleigh alive along with the entire district.

'We're coming home while we still can,' Dad said after a moment during which the sounds of China came through the line — chatter, traffic, industry — nothing at all like a country in crisis. 'We'll have to self-isolate for 14 days, but after that, you and I need to talk. I've been talking with a few investors over here, Richard. They're keen to strike while global markets are in shock. The opportunities in Australia are very exciting. I'm assuming you haven't found any work yet?'

That was when Richard closed his eyes and lay flat on the floor. Dad said his name but Richard didn't respond. He couldn't. He was pretending to be dead like the fish in his uncle's pond. After a few more attempts to summon him back to life, Dad gave up and ended the call.

Chika CHEE CHAA chika CHEE CHAA chika CHAA

Richard pushed further into Ashleigh's neck. But Dad was coming home and Richard had no argument to hold off the inevitable job order, no direction, no way to convince Dad he didn't want to be an accountant. He'd already knocked back the offer from Cedar Desk, telling Max he didn't have a future in advertising, telling him three times because the man wouldn't listen. There was dust in his room, on his table, on his pillow, in Ashleigh's bald scalp, and he was swallowing, swallowing again, disentangling himself from Ashleigh because her magic was tarnished. Searching for his ear plugs, he knocked over his bottle of mouthwash, heard Ashleigh sigh with quiet irritation, as the wattle bird outside kept hollering, barking, harassing, following him wherever he went, a flying piranha ensuring he'd never get up, never find his feet, never have anything to show for his ambitions but pain.

BANG!

The explosion echoed over the burnt forest outside, down the hill and over the creek below.

'What was that?' Ashleigh said, sitting upright.

Dogs barked. A car alarm at his neighbour's house bellowed. Richard put his hand on her back as the dawn broke in half and relaxed into the biggest 'fuck you' the world of piranhas had ever known. He giggled and felt Ashleigh tremble.

'That, my dear, is one dead fucking piranha.'

Richard kissed the side of her head and fell asleep.

THE RETURN

Eight months later Richard stood in the maternal unit of Flinders Medical Centre. There'd been no complications, no caesarean. Ashleigh's waters had broken at 1am and by 1:30am the ordeal was over. Now they were tired and excited, stuck in the childbirth zone of no sleep and a commitment to the great unknown suckling noisily away at Ashleigh's breast.

Richard was surprised how well he was coping. The blood, the sweat, the exposure of Ashleigh. He'd stood by her for the entire birth, feeling nothing but frustration for her pain, elation that she'd pulled through without problems, relief that their baby was healthy and strong-looking, much stronger than Richard thought possible for a baby one month premature. At one point, when he saw the remnants of amniotic fluid on his boy's head, he had a moment of fear, but just as quickly his new psychologist popped into his mind, her words, her training, the cognitive re-wiring of his mind forcibly drowning his anxieties, not because he could block them or stop them. That was impossible. But because he could think about the positives and squeeze the negatives from the room. He could focus on Ashleigh, a woman who loved him, who'd become a Quaker shortly after the Archibald Bushfire, who'd found a strange sense of serenity in the unorthodox movement, new friends in the old couple and their extended connections. He could put the past behind him, his misguided adventures in love, in advertising, the excited man on the radio who told him not to be 'bat-crazy' and to 'shop at YingCo', the easing pandemic, a mostly unscathed Adelaide population that had emerged blinking with too much toilet paper in their cupboards. He could focus on the part-time work he'd finally landed front-of-house at the re-opened Art Gallery of SA, a new direction that was humble yet on the right path, giving him enough to pay rent towards their city flat away from the tree trolls, his disappointed father, the dead fucking birds. He could focus on his art, a series focussed on fish in places they shouldn't be, in forests, in smashed up rooms, swimming in flames, in a police officer's hand, scaly beasts over which he'd finally found some control. He could stick at it until he got it right, until he became a master in his own right. There was no hurry, no rush. He had life and a lover. He wasn't his dad. He'd never be his dad and, as Richard had confidently admitted to Ashleigh only a few nights ago, he'd been feeling naturally happy for the first time in his life.

Richard's fingers caressed Ashleigh's luscious, recovered hair, sharing with her a moment nobody anywhere could ever hope to control.

The baby broke away from Ashleigh's breast. He rolled back and turned towards Richard, exposing for the first time a tuft of bright red hair above his little forehead, eyes un-focussed, looking up at what must have only been a smudge in a world of fluorescent light. The little baby moved its mouth, the edges of its lips curled, and Richard received a terrifyingly familiar smile.

Malcolm Sutton is an award-winning journalist whose work has been published Australia-wide and internationally. He lives in South Australia where he performs as a musician and runs a fringe theatre company that has produced works in London and Adelaide. Twitchers is his first published novel.